The
BROKEN
SPEAR

Endorsements

What a privilege to have the opportunity to be one of the first to read *The Broken Spear: Reformation Rising,* the first in a new series by the award-winning author Ruth Ann Ellinger. Historical fiction with a base in true history and family ties is some of my favorite books to read and from the first page, the reader is engrossed in the familial relationships and ties and potential adventure and strife that lay ahead. Ellinger is a gifted author of intrigue and drama.

MARIE A. GILMORE
Editor and Publisher of the award-winning *Osprey Observer* and
Christian Voice Monthly newspapers. Gilmore is a published author of
Open for Business! Now What?, a non-fiction small business book. She
speaks locally to small businesses and organizations.

The Broken Spear by Ruth Ann Ellinger sheds a bright light on the complexities of the Scottish Reformation and its effect on the clans and people of Scotland. History comes alive through her characters' struggles to make sense of the intrigues surrounding the Scottish court and the possible catastrophic effects those intrigues might have on Clan Carmichael. Faith and loyalty are tested and sacrifices must be made for the good of the country, the church, and most especially, for family. A fine read for fans of historical fiction set in Scotland.

CAROL UMBERGER
Author of *The Scottish Crown Series: Circle of Honor, The Price of Freedom,*
The Mark of Salvation, and *The Promise of Peace*

The BROKEN SPEAR

Reformation Rising

RUTH ANN ELLINGER

AMBASSADOR INTERNATIONAL
GREENVILLE, SOUTH CAROLINA & BELFAST, NORTHERN IRELAND

www.ambassador-international.com

The Broken Spear: Reformation Rising

ISBN: 978-1-64960-073-8
eISBN: 978-1-64960-076-9
Library of Congress Control Number: 2021939332

Cover design by Roseanna White Designs
Interior typesetting by Dentelle Design

Scripture taken from the King James Version of the Bible. Public Domain.

Quotes from chapter headings other than Scripture are from the hymnal, *Evening Light Songs*, Faith Publishing House, 1949, Gospel Trumpet Company, 1911. Public Domain.

AMBASSADOR INTERNATIONAL
Emerald House
411 University Ridge, Suite B14
Greenville, SC 29601, USA
www.ambassador-international.com

AMBASSADOR BOOKS
The Mount
2 Woodstock Link
Belfast, BT6 8DD, Northern Ireland, UK
www.ambassadormedia.co.uk

The colophon is a trademark of Ambassador, a Christian publishing company.

Dedication

To all my amazing ancestors, who provided the inspiration for this story lifted from the archives of Carmichael history and to lovers of inspirational and historical fiction the world over.

Acknowledgments

MANY PEOPLE ARE INVOLVED WHEN writing a historical and inspirational work. To name them all would take pages, but there are a few that deserve mentioning for their help and encouragement while I wrote this inspirational series. First, I would like to thank my husband, Wright, who long-suffers with me through the ups and downs of writing and encourages me when I feel overwhelmed with such a daunting project. He is my constant reassurance.

Thanks to the rest of my family, who never fail to ask, "Are you finished yet?" That one question keeps me on task.

Appreciation and thanks to Richard Carmichael of Lanarkshire, Scotland, Chief of Clan Carmichael. He offered sketches of clan history, pointing me to Mont St. Michel, Normandy, where one of my protagonists, Peter Carmichael, was incarcerated. I gained a good understanding of this historical site when it was a prison.

Thanks to my publisher, Ambassador International—the editors, project managers, and staff who have helped in publishing and promoting my books these many years. Thank you and God bless you all. Finally I thank Jesus, my Lord and Savior, the One Who inspires me, believes in me, and loves me. Thanks be to God for His unspeakable gift!

Note to My Readers

SOMETIMES, I THINK I MUST be crazy for writing books with such detailed historical content. I uncover the lives of those long dead and forgotten, discovering stories that should be told but are hidden beneath mind-numbing historical facts. I write what should be told—stories and events that, at times, altered the course of history.

In the *Stone of Destiny* series, book one is set in sixteenth century Scotland during the onset of the Protestant Reformation. It is a tale of tragedy and triumph, of heroism and bravery. Using historical facts, I include my own ancestor's involvement in those extraordinary events of the Protestant Reformation.

Lifted from the pages of history, we meet the dynamic activist, William Carmichael, a vibrant and forceful character, and his son, Peter, and his beguiling first love, Jenny. Peter's uncle, Sir John Carmichael of Carmichael, chief of a Scottish clan of influence in the Southern Uplands, holds the family together as they face the perils of the ongoing religious uprising.

The story is recorded in history, but historians record mere fact, not the emotional life and human aspect of the characters.

I, the writer, envision the impacting scenes that happened between the lines, pen those tender and stirring words never recorded in history, remember love known only in secret, and write about the honor and integrity of those whose brave deeds and undying love were never valued or remembered . . . except by God.

Chapter 1

Lanarkshire, Scotland

1531-1533

I was a captive, but mercy released me
I was in darkness but now I can see.

Evening Light Songs

PETER'S EYES BURNED WITH INTENSE heat—searing heat that rolled about him like the relentless waves of a fiery sea. Flames licked at his feet and his clothing, eager to devour whatever part of his body they could reach. Gritty ash rose in a thick, dark cloud over his head as smoke from the burning wood filled his throat with caustic choking fumes.

He struggled to pull free from the bonds that held him fast to the solidly planted post. He repeatedly strained at the cords with every fiber of his remaining strength, but his efforts were futile. He was no match for the strong hemp bindings.

Opening his mouth, he pushed the last vestige of breath from his lungs, attempting to call for help. No sound came from his parched throat—only a dry wheeze, like the rasping sound of a dying locust.

He could feel himself slipping into darkness, a darkness filled with heat and smoke and flames.

Was this how he would die? Was this the horrific way he would meet his end? If so, the sooner he slipped into that dark abyss pulling him down toward oblivion, the better it would be. Then, he would no longer feel the flames, no longer remember how he had come to this.

Then suddenly, miraculously, strong arms reached for him, tearing the bindings away like rotten threads, grasping him in a vice-like grip and pulling him away from the flames and from the yawning darkness sucking him down into nothingness.

"Peter! Peter! Wake up, lad! Ye are dreaming."

Peter bolted upright, drawing in a ragged breath as though it were his last. The abrupt jolt to his senses startled him to wakefulness, and he shuddered involuntarily, looking around at the bed clothes that lay on the floor in a tangled heap.

His nightshirt was soaked with sweat, and he blinked rapidly. Then the fog began to clear from his eyes. Glancing quickly around the small room, he relaxed, sucking in a deep breath of welcome relief. The dream had seemed so real. He could almost smell the smoke and feel the heat from the flames scorching his skin, but . . . It was only a dream, a nightmare sent by Satan to torment him.

His father, William Carmichael of Carmichael, brother to their chief, was bending over him, an anxious look creasing his rugged features. He was the only other person present in the sparsely furnished rooms attached to the stable where Peter worked and lived.

He released the firm grip on Peter's arm and sat on the edge of the bed, his keen eyes sweeping over Peter and then over the sparse orderly room as though he was searching for an enemy.

For a long moment, William studied Peter's trembling form, taking in his every movement, his every breath. Slow hot anger flamed inside him, creasing his craggy war-like features. Peter must not see his agitation. He must never know the deep anger he felt toward those men who had caused his son's night terrors.

With great effort, William gathered his churning emotions, his countenance softening. He retrieved the coverlet from where it had fallen on the wide plank floor and, folding it carefully, he placed it on the bed. He said nothing, waiting for Peter's agitation to subside and for his own burning anger to cool.

Cradling his head in both hands, Peter methodically breathed in and out, attempting to calm his strained nerves. He spoke to his father then, his voice agitated and tremulous.

"When will these cursed nightmares ever end, Father? Why can't I rid myself of this awful torment?"

An odd combination of pity and anger rose in William's breast, causing his piercing green eyes to burn with an unnatural light. He glanced at Peter's sweat-soaked nightshirt and the tangled bed coverings. He decided to wait for several moments before answering, and he began praying for compassion to outweigh his anger. Shrugging his broad shoulders, he chose a safe response to his son's perplexing question.

"I canna say, son." William turned to look through the small window where he could see the morning mist hovering just above the tree line. His face was an indiscernible mask, for he was long-accustomed to hiding his feelings.

Peter's nightshirt clung to his bare skin in lumpy folds. He felt the pungent dampness and shook his head in disgust.

"Just when I think I'm over these dreadful dreams, they return with a vengeance to haunt me, to mock me, torment me!" Groaning aloud, he ran his strong fingers through his dark hair, leaving deep furrows like a plowed field. "They come without leave, like some demonic presence to plague my mind!"

William gripped his son's arm and spoke with an assurance he did not feel himself. "Someday, lad, they will cease. Time is a healer, has a way of curing a troubled mind haunted with evil dreams. Dinna fash yourself overmuch, lad, and be out o' bed wi' ye. The horses be waiting." He turned to the half-open window again, where the soft muted whinny of a horse caused his lips to curve in a rare smile.

"Aye, lad, do ye hear the noble beasts calling ye? Remember this, son, a busy mind with a brawny back will help ye forget your troubles, problems that cause ye to want an answer when there is no answer, mysteries that haunt the human mind."

Considering his father's words, Peter wondered if his reclusive and reserved father had ever experienced a moment's fear. If William Carmichael had ever lacked for courage, Peter had not witnessed it.

Nodding benignly, Peter wished only to change the subject. He was weary to the bone of fighting something he could not understand, something he could not resolve. He forced his mind to focus on the present.

Noting William's travel attire, he said, "And what are ye about today, Father? You look like you are making ready for a long journey. Are the horses needed for the king? No word came to me that they might be moved, so I didn't make ready."

"Nay, no horses for the king today, lad. The stable of the king's favorites won't be moved until the autumn festival. Today, I'm riding with your uncle John to Edinburgh." He hesitated, not wanting to fully explain.

"Ye remember the trouble with the Douglas? Going to see about it, that's all. Be back in a week or so. Came by this morning to let ye know . . . the Privy Council has convened and . . . " William stood then, as if he could no longer remain still, the words on his lips left unspoken. "I want to caution ye—be mindful of the horses. Keep a close eye on the stables. Ye know, son, times are unsettling, aye? Been scouting the borders of our lands with me men."

Peter nodded, his eyes holding questions.

"Saw some Border Reivers hanging about, scouting the region for cattle and sheep or whatever else they might pillage. Appears they're up to no good. If trouble arises, gather our men and protect the stables."

"Not to worry. I will protect the king's mounts and our own horses as well." Peter felt his father was avoiding the true reason for his departure for Edinburgh. "So then," Peter persisted, "you and Uncle John plan to be present at the inquest?"

"Aye, lad, we'll be there—if we are not stopped by the royal guards. All the clans in the Southern Uplands are concerned, and their chiefs will make an appearance."

Peter understood what that meant, and he didn't like the sound of it. The king's men would be watching for any opposition to the inquest. His father had not come by merely to remind him of his duty to the king's stable mounts. He wanted Peter to know where he was going without duly alarming him. If something unforeseen did happen, Peter would understand.

"Isn't that making a rather bold statement to the papal hierarchy, not to mention the Privy Council? It seems extremely dangerous, Father."

"There will be a vast mix of clans and sentiments among those who attend, Peter. Far too many to assign sides in this inquest. We have long been friends with the Douglas clan, so I dinna suppose it will seem strange that we attend. And . . . " he said smiling, "we do hope to make a statement—our chief is strong, respected, and won't be daunted by those who would hope to intimidate our people."

"Father, be careful; I beg you." Peter could not bear the thought of his father coming to harm.

William waved his hand in a careless gesture. "Ye know me, Peter. I be the soul of caution."

Peter shrugged his shoulders at this statement, knowing his father to be a risk-taker if duty called for it. His eyes swept over his father's accoutrements for the journey, an indication of what might be waiting for the Carmichaels in Edinburgh. His father's offhanded words did not match his traveling gear.

A broad sword was sheathed at William' side, and a razor-sharp dirk was hidden in his boot. Hanging from his belt was a battle axe with the clan crest etched on the grip of the handle. William was a Carmichael, a "Man of the Broken Spear," a man not given to thoughts of defeat. He feared no man. Because he knew this, Peter was unconvinced that this venture was just a routine journey to aid the Douglas.

Observing Peter's scrutiny, William smiled ruefully. "Och, lad, we be going to show up dressed like we mean business, that's all." William slapped Peter on the back. "Maybe put the fear of God in some of those corrupt councilmen a wee bit, aye? No worries, Peter."

For as long as Peter could remember, his father battled the forces of evil existing along the Scottish borders. Fierce border clans, known as Border Reivers, robbed and pillaged neighboring clans as far north as Biggar.

The Reivers struck at night, raiding, burning, and killing as they went. Their swift Galloway ponies carried them through the boggy and desolate landscape known as the disputable lands, the area bordering Scotland and England, then on to safety and their own fortified strongholds, where they hid their stolen cattle and booty.

William, "Man of the Broken Spear," endeavored to keep the peace while protecting the southern borders of Carmichael lands from the constant threat of the Border Reivers and other lawless characters. The struggle for control of the border lands was centuries old, as ancient as the land itself.

Animosity between the Scottish and English Reivers was ongoing. Throughout the years, William Carmichael's life was marked by battles—some for Scotland's freedom, others when settling clan disputes, a constant source of disturbance to the peace of the Clyde Valley and the Southern Uplands.

In recent years, however, William's austere and reclusive nature found a cause worthy of his leadership. After studying the sacred Scriptures for himself, he became disillusioned with the Holy Mother Church. The practice of reading an English translation of the biblical text was strictly forbidden by the Pope; but for William, this was the catalyst that caused him to share loyalties with the religious enlightenment sweeping across Europe, reaching even into the Highlands of Scotland.

A rising had begun, and the simple Scripture "the just shall live by faith" was sweeping across Europe in a great awakening that challenged the long-standing domination of the Holy Mother Church.

In retaliation, the Christian believers were subjected to persecution of the most insidious nature.

This nonconformist message brought with it a different kind of warfare, a warfare William Carmichael was not familiar with, a warfare not easily fought or conquered by the literal sword. The protesting Reformers were unclear as how to proceed, how to obtain victory over the religious powers that had kept entire nations under tyranny and darkness for over a thousand years.

The rising had indeed begun, and Scripture-believing Christians breaking away from the papal Church—those who understood what it meant to be free from man's rule and tyranny—were a threat to the all-encompassing, all-powerful seat of the politically organized Church of Rome. To gain freedom from papal rule, the free-thinking Christian zealots were ready to spill blood if necessary. They gathered their weapons and made ready for a religious war.

Although William never spoke of this to Peter, he knew many Reformers were preparing themselves for a physical conflict. William Carmichael of Carmichael was among them.

"Aye, lad," William said, pulling on his riding gloves. "God willing, we'll be at the inquest, but dinna fash yourself, son. Your Uncle John has influence, and we ride with Clan Lesley, Elliot, Hepburn, and Douglas."

Peter's throat tightened. "Be careful, Father. The Douglas is not well-liked by the king; his stepfather is—ye know this—a Douglas, and the king has hated him ever since he kidnapped him and held him captive."

"Aye, I know this, lad." William softened. He understood his son's concerns and wanted to ease his mind.

Peter spoke as though to an equal. "I want ye to return . . . to continue as we always have." He knew his words were unnecessary, but he needed to say them just the same.

Outside the small window, the sun began to pierce the hazy mist of early morning that surrounded the Valley of the Clyde, leaving a heavy dew that sparkled in the pale sunlight like thousands of diamonds. Peter turned to his father, looking long into his expressive green eyes.

"We have connections with the king, aye? Perhaps he can negotiate a lesser charge for those facing inquest. He is a peaceable man, I believe."

William laid a hand on Peter's shoulder, a comforting gesture intended to ease his fears. "I know. Ye have been friends of the king since ye were all bairns, like all who live in the southern border lands."

"But it has been far different now," said Peter, "since Jamie is now King of Scots."

"Aye, that's so. Even after the young king's escape from his mother's husband, life for him has changed. But remember . . . he is influenced by those who advise him, those who ignorantly support the edicts of the Roman Pope. Jamie's mother, the Queen Mother Margaret, will not defy the divine authority of Rome, especially when she seeks a divorce approved by the Pope."

William rested his hand on the hilt of his war sword, the gesture conveying an unspoken message. "I do not expect young King James to sanction this present reformation, Peter. He is young, inexperienced, not wanting to risk the disapproval of the Pope. A difficult place to be, aye?"

At his father's words, a mounting fear began to hammer Peter's mind, but he lifted his head in a show of confidence. He did not want his unease to show, not when his father was going to Edinburgh to be present at the inquest of their Douglas kinsman.

Dropping his head in resignation, Peter sighed. Nothing he could say would alter his father's decision to attend the inquest. "Don't worry over the horses, Father. I can manage well enough. Just be safe and come home . . . home to the Clyde." Och, he could manage the horses al right; but what he feared most was that he couldn't manage life without his father, and he wasn't at all sure he could survive the pressures of the coming Reformation.

"I know ye can handle the horses, lad." William hesitated, sensing his son's uneasiness at his departure. "And I will come home, naught to fear. I'll see ye at the back of seven days."

"Aye, Father," Peter said in a brisk tone. "At the back of seven."

William Carmichael, second-in-command of the lands of Carmichael, felt this leave-taking more keenly than at other times. His only son had grown into a man, a son to be proud of, and now . . . he must leave him to manage alone. William knew Peter was an able leader, tall and strong like his Carmichael ancestors. He could count on him to be honest and trustworthy.

Since the day Peter had been made to watch Patrick Hamilton die a fiery death at the stake, William felt in the very marrow of his bones that God would use Peter for the cause of Reformation in Scotland to be a spur, a thorn in the side of the clerical powers opposing reforms of the Holy Mother Church. But secretly, he hoped his premonition was wrong.

This rigid and dark stone of offense had held entire nations captive for over a thousand years. It must be shattered, broken apart, exposed. But who could do it? How could anyone challenge the long-held stronghold of men?

Chapter 2

Some trust in chariots, and some in horses:
but we will remember the name of the Lord our God.

Psalm 20:7

AT THIRTY-EIGHT, WILLIAM CARMICHAEL WAS still a handsome figure, masculine and rugged in bearing. He was the second son of John Archibald Carmichael, second of Carmichael, and brother to Sir John, third of Carmichael, illustrious soldier of many battles, the eldest son and heir of a barony nestled in the picturesque Southern Uplands of Scotland, where the great River Clyde meandered lazily to the sea, emptying into the Firth of Clyde at Glasgow.

William guarded the Lands of Carmichael with a shrewd sagacity. Years of feudal battle in order to protect their lands and herds—lands won in feudal conquest—was not about to be put at risk, not on his watch.

Sir John depended on his younger brother to secure their lands from border raiders and cattle thieves who harassed the border regions and beyond. For years, William and his handpicked clansmen had successfully guarded and maintained the Carmichael holdings. William rode his black stallion, Shadow, over the countryside overseeing clan activities. He did so with a fierce determination.

During the early years of the sixteenth century, times were perilous and dangerous, and tempers were hot.

William' skill and expertise with horses came to the attention of the young King James V, only two years older than Peter. In his formative years, the youthful heir to the throne of Scotland was a frequent visitor to Carmichael House, quite unaware of the power he would someday acquire as king of Scotland. He was a simple youth, seeking companionship with the neighboring young people living in the Valley of the Clyde.

Young King James V of Scotland was born at Linlithgow, only half a day's journey from Carmichael. The king maintained and staffed several stables in the lowlands. William managed a smaller stable near Biggar, close to Carmichael in Lanarkshire. Here he taught Peter every facet of equestrian riding and training. Father and son directed events that required the king's horses in attendance.

When only one year old, the infant king ascended to the throne when his father, James IV, was beaten by the English at Flodden Field. During James' infancy, the Scottish nobles fought for power, and James was held a virtual prisoner by his mother's husband, a power-hungry Douglas, Earl of Angus.

After his escape from his reviled stepfather, the king kept horses at the ready should he find it necessary to flee from this ongoing power struggle. He was fond of blooded horses and bought and sold the various breeds as a rather expensive hobby, but also as a necessary means of escape should his enemies try to overthrow him.

When the king was in residence at Linlithgow, William and Peter were often at the stables there. Peter cared for the horses and stables near Carmichael, working with the resting mounts and training the new foals, overseeing and exercising the king's equestrian obsession.

Caring for the horses was second nature to father and son. They were quite content with this lot assigned to them by the king. But now, William Carmichael prepared to ride to Edinburgh in defense of a Douglas crofter and clansman. Just the name Douglas could raise a prejudice in the king; albeit, the people of Clan Douglas had little to do with the Earl of Angus and his kidnapping of the youthful King James.

William gripped Peter's broad shoulders, a farewell gesture that needed no words. His confidence in his son's ability to care for things in his absence was evident. He exited Peter's room and untied his mount that was secured to the fence. The great horse waited impatiently, pawing the earth, resplendent in the early morning mist. Drops of moisture clung to his mane like little silver beads, and the stallion whinnied loudly, eager to run.

Peering through the small window overlooking the approach to the stables, Peter lifted his hand in farewell, watching his father mount the black stallion with graceful ease. The horse reared slightly in anticipation of the journey, shaking his great head until his dark mane cascaded across his broad neck. Before proceeding to Edinburgh, William would ride to Carmichael House to meet with Sir John, then ride with the clansmen to the inquest.

Seeing Peter at the window, William caught a glimpse of his young wife, her likeness framed in the handsome face of his only son. It seemed it was Maggie who smiled at him, blue eyes soft and warm with love. Maggie had given him Peter—all he had left of the laughing wife he had adored.

Even now, so many years after her death, a mist rose to his eyes when he thought too long on her passing, leaving him alone with a hole in his heart that was never filled. Memories of Maggie—unbidden and uninvited, bittersweet with longing—still tore at his heart. He must not think of those lost happy days. He would stay focused on the task before him.

William waved a farewell to Peter and offered a smile of confidence, then turned his prancing mount and nudged the steed forward. The eager stallion sprang at his master's touch, and William rode away from the face in the window, not looking back, dismissing the sad thoughts that kept him lonely and solitary for too many years. He did not wish for Peter to see the pain that gathered in his eyes. He was not fearful for himself, nor of dying, or even of what the future might hold, but only of leaving Peter.

Guiding his mount along the rough trail to Carmichael House, William knew there was no reversing the onset of Reformation, no turning back. It was like a tidal wave, uncontrollable, irreversible, catching up everyone in its wake—those who were zealous for the cause of the Reformation, and those who were not. Lines were drawn; sides were chosen; and only God knew how it would end.

It was simply the way of things, of rebellion, of revolution and bloodshed and war. He preferred to think of this awakening as "restoration of the truth of the Gospel," but the political powers of the day would label this religious awakening as pure rebellion to the monarchy and to the Holy Mother Church.

And because of this, the people of Scotland were under threat of inquest if suspected of heresy. The papal seat in Rome was a stronghold, an undisputed, politically organized power, whose authority had been unchanged and unchallenged for over a thousand years—until now, that is.

Peter understood the danger his father faced as he rode to meet with his uncle, Sir John Carmichael of Carmichael. He was still unnerved by the vivid memories of last night's dream and thoughts of the impending inquest. If not detained by the Royalists guards, the strongest and most able men of Clan Carmichael would be there, listening to the council's decision. The outcome was uncertain. It could turn ugly, even disastrous. Then what would his father do?

In a covert alliance with other secret Reformers, William warned those under suspicion of heresy, hiding them in several underground locations and assisting them in avoiding the royal guard. This was a dangerous undertaking for William, but his resolve was sealed with the death of the young Scottish Reformer, Patrick Hamilton.

For the past twenty-five years, Christian Reformers were proclaiming a new message of spiritual freedom—freedom from the papal corruption long hidden from the people of Scotland. This corruption included selling masses and indulgences for sin and for the souls languishing in purgatory, requiring self-punishment or penance to escape or shorten the time spent in an imagined terror-filled torment.

These strongholds of the people's minds garnered an amazing amount of money from the very poor to the affluent, a lucrative cash flow for the Roman Church. William could not sit idly by. He was not that kind of man. He must act.

Chapter 3

There's a mighty Reformation sweeping over the land,
God is gathering His people by His mighty hand.

Evening Light Songs

THOUGH ONLY EIGHTEEN, PETER CARMICHAEL was a man in every respect. William had educated his son with the clan children and his cousins who could spare the time and means to learn to read and write. He had hired tutors in Greek, Latin, and the European languages.

Mathematics and the study of architecture began at an early age. It was William himself, however, who taught Peter the honest hard work of managing and maintaining the health and welfare of the king's horses, the essential hands-on expertise of an equestrian.

The hours spent in the stable under his father's instruction taught Peter the practical value of hard work. William not only wanted his son to have a good education, but he also desired that Peter be a man of honor, a man who would respect his fellow man and be mindful of the weak and suffering among them.

As William worked beside his son in the pungent oak-lined stalls of the stable deftly tending the horses, he recounted tales of their illustrious forbearers, men who had suffered for freedom—those who had fought for common human decency. William had promised Maggie . . .

Unlike his father's rugged warrior-like appearance and bold demeanor, Peter bore the aristocratic features of his mother's people, but he possessed the courageous heart of his warrior father.

Over six feet tall, Peter was lean and muscular with thick wavy hair, black as a raven's wing. He kept his unruly locks trimmed short for ease and comfort. His keen eyes were deep blue, fringed with dark lashes and thick brows set in a broad forehead that gave him a resolute appearance, adding years to his actual age.

After the hoof beats of his father's stallion died away in the distance, Peter dressed quickly and hung the kettle over the low peat fire in the corner fireplace. A strong mug of tea revived his spirits, and a bowl of porridge and oat bread completed his simple breakfast. Every three days, the cooks at Carmichael House sent a quantity of food for his use. Anytime the king's horses were required, Peter received generous supplies of food from the king's kitchens at Linlithgow. There was no need for concern over this daily necessity.

Peter groomed and fed the horses, his scattered thoughts keeping pace with the brush strokes. Closing the stable door, he glimpsed a figure riding across the field on horseback. A billowing blue gown was partially tucked beneath the rider, who straddled the horse like a young lad. Her hair was the color of sunlight and blowing free in the wind. She rode astride a Galloway pony that, for all appearances, seemed to be galloping out of control across the gentle rise and fall of the horse pasture.

Peter smiled to himself. It was Elizabeth Katherine, his cousin, Uncle John's daughter and his childhood friend and confidant. She rode at breakneck speed, not heeding the often-repeated reprimand of her father to "ride like a lady."

Katherine reined in her horse a few paces from where Peter stood, sending muck and dirt from the sudden stop flying in all directions. Peter grabbed the mare's bridle, brushing a portion of the stable yard from his hair and tunic. Resting one hand on his hip, he gazed at Katherine, shaking his head in bewilderment.

"What on earth, Katherine!" He attempted to calm the overheated horse with soothing words.

Katherine ignored his exclamation and slid from the saddle, landing with a solid smack of her boots next to Peter's tall frame. She smiled up at him, eyes shining.

"Well, Peter," she said, clasping her hands together. "Since both our fathers are, at present, on the road to Edinburgh and won't be home for perhaps a fortnight, I stole away to spend the day with you. Ha! But don't worry; Coira knows where I am."

"That sounds about right for you," Peter added in feigned disgust.

"Och, Peter, don't be such a grump. It's a bonny day, to be sure. Why, we can do as we please with no one to scold us!" Her eyes fairly twinkled with mischief.

Peter laughed at the impish look on his cousin's face. Katherine was his favorite cousin, a beguiling lass with sun-streaked hair and deep expressive brown eyes. She was a few months younger than Peter; and from childhood, he had assumed a brotherly protectiveness over Katherine. She was like the sister he never had.

"Well, cousin," he said, addressing the slight form that only reached to his shoulders, "That's some greeting this fine morning." He patted the long face of her mare now stomping and snorting in protest of the brutal workout, throwing back her head and blowing clouds of steam from her flaring nostrils.

Peter shook his head, then bent to kiss Katherine's cheek. "And what mischief are you planning today? Did I hear you say you were running away?"

"Aye, I did say that."

"Well, that's an intriguing thought, to be sure."

"It will be great fun, Peter, to do as we please."

"Och, lass, you always do as ye please, I be thinkin'. But we'll not do anything today until we rub down your poor mare. She's about to collapse. You'll ride her to death someday, Katherine."

"Nonsense!" Katherine exclaimed with a flourish of her hands. "Duchess loves to run. Why, I'll wager we could ride our mounts and catch up with Uncle William and Papa if we had a mind to."

"Och, lassie, we're not going to try to catch them—not today, anyway. You do come up with some novel ideas." Peter lifted the reins of the sweating pony and looked toward the northern road to Edinburgh.

Katherine pulled a face at Peter. Then retrieving a rather faded ribbon from her pocket, she tied her wind-blown locks at the nape of her neck and brushed strands of golden hair from her face.

"Nay," she said sighing, "I didn't expect we would, but it did cross my mind. Thought it might be fun to go to Edinburgh. We are so . . . so out of touch, Peter. It would be a welcome change to our life in the country, don't you think?"

"I like my life in the country just fine." He hesitated a moment, searching his cousin's face. "You do understand, Katherine, that your father and mine are riding to Edinburgh to attend the inquiry before the Privy Council?"

"Yes, so I've heard."

Peter continued rubbing down the mare, his blue eyes studying Katherine over the back of the pony. "Wouldn't want to be present at the inquest, anyway. Always an ugly affair. Dangerous, too. Not a good place to be at present."

Katherine exhaled. "Aye, Peter, Papa told me of their intention to be at the inquest, but he offered no details, and he didn't seem worried. Surely, it will all work out for the best. No one would dare harm a Douglas simply because he is a Douglas and a clansman . . . would they?"

Shrugging his broad shoulders, Peter did not respond at once. He spoke softly to the mare as he worked, meticulously grooming Katherine's mount from head to foot, then feeding her some oats and giving her some water to drink.

Katherine frowned; her good humor dampened by Peter's somber mood. She sat on a nearby stool, watching Peter groom her weary mare, sensing the melancholy tone in her cousin's words.

"Don't pout, Katherine."

"I'm not pouting."

"Aye, cousin, you are." A half-smile curved his lips.

Katherine glared back at him. Her riding frock was smudged and damp from her ride through the early morning mist. Her fingers were idly plucking at the mud spatters on her skirt, hoping Peter would share his thoughts. They had always shared their secrets; but in recent months, Peter had grown serious, seemed more reserved.

A sudden, icy feeling caused her body to tingle with an unusual feeling of dread. She did not fear for the safety of her father or clansmen, but something more ominous, more urgent and alarming, clutched at her heart with chilling fingers. For as long as she could remember, Peter had been her champion, taking her part, shielding her from danger, watching over the motherless girl with brotherly concern. He understood her as no other could possibly understand. He was more than a cousin or brother; he was her constant and loyal friend.

Katherine tugged off her riding gloves and stood to face Peter. She placed a small hand on Peter's arm. "Stop a wee moment from your work, Peter. What is wrong?"

Peter paused and placed the grooming brush on a shelf. "Wrong? Well, since ye have chosen to run away this fine day, why don't we go to the loch and shoot some fish for supper? We can talk there—away from any who might happen along, aye?"

Katherine nodded in agreement, still troubled by Peter's serious manner. She had hoped to keep the atmosphere light today, but the weight of their neighbor's inquest hung over the day like a wet cloak, damp and ominous, cooling the warmth of the morning sun.

The blue mist hanging over the valley seemed to linger on the floor of the glen as though reluctant to rise, sheltering the two young people from something yet unseen. Katherine's mind raced ahead, remembering the true reason for her errand, news that would be hard for Peter to hear.

"Aye, cousin," Katherine agreed. She made a valiant effort to appear enthusiastic. "Let's go to the loch—catch some fish and talk of happy times." How desperately she wanted this day to be acceptable for Peter.

"Like old times, aye, Katherine?"

"Aye, indeed, like those good old times when we were children with all our cousins rambling about." She turned away, her brown eyes welling up with sudden tears, tears that she did not want Peter to see.

Chapter 4

. . . and who knoweth whether thou art come to the kingdom
for such a time as this?

Esther 4:14b

AFTER KATHERINE'S MARE WAS SETTLED in a stall, Peter retrieved his bow from the work shed, where he kept his weapons and hunting gear. Katherine packed a basket with bread and cheese and a bottle of cider from the store of provisions in Peter's room.

The two cousins walked through the dew-drenched barley fields glistening in the morning sun like a thousand tiny stars had fallen from the heavens. Sunlight streamed through the mist until it began to shift and fade away.

Katherine held her skirts high, attempting to avoid the long wet grass. Leaning lightly against her shoulder was a net made of hemp that fastened to a long pole. Peter had made the fishing net for her many years ago; and although it required skill in its use, she preferred the net to other methods of fishing.

She laughed up at Peter as he led the way through the sparse woodland dotted with wild bluebells swaying in the wind. Spring flowers carpeted the open areas in a vivid profusion of color, lifting their wee flower heads in search of the warm morning sun.

Like a playful young lass, Katherine hopped on one foot, then the other, a game they had played in childhood. A narrow, winding deer path led them over a grassy slope to where a narrow glen sheltered a picturesque loch hidden from the view of travelers. The loch, shining silver and green with tiny ripples, sparkled and flashed in the morning sunlight. It was fed by a small burn and was surrounded by a thick forest of oak, pine, and ash trees. The loch was alive with leaping brown trout and perch.

The Carmichael cousins often resorted to this lovely glen, a place where they talked and fished and dreamed of a future where life was simple, where tyranny and discontent no longer existed. But today, the menacing undercurrent fueling the fires of religious Reformation threatened any dream of a pleasant and tranquil future.

The cousins positioned themselves on the sloping bank of the loch, fishing in silence, careful not to disturb the fish that were so easily surprised by noise or sudden movement.

Katherine lay on a blanket, flattened against the bank, her head barely visible above an overhang where unsuspecting trout nudged curiously at the woven net bobbing gently in the clear water. Adept with using the fishing net, Katherine lay prone against the bank, waiting. With uncanny skill and a generous amount of patience, she suddenly jerked and twisted the net, capturing a large wriggling trout, open-mouthed in surprise, thrashing crazily against the constraints of the net.

Covering her mouth to keep from laughing, Katherine rolled over and held up her catch for Peter to see, boasting that she had certainly caught the largest fish in the loch and declared herself winner for "catch of the day." In years to come, Peter would remember Katherine in this way—young and laughing, her eyes sparkling with delight and wonder. From a tiny lass, she found joy and pleasure in the simple things that surrounded her world.

By noon, Peter had speared several more fish with his bow, and the cousins quit their fishing sport. Peter cleaned the fish, while Katherine spread a blanket on the top of the bank and retrieved the covered basket. She tore apart the fresh bread and sliced the rich goat cheese.

After consuming their simple luncheon, the cousins lay on the blanket, gazing into the brilliant blue sky, watching finger-like clouds scurry across the heavens to form and re-form into cloud figures of animals, angels, and old men, then fade into the distance.

Katherine braced her head on one hand, her elbow resting on the blanket. Looking at Peter's long, muscular form lounging lazily against the bank, she posed a question that now troubled her mind as a result of Peter's grim manner.

"Peter, will your father take up arms? I mean, will he fight to save the Douglas at the inquest, do you think?"

Peter's face darkened with concern. He crossed his arms behind his head and looked up at the ever-changing patterns in the slowly drifting clouds. "You know, Katherine, inquest waits for any who defies the edicts of the Romish Church. Real danger has increased considerably . . . since . . . since Patrick's death." A steely light rose in his eyes, and a shadow passed over his countenance.

"I don't expect the present inquest to relax their purpose to silence Christian believers," Peter continued. "With the increase of those wishing to join fellow Reformers in this cause, persecution is also on the increase. But rest assured, sweet lass, Father will be careful. After all, he keeps the king's stable." A rueful smile curved his lips.

"True enough," Katherine agreed, "but after the young king escaped his stepfather's hold on him, he forced the influential branch of the Douglas family into exile. Remember, Peter, Jamie's stepfather is a Douglas whom he hates with a passion."

She dropped her head, a troubled expression crossing her features. "He won't have much mercy on any Douglas, even the lowliest of clansmen."

Peter shrugged. "Father is aware of that. I'm thinking his presence at the inquest is to understand how things are developing, to show support for the Douglas in question, and not to take up arms against the judgment of the council. 'Carmichael of the Broken Spear' is making a statement, that's all."

"Pretty strong statement, if you ask me," Katherine said. She sat up, hugging her arms around her knees.

"Well, I suppose I could be wrong. He was carrying quite an impressive arsenal with him. You know, Kate, Father hates tyranny and is weary of all the burnings. Something must be done to stop the bloodshed. Remember, *Tout Jour Prest* is the Carmichael motto."

"Always ready," murmured Katherine softly.

"Aye, lass, we must be ready."

"But Peter, how can we lowly Scots change the course of such a mighty religious power?" Her brow furrowed in perplexity.

Peter shook his head and sat up, and choosing a smooth stone near the blanket, he threw it across the clear waters of the loch. It skipped over the surface several times before sinking beneath the rippling waves.

"We are like the wee stone, Kate—small and insignificant as it passes over the surface of the deep water, but see the ripples it makes? The firm and solid impact of the wee stone is felt to the farthest shoreline. Oh, aye, we can make an impact in the grand scheme of things."

"Och, aye, if only we could see the purpose in the grand scheme of things," Katherine said wistfully. "But surely, Peter, our families have done nothing to warrant an inquest."

"Nay, not yet, anyway. You know of Father's secret and covert attempts to aid the Reformers. Because of our family's influence, the council will be hesitant to implicate our clan for the simple reason that the king holds a previous connection from our youth. But a Douglas? Well, he might not think twice about sending a Douglas to the stake, innocent or guilty."

"If the Christians seeking radical reform take up arms, how can they expect to win over Rome? Aye, they might free a fellow clansman, but they will eventually be hunted down and exiled or executed for heresy. It is too dreadful to think of."

Peter rolled onto his stomach and plucked a tall stem of orchard grass growing next to the blanket. Placing it in his mouth, he chewed thoughtfully. "Aye, that's true. The 'Mother Church' is far too powerful and is determined to squelch this Reformation movement."

"Then, there must be another way, Peter."

"Are you thinking of our illustrious great-grandfather who fought in France to aid the French against an English invasion?"

"Not exactly."

"Well, I think my father thinks about that battle. He is forever reminding me of how Sir John rode into battle and unhorsed the English commander, breaking his spear in the process."

"Aye, Uncle William is truly a 'Man of the Broken Spear.' And, Peter, there are many like him, ready to fight for religious freedom." She studied her hands, sadness marking her features.

"I'm afraid it may come to that, Katherine."

"We cannot take up arms and fight Rome," Katherine protested. "That is ridiculous! They mark any who even dare speak about reforms in the Holy Mother Church. Even talk of corruption among its leaders will not be tolerated." Katherine's dark eyes swept over the sun-dappled clearing, assuring herself that no one was about to hear their conversation.

Peter sighed deeply. "Understand this, Katherine—there are hundreds who are ready to fight for religious freedom. Your father and mine are among them. You must be prepared to accept this."

"I cannot accept going to war, Peter, and I don't believe my father is for taking up arms either. He says to subdue an enemy without fighting is the greatest of skills. Coming from a soldier who fought many battles, I believe him. I have said before, there must be another way. Diplomacy is always an option."

"Really, Katherine? Diplomacy does not appear to be an option at this point. That time has passed. I know that taking up arms will surely cause more persecution for the Christians; and I know Sir John wishes for a peaceful resolution between the Reformers and the Church, but I don't see that happening. If push comes to shove, Sir John will fight."

Peter sat up, then plucked several more longs stems of the fragrant grass from the soft earth at his feet. He pointed the stems at Katherine. "Do you have any better ideas? I think diplomacy and taking up of arms have lost the vote."

Katherine stood to her feet. Her eyes were brilliant and hopeful. Turning her full attention to him, she said, "As a matter of fact, I do."

Peter laughed. "Oh, really? Then say on, lass."

Hesitantly, she began. "You're not going to like this." She turned her head away, not looking at him, her lips trembling with undisguised emotion. "Truth be told, Peter, I came purposely today to tell you . . . tell you that Jamie . . . that our Jamie has offered for me."

Peter stood to his feet to face her. "Offered for you?"

"Yes."

"Jamie? Offered for you? What are you talking about? What do you mean . . . an offer?"

"You heard me, Peter."

Shock registered on Peter's face. "The king? James Stewart? He has offered for you?" Incredulity was written plainly across his handsome features.

"That is preposterous!" Peter exclaimed in disgust. "He can't do that, Katherine. He must be daft! Jamie must find a queen from the royal bloodline. He will seek a political alliance that will benefit and further the kingdom. That's the way of it, the way it has always been. If he has told you differently—and you believe him—then he has deceived you. His offer for you is just a bunch of political blather."

Katherine's expression altered, and the light went out of her eyes as though the sun had gone behind the clouds and only shadows remained. She shook her head in consternation.

"I don't think you quite understand. Jamie has spoken with father . . . at length . . . told him that he wishes for me to be . . . to become . . . " Katherine's voice dropped to a whisper, and her hands fluttered nervously at her side.

"Jamie spoke to your father. Well," Peter scoffed in a contemptuous tone, "Sir John will set him straight on that account."

"Peter . . . I don't think you understand. Jamie wants me to be . . . to be his . . . his mistress, not his wife, not his queen. He made it clear to Papa, that if his royal request was not accepted, he would mandate his wish for me; issue a royal command that could not be refused."

Peter jerked as though someone had slapped him, his eyes burning with shock and unbelief. "What? His mistress! That is outrageous, ridiculous! Is he daft, out of his mind? Surely your father denied him, refused him."

For a long moment, Katherine remained silent, desperately trying to hold back her tears. When at last she spoke, her voice trembled. "At first, Papa was grieved and not a little agitated with his royal request, unwilling to consent to his offer. Yes, Peter, Papa did refuse, but . . . Jamie is also the king, and a summons from the king cannot be denied. He made that clear."

"The king!" Peter interrupted. "Have you forgotten, Katherine, the king is also the friend of our youth? Jamie Stewart is not just any king! How can he ask this of you? How *dare* he ask this of a friend? If he weren't the king, Jamie would not dare place you under a royal order."

He threw the grass stems away with unnecessary force, as though they were loathsome to him, then pointed an accusing finger at Katherine.

"Never mind, Katherine, I will speak to him myself, will shame him for even thinking he could have you by exercising his royal authority. You will remember, Katherine, when he attended Margaret Somerville's wedding at Cowthally Castle, he knew very well you were there. He pursued you without leave from Lady Somerville. He uses his power to beguile you, and when that doesn't work, he issues a royal command."

"Perhaps he did but know this—I did not seek him out, Peter. In fact, I avoided him, ignored his attention."

"Avoided him, Kate? Lady Somerville said herself that Jamie was a frequent visitor at Cowthally, playing his lute, hanging about all last summer while you were under her protection. He claimed to be hunting, but now I see he was hunting a beautiful lass such as yourself for his own carnal purpose."

Katherine faced him, placing a hand on his arm, willing him to listen. "Please, Peter, please listen to me. I have known for some time that Jamie would send for me. You know . . . he has always admired me . . . cared for me. I avoided him because I felt that someday, he would seek me out for his own pleasure. Now that he is king, he makes his request known."

Peter raged inwardly, his face reflecting indignation, his hands forming tight fists that clenched and unclenched at his side.

"Not a request like that, Katherine! Not like that. You know it will be a ridiculous farce, a sham. You don't love him. I know you don't. For heaven's sake, Katherine, you are only sixteen!"

Lifting her arms in a beseeching manner, Katherine met his disapproving gaze. "You are assigning blame to me, and I am not to be blamed, Peter. I am shocked, just as you are now; but, Peter, I continually refused his advances. When I was at Camwath under Lady Somerville's protection, he sought me out many times. Lady Somerville resisted his pursuit of me, but what do you say to a king? I knew this would get ugly."

Katherine twisted her hands together in distress. "And, aye, it's true. I do not love Jamie in that way, but he is a friend—a friend we have both loved since childhood. You can't deny that. At least he is not some repulsive, sovereign authority we do not know."

Peter turned his face away, not daring to look at his cousin. He could barely control his outrage, his anger. His fury over her news was boiling near the surface, ready to spill over into words he might regret. Katherine had not seen him so angry, not since Patrick's death.

"The more I thought on it," Katherine continued, hoping to soothe Peter's hot anger, "and with Rome sending their most persuasive officials to try the dissenters for heresy, I thought of my situation in a different light."

"In a different light?"

"Aye, since I will have no choice unless the king withdraws his request, perhaps this will be an opportunity to influence the king, be close to him, to persuade him to use his power to spare the Christians. I realize that some feel this is a high honor to be . . . to become the king's mistress. I do not feel honored, Peter. I feel desperate to make the best of my situation."

Peter could not believe what he was hearing. "And do you feel you can make the best of such an appalling situation, Katherine? How on earth can you become just another mistress in Jamie's growing line of consorts? Raising his bastard children?"

"I will have no choice, Peter, and since I do not, I must find some kind of peace until God releases me from this dilemma."

Katherine laid a small hand on Peter's arm. "Remember Queen Esther in the Scriptures, Peter? I have thought of this so many times since Jamie sent his request. Do you remember her uncle Mordechai's words?"

> Think not with thyself that thou shall escape in the king's house, more than all the Jews. For if thou altogether holdest thy peace at this time, then shall there enlargement and deliverance arise to the Jews from another place; but thou and thy father's house shall be destroyed: and who knoweth whether thou art come to the kingdom for such a time as this?

"Ha, cousin," Peter mocked. "And you—do you believe that you will save the Christians from inquest and martyrdom?" Peter laughed cynically.

"Perhaps, I can help," Katherine said in a serious tone.

"Will you, my own sweet cousin, sacrifice yourself to be used by the king . . . simply for influence? Aye, and trust me, you will be used, then thrown aside as soon as the king chooses a queen."

Peter's censure and scorn was palpable. Katherine felt the sting of his disapproval to her bones. She grabbed both his arms, turning him to face her. Then holding his face between her two hands, she said, "Look at me, Peter Carmichael!"

Katherine's eyes burned with passion as she held his gaze, forcing him to look at her. "What am I to do, Peter? I have no choice in this matter. I have prayed that God would make a way of escape, but no door opens. We don't know if any of us will live through these dreadful times. The king—our own Jamie Stewart—knows how we feel, and he has turned his head . . . because . . . because he loves us. Who can say if this door has not opened to me for this purpose?"

Peter spoke again, his voice shaking with feeling. "It seems ye have accepted Jamie's request as your fate, lass. What more is there to say?"

"Aye, Peter, I have settled this in my mind. It is the only way I can survive this, and I must survive." She threw her hands wide in appeal. "It is not as though we don't know Jamie. I trust him to be kind to me, to be . . . to love me if that is possible."

"Love you?" Peter laughed in derision. "And what of the man you truly care for, the one you truly love and to whom you have been promised? Have you thought of him? Don't you think Robbie Somerville will feel quite betrayed by the king's decision to take you from him? Have you even told Robbie?" He paused to stare at Katherine as if seeing her for the first time.

"I will tell you this, Katherine," Peter said with conviction. "I could never abide such disloyalty in someone I loved. Nay, not for any cause."

At Peter's unkind words, Katherine broke down, unable to hold back the hot tears. She turned from him, her body shaking with heart wrenching sobs.

"You do not understand, Peter," Katherine said between sobs. "How can you think so ill of me? All our lives, we have been like brother and sister—two motherless children, taking comfort in one another, dreaming of a future where we can be happy and secure. Your words are too harsh, Peter, too accusing. You cannot fault me for what I cannot help."

"You have chosen to accept this outrageous request instead of fighting for yourself, Katherine. Life at court will change you . . . forever."

Katherine wiped at her tears with the sleeve of her gown. "You are right about one thing—the king's request will cost me dearly. It was for peace—peace and security for our family and for our people—I can see no way out. The king has summoned me."

Peter softened. His hasty words and rigid attitude had cut Katherine deeply. She was pleading with him, her face crumpling into wordless grief. He had always been so gentle with her, unable to bear her tears. Not in all the years, not until now, had he been so unfeeling with his words.

This was no time for harshness, and he had been unforgiving in his manner, unwilling to understand her purpose. She did not choose this course, and since it was inevitable, she desired to have an influence on the king, to spare their family and the Southern Upland clans who were daily joining the Reformation movement. But still . . .

With a deep, ragged sigh, Peter reached his strong arms to his cousin, gathering her to himself, comforting her with meaningless words. He regretted his impatience, his bad temper, and unkind attitude, but inwardly, he refused to add his approval to the king's bidding, even though it was a royal command. He could not sanction such a demand from Jamie Stewart. He wanted to call him out, to challenge him.

Peter attempted to calm her, to lessen her grief and stop her tears. But deep down, Peter knew Katherine's call to court would change her from his cherished cousin to a woman with a complicated life. He could not think about it now.

The two cousins held each other close, conscious of one thing: their youth was slipping away, like sand spilling through an hourglass, and they could not staunch the flow. The tide moved swiftly along, carrying them with it. The happy, carefree days of innocent youth were over. They must face an uncertain future filled with unbelievable treachery. How would they ever get through these terrible times? And now, they would be separated by the unthinkable—Jamie Stewart's royal privilege.

But in the midst of this great spiritual darkness, a fiery sword was raised, piercing the very head of the serpent. This flaming sword dared to challenge the greatest religious power in the known world—Rome, an ancient religious tradition veiled in ignorance and superstition. Would this governing power that held its people in bondage bring Scotland to its knees through the fires of inquisition? This tidal wave of revolution had begun in earnest, and there was no turning back from an inevitable spiritual conflict.

Lines had been drawn in the sand. It became more and more apparent that those who lived in the misty shires of Scotland—the ancient clans, their chiefs and people—could not remain neutral in the approaching religious cataclysm. They would be forced to swear allegiance to the papal powers of Rome or face inquest.

At length, Katherine's sobs subsided, and she grew quiet. That unforgettable and haunting moment in time—a moment rooted forever in memory—became for Peter and Katherine a turning point in their young lives. They stood trembling, holding to each other like frightened children lost in a dark forest.

The wee loch hidden in the quiet glen witnessed their distress, and the birds stilled their singing while the cousins pondered their future, what might be their part in the events now unfolding before them. They understood one thing—the peaceful, happy life they had known as children would never be the same . . . never again.

Chapter 5

Christians all should dwell together in the bonds of peace
All the clashing of opinions, all the strife should cease.

Evening Light Songs

AT THE END OF JAMES IV's reign in 1513, those who rebelled against Rome's religious and political practices were increasingly threatened with inquest. No one dared voice an opinion on the many abuses suffered by the common unlearned people. Betrayal by royalists was rewarded with money and position, and the non-compliant were swiftly silenced. Rome insisted the Scottish people be accountable for their free-thinking ways.

Now, after years of relative peace, the carefully guarded sanctuary of the Southern Uplands was under threat of treason. The threat came from both the reigning monarchy and the churchmen of Rome keen to stop the Reformation movement. Because of the close proximity to England, the border clans strived to remain neutral in their political and religious alliances.

It was a continuous tap dance that required vigilance and skill. For years—even centuries—Clan Carmichael, along with other influential clans living in the Southern Uplands, had engaged in this political maneuvering, and at the same time, had guarded their own lands from Border Reivers.

At the inquest in Edinburgh, the Douglas in question, kin to the Carmichaels, was acquitted and released. Though still under suspicion of the Privy Council, Clan Douglas and their compatriots were still too powerful to consider burning one of their clansmen for heresy. For centuries, Clan Douglas had wielded a dominant influence in the Southern Uplands.

Sir John Carmichael, William Carmichael, and several influential clan chiefs living in the border regions, left the Privy Council feeling their presence had sent a message. They returned to their homes, relieved that they did not have to make any hard choices during this particular enquiry.

The Church of Rome was not vigorous in burning Protestants in Scotland, perhaps because they felt this northern region of Britain too insignificant, and only a small number of people were punished for heresy. Punishment might include excommunication or extreme penance, but burning a dissenter was viewed as an act of violence even among non-believers.

Indeed, some clergymen sympathized with the activists' ideas and encouraged reforms in the Church of Rome. But this supposed lull in aggressive actions by the Holy Mother Church would not last long.

The clansmen returning from the inquest in Edinburgh marched wearily along the wagon road to their cottages and to a steaming supper cooked slowly over low peat fires. Smoke from nearby villages drifted to the edge of the roadside, mixing with the misty gloaming now settling in, signaling the end of day.

As his stallion drew closer to home, William thought of Peter. News of the outcome of the inquest would be uppermost in his thoughts. Love for his only son welled up in his heart, taking his mind back to the day when Peter was born. It was a day forever etched in his memory, a day when the woman he loved had left so suddenly, so unexpectedly, never to return.

At times like this, when the world weighed heavily on his mind, it seemed Maggie lived again, her image smiling at him in the likeness of their son. Despite the tragedy occurring at his birth, Peter was a gift from God, the last gift Maggie had given him before she reached her arms for the wee babe. She placed a kiss on the infant's soft cheek, her blue eyes holding no regret. As she felt her life ebbing away, she smiled softly, then handed the infant to William as though the wee babe were a gift.

William could still feel the helplessness of that moment when, with her last ounce of strength, she begged him to care for their infant son, to raise him to be noble like himself, and to love him as he had loved her. As though in a dream, he had promised to carry out her wishes, to raise their son to be a strong man. He assured Maggie that he would love the tiny infant as he had loved her—unconditionally, completely. He had not thought she would truly die. How could that have happened?

But his promise was only words, spoken in grief. That grief had been deep, weighing down his spirit with unrelenting sorrow, stealing away the joy of living. The only bright spot in his life was his love for his ancestral lands . . . and for Peter.

His promise to Maggie still seemed unreal, unimaginable. At times, the horrors of that day haunted him, replaying over and over in his mind. Then, when grief became too heavy, he would saddle his horse and ride through the countryside until he could reconcile himself to his circumstance.

In the years following Maggie's death, he grew taciturn and silent, spending days away from home, where his adoring son waited for his return. He arbitrated clan disputes for his chieftain brother and managed the needs and complaints of the tenants living on the fourteen-thousand-acre estate. The work was demanding, but it took his mind from his incessant sorrow.

William took pleasure in his only son and in his exacting care of the Carmichael Estates. He felt that Maggie still lived on in the spirit of their son, the incredible parting gift born of their mutual love. This farewell blessing, a babe to love, caused William to hold his son close to his heart.

At length, his painful loss found a purpose in the ongoing Reformation movement. This resolve, to reform the papal church, challenged his faith and offered hope and healing for his grieving heart. William left Edinburgh with renewed faith in God and in his ability to shield their people from the ravages of the inquisition.

Chapter 6

And power was given unto them . . . to kill with sword,
and with hunger, and with death, and with the beasts of the earth.

Revelation 6:8b

AS THE REFORMATION GAINED IN strength in Europe and Scotland, William became friends with the young Patrick Hamilton, a zealot of uncommon intelligence who took the Pope of Rome and the many papal injustices to task. The young Reformer spoke with such eloquence and passion that many of the underground and covert believers joined forces to proclaim the truth of the Gospel as it was written, coming out of their long-imposed silence to renounce the tyrannical rule of the Romish Church.

The Holy Scripture was now made available for the common man, translated into English from Greek and Latin by the daring English scholar, William Tyndale. This one translation brought light and hope to a world shrouded in spiritual ignorance and gross darkness.

Now, as the tides of insurrection swept over the land and hostilities against the Mother Church increased daily, William was eager to join with other clansmen to confirm their stand in the coming Reformation.

However, Sir John was hesitant, troubled, uneasy, and the clan was restless. The inquisition was coming too close to home, and the clan leader was responsible for the safety and welfare of his people.

On the return trip from Edinburgh, the two brothers sat astride their mounts, pausing momentarily along the roadside, waiting while the rest of their party proceeded to move around them, each to his own home, thankful that their journey was nearly over.

Sir John reined in his mount, preparing to turn onto the road leading to Carmichael House. He was the eldest son, the heir, and handsome in a rugged, steel-faced, solid sort of way. He wasn't superior in his manner but had about him the aura of a leader. He had the ancient, wise look of an old clan chief, a veteran warrior, but timeless in his features, with clear, keen, blue eyes and a graying beard.

He turned to William and said, "The council was lenient, even somewhat sympathetic. The Douglas clan can rest peacefully tonight, at least. Who can say what will happen next?"

William stretched his back, turning this way and that, weary from the long ride from Edinburgh. "Aye, 'tis so, but remember, a black hand can carry a bright light, aye, John? God can use evil men to do His pleasure if He so chooses."

The two brothers smiled warily, but there was no comfort in the comment. An uneasy silence followed the attempt to lighten the moment. Although the Douglas had been released, the brutal questioning of their close neighbor had left a cloud of doubt over those clansmen present at the inquiry, including the chief of Clan Carmichael.

Sir John shifted uneasily in the saddle. "Ye know, William, this is not the last of it. Aye, in truth, it is doubtless the beginning of increased papal scrutiny for our people. We had to be there, that's all. Hopefully, the council will view our presence at the inquiry as a show of support for our close kinsman, not as an aggressive action."

Seeing Sir John halting along the roadside, the accused Douglas clansman approached, then grabbed hold of the ornate leather bridle of his chieftain's horse. Removing his hat, he smiled broadly. "Good day to ye, Sir John, and God bless ye."

Sir John touched his hat and smiled. "Be of good courage, Thomas, and remember this day—a day of great victory for ye and for Clan Douglas. But remember this." Sir John leaned over in his saddle, looking directly into the clansman's eyes. "Be wiser in the future. There are spies about, ready to use their office to bring any who is dissatisfied with the Holy Mother Church before the Privy Council. This will not be the end of it, I'm afraid, so take heed."

The old clansman twisted his hat in his gnarled work-worn hands, the memory of his blunder still burning in his mind. "Aye, me lord, I will remember, and I am sorry for the careless words. I meant no harm—not to ye, Sir John, or to me clan."

"Learn from this, Thomas. As your chief and leader, I am responsible for my people. If words of dissension are spoken in haste or passion, the authorities look for the head man to accuse."

"Aye, Sir John, I will respect your wishes and follow your council . . . in all matters." The acquitted clansman moved away then, knowing that the warrior chief spoke the truth. He must take heed to his words.

Although hungry, dusty and bone-tired, the remaining clansmen stopped in their weary journey, expressing their gratitude and thanks for their chief's show of support, for his courage to risk his good reputation for those who had none to speak for them, no advocate to plead their cause.

Sir John nodded warmly to each of them, bidding them Godspeed and to pray for wisdom from the Almighty. The timeworn chieftain sat straight in the saddle, watching solemnly as the weary men moved around him in the road, his dappled war horse prancing in place.

Just as I am, he thought, *prancing in place, dancing around the ecclesiastical fires, wondering how I can ever lead my people through this spiritual maelstrom, this darkness that holds Scotland in chains—shackles that hold the human mind captive, enslaved to the will of men.*

He pictured his beautiful daughter, his Katherine, her honey blonde hair falling about her shoulders, her brown eyes twinkling with mischief. Pain pierced his heart like a dagger. He pushed the dark thoughts from his mind. He must think of other things. To dwell on Katherine's situation was too much for this day's work.

Once again, he turned to William. "Let's go home, brother. Much we need to talk about, aye, much to consider."

William hesitated, then turned his stallion in a tight circle to face Sir John, his horse pawing the ground, eager to return to the trail.

"Vera well, John, but tomorrow, I must see Peter." Looking toward the south, he continued, "When I left for Edinburgh, he was much bothered. Been dreaming again . . . and . . . " William paused, looking away, not certain how to explain.

Sir John nodded knowingly. "Peter is strong, William . . . like his da'. In time, this, too, will pass. Dinna fash yourself over the lad. Had my young sons lived, I would wish them to be like Peter."

Lifting his head, William nodded, remembering the two small graves where Sir John's infant sons rested under the oak trees. The last wee lad lived only a few hours, and with Katherine's birth, her mother soon followed. His only remaining son was a soldier like his father, stationed at a garrison in the far north of Scotland.

Sir John handled his sorrow as he did other battles, with shrewd sagacity that carried him forward. He was a private man; and if he harbored deep sorrow, he held it close to his heart, refusing to abandon himself to senseless grief, but handled his heart with kindness, knowing that life at best is unpredictable and he must be merciful with himself.

The years had given him a philosophy that he carried with him, knowing that life had its dark side and he must understand how to face it with courage. Heartfelt grief was the price he paid for loving Gwendolyn. And he paid it, knowing the years they shared together and the memories he now cherished would be enough to last a lifetime. He had loved. It was enough.

Chapter 7

Though tried and pressed, yet I will trust,
This one thing I can do.

Evening Light Songs

THE TWO BROTHERS TURNED THEIR mounts onto the road leading to the ancestral seat of Clan Carmichael. The ancient castle house was well-hidden, safe from wandering clans or border outlaws, and preserved since the eleventh century by its impregnable location in the Southern Uplands.

The road meandered through a virgin forest of beech, sycamore, oak, and ash trees. The trees were ancient, huge, gnarled, and heavy with lichens and fungi. A smaller lane sloped upward to the right of the main road and was protected by iron gates set in stone pillars. This smaller road circled the base of a gently rising hill and a grassy meadow where cattle grazed.

The brothers rode slowly to the imposing stronghold where the Carmichaels had resided since the eleventh century. The castle fortress was nestled in a narrow glen with the forest on one side and the gentle rise of the hill on the other. Tinto Hill rose in the distance, the high peak surrounded by clouds and the misty gloaming of evening time.

The three-story house was secreted from view of inquisitive wayfarers or, worse, border outlaws looking for straying cattle or whatever else they could pilfer from the estate. Along the gentle rise to the west of the house were terraced gardens, the butler's house, the coachmen's house, and the main laundry. For convenience, the stables were in close proximity to the west entrance. Small, neat cottages dotted the surrounding area and served as living quarters for those who worked the land and maintained the estate outside the main house.

The two men arrived weary and ready for a hot meal. Servants came running to tend to their needs and hear news of the outcome of the inquest and how their fellow kinsman had fared.

From the early days of Robert the Bruce and the Wars of Independence, Clan Carmichael had been strong allies of the powerful Douglas Clan. Marriage among the two clans was not uncommon. Over the years, they had remained friends and supporters, assisting each other in all manner of clan disputes.

Stable lads led their horses away to be groomed and fed. Sir John and William entered Carmichael House through the ornately arched double doorway of the central tower. Two wings, one on the east and one on the west, were connected by a wide hall and central tower house that served as the main entrance.

The east wing housed a study and library, a gun and weapons room, and a privacy alcove. This wing was often referred to as the "lairds' wing." A narrow, winding staircase led to upstairs bedrooms overlooking the lovely Scottish gardens. The west wing contained the drawing room, ladies' sitting room, and the dining room, reserved for important guests and for the ladies. At the back of the east/west wings were the kitchens and servants' quarters.

After a hearty meal of venison steak, turnips, and a variety of root vegetables, the brothers resorted to the study in the east wing. A fire had been laid in the great stone fireplace, and a table of sweet meats and hot cider filled the room with a comforting fragrance.

Without regard to the customary small talk before matters of a serious nature were discussed, William went directly to the heart of their present concerns.

"What next, John? How in the world can we shelter our people from the backlash of this Reformation? We cannot stay neutral forever. More and more dissenters are gathering in private meetings, the number growing every day. The Douglas clansman was only the beginning for our people."

Sir John leaned his head wearily against the worn tapestry chair. He spoke in a low voice, gravelly with years, weary with conflicts, war, and clan struggles. Shaking his head, he said, "I dinna kin, William. All I can do—all any of us can do—is ride out the course of events as they happen. After all," he said resignedly, "we are only men."

"Aye, John, we be that, but we are also men of action. For years now, we have studied the works of Wycliffe, of Hus, Luther, and others who have dared to speak out. With what is coming to our land, we must declare ourselves and join with the Reformers. It is time for the hidden Church to come out of hiding!"

"And what has such action cost the Reformers, William? Wycliffe was excommunicated, denounced, his works destroyed, his body dug up, his bones burned. And Hus? A brutal, fiery death at the stake. What of our own young Patrick? Now there is Luther, Tyndale, and we have those rising in our own country. In time and with patience,

William, perhaps a lifetime, we will see change. In our patience possess we our souls."

"Ye are afraid then? I canna believe that ye, me own brave brother, fear what might come if the believers remain steadfast." His frustration was evident.

Sir John sighed. "I am no coward, William. Ye know that. I don't just think of meself. All me life, for years, I spent in the middle of some battle fray. I be weary of it. Now, we must pray to stay in the king's favor, yet hold to faith. It is a precarious balance indeed. I do know this, William—we must endeavor to remain unattached, unaffected; or in the near future, we may yet see our people, including Peter and Katherine, face the Privy Council."

"I fear ye are right, John. Ye know," he said softening, "our best days be past—a truth we face without fear—but ye be right . . . there is Peter and your Katherine. For their sakes, we must find a way to help them through this, to survive. Peter is still affected by Patrick's death. I be certain ye know this. It pains me to say it, John, but I don't know how to help the lad; and truth be told, this next generation may witness worse than burnings."

Sir John rose wearily from his chair and walked to where William sat on the opposite side of the stone fireplace. He placed a comforting hand on his brother's shoulder. "The lad needs time, William. He will come through this. He loved Patrick, should never have been made to watch him die. Nay, it was done to strike fear in all of us who have not taken a definite stand."

William clenched his fists, a look of intense indignation causing his features to redden. "Aye, it did that! But remember this: Patrick's death also brought courage and strength to others who face the same fate for the Gospel. Nay, Patrick's death . . . it was not in vain; neither was the earlier Reformers you mentioned. As bloody as those deaths were, God has used it to spread the Gospel. Ye canna deny it, John."

A slow smile spread across Sir John's face. He strode purposefully with his usual steady gait to stand by the blazing fire, resting one hand on the oak beam that served as a mantel. Beeswax candles burned brightly in pewter candlesticks, lighting his rugged face. Turning to William, he resumed.

"That one burning of a Reformer has set the whole of Scotland on fire, I'll admit. Cardinal Beaton's friend and our esteemed priest, John Lindsey, stated it truthfully: *My Lord Beaton, if you burn any man except you follow my counsel, you will utterly destroy yourselves. If ye will burn them, let them burn in low cellars, for the smoke of Patrick Hamilton has infected as many as it blows upon.*"

"Aye, and it has blown upon all of Scotland," William said. "Since twenty-four, when the law forbidding the reading of Luther's writings was enacted, people are begging for smuggled copies of his works. Quite the reverse effect, aye?"

"Indeed, that incident only served to strengthen the Reformation." Sir John looked at William with a penetrating gaze. "But we must be cautious, act wisely with discretion. We have much to lose, much to consider. I know how you love these lands—our lands—but we can lose them in one foolish act of open rebellion."

"We have close ties to Clan Douglas," Sir John continued, "so our presence at the inquiry was an observation, not a threat or act of disloyalty. It must remain that way, William. Far better to resist the papists by secret warfare rather than overtly disputing their resistance to the Protestant Reformation."

A disgusted look clouded William's handsome features. "I highly doubt that everyone saw it that way, John—as merely an observation. Think ye that we can remain neutral and unaffected, unchallenged by the papists, the Privy Council?"

Sir John shrugged his shoulders, shaking his head in consternation.

"As in the case of the Douglas," William resumed, "it matters little that the Holy Mother Church and the Pope strictly prohibit the importation of all Protestant writings and forbid all public disputations about the heresies of Luther and Tyndale's translation of the Gospel."

William ran his hands through his dark hair. "Aye, the papal fear is not unfounded. There is great reason to think that some of these Protestant writings have fallen into the hands of our people as it did Patrick's. Even Patrick, a youth of royal lineage, was by his own choice, a chosen instrument, the bearer of light, one shining candle in the mist, the smoldering beacon of eternal truth."

"Aye, indeed," said Sir John. "Patrick broke apart the stone of darkness and deception."

"How then, John, can we as believers of biblical truth, remain independent of this cause? Change does not occur unless ye are ready to be the catalyst. Action matters, not our inaction."

"Ye be too impatient, William," Sir John said with his typical chieftain's authority. "Aye, at present, I will remain undeclared. Truth be told, I do not understand how to proceed, but I do know this; we dare not act on emotion, nay, nor on fleshly zeal, the passion so easily stirred to the action ye speak of. Let us pray and wait on God to direct us, William. But now, I have a more urgent matter to discuss with ye."

William looked annoyed but acquiesced to this change in their discussion. Sir John returned to his chair and sipped his hot cider. "I wish to tell ye about . . . about Katherine's situation."

"Katherine's situation?" William sat up straight and lowered his cup. "Is she going abroad? I thought perhaps she should leave Scotland for a time, perhaps go to England. The Tudor king is favorable to the Reformation, and Katherine has been taught by her English governess. She would fit in . . ."

"Nay, brother," interrupted Sir John, "she is not leaving Scotland. Quite the contrary. The king has sent royal orders for her. He wants her for his . . . his mistress."

"What! His mistress! Jamie Stewart? How would he dare to summon her for his mistress?" William sat his tumbler on the table with a sharp thud. Disbelief cloaked his features.

Sir John shifted uneasily in his chair. "Jamie Stewart is also the King of Scots, remember? He is our sovereign."

"Aye, he is that now, but he is also Jamie Stewart, the lad who grew up among us, played with our bairns, and took supper with us betimes." William Carmichael shook his head as though to shake the unwelcome news from his head. "Ye refused the summons, didn't ye?"

"Aye," Sir John answered, "that I did, but Katherine feels it is of no use." He dropped his head. "After much thought and much prayer, Katherine . . . she feels her refusal to obey the summons would make matters worse. This unfortunate circumstance may be from God, she says." Sir John smashed one fist into the palm of his hand. "I hate it, William, hate it like the bloody thing it is, but I can't stop the lass. She is determined."

"But why obey the king's summons? He is her friend and early playmate. I daresay he wouldn't cut her head off!"

"Nay," Sir John agreed with a scornful laugh, "I dare say he would not, at least not now. Later, when the king chooses a queen, it is hard to say what will happen. I would send her away to live in exile, but she refuses to leave Scotland. Katherine feels if she must obey the king's summons, she can influence him, be useful for the cause of the Reformation. She will be in a place of import, will have a voice."

"Aye, she may have some influence, if she is not slain or cast aside when another takes the king's eye." William shook his head in negation.

Rubbing his temples to ease the tension, Sir John said. "I agree. The young profligate will seek out pleasure with whom he chooses. 'Tis a dangerous game for the lass."

"You know how it is, John . . . " William picked up his tumbler and shifted his eyes away from his brother. "Most often, a mistress is of short-time service, unless she is a favorite or until the king chooses a queen. So sorry to remind you of this."

"Dinna ye think I be knowing this," John said indignantly. He flinched as though he had been struck. His face grew pale, the words too harsh for a father's ear. He stood, pushing his chair aside and pacing the wooden floor in front of the fire.

Clearing his throat, William searched for words of comfort, but he could find none. He had not wished to trouble his chieftain brother, but he could not help knowing his words had pierced John's heart like a dagger.

"I'm sorry, I dinna mean to twist the dirk," William offered. "A terrible, ugly thought, I know, but true, nonetheless. Katherine is like a daughter to me, a sister to Peter. Think ye, John, Jamie Stewart is barely twenty years and has already fathered two bastard sons by two different mistresses—Elizabeth Shaw and Margaret Erskine, more's the pity! So why does the young profligate need our Katherine, I ask ye that? She is but sixteen summers."

"Because of her childhood friendship with Jamie, I suppose . . . and because of her lovely, winsome ways. Who could resist the lass if it were in his power to claim her?" Sir John breathed deeply, leaving out a long, slow sigh. He resumed his pacing, stopping in front of William to speak.

"Jamie Stewart was encouraged in his debauchery by one of his regents, but then, he has acted as king since age sixteen. How foolish is that? Do ye think he acts on his own? I tell ye . . . nay! He is the product of those who influence him."

"What can I say, John? Debauchery and dissipation, along with the illegitimate children that kind of life produces, have long been a royal privilege. I might add . . . the bishops and cardinals also lay claim to that prerogative, while wearing priestly habits. Need I say more?"

"Young James came by it honestly," Sir John said. "Look at his father, his grandfather, and even his great grandfather, all named James, boy kings with the same issues. Katherine feels she must take that risk."

"Nay, John. It is too great a sacrifice, and far too dangerous. Ye must stop her! The lass isn't thinking of how this will affect her future. She's not thinking clearly."

Sir John halted in his pacing. "I'm afraid the lass is thinking . . . thinking about the future of all Scotland. Not for love's sake does she intend to obey the king's summons. Ye know she wouldn't do that. I believe she fears that the political powers are casting eyes upon the Carmichaels, and she wants to protect us with this unholy alliance."

Sir John absently rubbed his forehead with thumb and forefinger. "Jamie will be good to Katherine—I have no fear of that—but ye are right, he will marry a queen, a political alliance sometime in the near future; and if the queen is a papist, Katherine will definitely fall from favor."

William rose from his chair and walked slowly to the small oak table to fill his cup. "If she were my lass, I would send her away, against her will, if necessary. The king will marry a papist—that is certain—and Katherine will be just another castoff, another discarded mistress of the king."

"Ye have voiced my worst fear, but I will not send her away and incur the wrath of the king and bring down trouble for all of us. Katherine refuses to leave Scotland and is resigned. I do not see his summons as an honor, as the king does, as many do. It is the way of the royal house, always has been."

William turned to his brother with an expression of incredulity. "Hard to believe God would be in such a royal request, aye?" He shook his head in consternation. "Does Peter know . . . does he know about this . . . the king's summons?"

"She was going to tell him when we were in Edinburgh for the inquest." Sir John shook his head and continued to pace.

"Peter will not like this, John."

"Do ye think I like it?" Sir John thundered. He threw his mug with excessive force into the stone fireplace, shattering the pottery into a thousand pieces. "There is no help for it, William. Blast it all! Someone will sacrifice themselves to support a cause. Someone will pay the price, and unfortunately, Katherine is the one who will pay, obey when there is no way to escape."

"Aye, tis true, but must it be Katherine? She is so young, so innocent." William could not help thinking of his own young wife, so young when she died.

Sir John threw his arms wide. "When God is moving, someone will rise to the occasion; and when that happens, we canna stop it. If this be the will of God, I do not understand His way, but I dare not interfere. Katherine says God must be using her like Queen Esther . . . come to the throne for such a time as this."

The clan chief's throat tightened. His heart felt like a rock, heavy and inconsolable. He turned his face away from William. For once, he could not look at his brother. He gazed fixedly into the leaping flames now eating away at the logs in the fireplace. Shards of the pottery mug lay among the ashes and seemed symbolic of his present feelings. The craggy lines around Sir John's eyes deepened, and he found it difficult to speak. His voice, raw and raspy, grew low and poignant with emotion.

Finally, he turned to look at William, his heart showing through his normally calm demeanor. "Katherine is my only beloved daughter . . . my babe, her mother's sacrifice of life . . . " He left off speaking, not able to continue for the tears welling up in his blue eyes. His voice was broken, shattered by this unexpected turn of events.

Seeing his brother's brokenness, William said, "Then may God grant that . . . that it may be as well with Katherine as it was with Queen Esther." He rested a comforting hand on John' shoulder.

"William, what more can I do?" John said cradling his head in his great strong hands, hands that could hold a sword without wavering, steady and sure; but just now, they shook and trembled with a mind-numbing sorrow—sorrow for his country, for the perplexing events that would change their lives, and for Katherine, the daughter he loved more than life itself.

"John . . . brother, there is nothing ye have done to bring this about. Much as I hate hearing of this, Katherine's decision to obey the king's summons is her way of surviving, managing a difficult problem she canna resolve."

"We must continue to pray, William. Pray that God will somehow make a way of escape for her."

Taking a deep breath, William said, "She has obviously given this much thought and prayer. We must trust her instincts, aye? The lass has a good head on her shoulders, just like her da'. Even though we don't understand, and if the lass must go, ye must take comfort in this: Jamie has always been fond of her and been considerate of the lowland clans with all their problems. Perhaps she will be of some influence as she has hoped."

Gesturing with his cup, William continued, "I believe the king's campaign to rid the Southern Uplands of Johnnie Armstrong and his outlaw raiders last year was a show of support to the border clans. I'm certain his regents didn't suggest that move."

Gathering his overwrought emotions concerning Katherine, Sir John said, "I feel the same. I was encouraged by his decision to rid the borders of those thieving outlaws, no doubt prompted by his long connections with the upland clans. Hanging Armstrong and his fifty men shows the young king can also be a sovereign of strength, uncompromising when it comes to his own will. Pray his heart will not harden, that he will listen to Katherine if she indeed answers this summons."

"What of young Somerville, John? Will he be able to bear this? He has loved Katherine—planned a future."

"The king's law concerning such things can be absolute, William. Ye know that. If King James bids Katherine to come to him as his mistress, and she goes to the court, there is nothing Somerville can do." Sir John returned to his chair, seated himself, and continued. "Nothing could have prepared me for this."

"I am so sorry, John. I would that I could do something," William said.

"Unfortunately, there is nothing any of us can do," John sighed. "Katherine is willing to obey, and that will certainly be difficult for the lad to accept. Somerville loves her, but even so, like all of us, he must honor the king's request."

The two brothers talked long into the night, hoping to arrive at some plausible scheme, some strategy that would offer them a way through this morass of spiritual and political posturing. The impending future of Scotland, even the future of their children, lay in this unequal set of papal scales, of spiritual wickedness in high places. Sir John would seek a balance, but William would seek reform.

The fire slowly burned to ash, and even after much talk, the only possible conclusion for Clan Carmichael and their people rested in an invisible Sovereign, that unseen and obscure spirit that for so long had been hidden from them. Who could guide them through this quagmire of betrayal and deception?

Their enemies were many, their allies growing fewer with every passing day, but light was breaking, clear and bright, an all-encompassing truth that would enlighten a world sinking in spiritual darkness. The dawn of the great Protestant Reformation had begun in earnest, and throughout the length and breadth of the upland valleys, the Carmichaels of Carmichael could hear the pulsating blast of the trumpet, a call to arms. But this battle was unlike that of any they had ever faced in their long, passionate, and blood-soaked history.

Chapter 8

And the Lord answered me, and said, Write the vision,
and make it plain upon tables, that he may run that readeth it.

Habakkuk 2:2

THE SKY WAS DARKENING, THREATENING rain. Jenny pulled the hood of her thick, woolen cloak over her head, fastening it snugly under her chin. She was miles from shelter, miles from the warming fires of Shieldhill Castle. She had fled the only home she had ever known, unable to endure one more dreadful confrontation with her father. Nay, not one more!

Instead, she had saddled her mare and escaped from her father's imposing presence, riding unaccompanied through the open countryside. She avoided the main wagon roads, not wanting to meet travelers who might question her journey over the moorlands. By now, her flight from Shieldhill would be discovered, and her father would have dispatched the servants to bring her back.

At first, Jenny didn't care where she was going, just so it was away from her father's unreasonable demands. Her father, Edward Chancellor, was the powerful Laird of Shieldhill Castle at Quothquan and a vigorous opponent of the present Reformation movement sweeping across the borders of England to Scotland.

Chancellor was also a devout follower of papal Rome. He had discovered Jenny reading the Scriptures from a copy smuggled from England by her governess, Jane MacDougal. Jenny had begged Jane to allow her to read Tyndale's English translation taken directly from the Hebrew and Greek, made available by the invention of the printing press.

However, the unlicensed possession of the Scripture in English held a death sentence. But despite this grim threatening, Jenny had acquired her own forbidden copy. When a servant had caught her reading the outlawed book, this same servant reported this to the laird, and the result was a sound thrashing from her father and the dismissal of her governess.

The rain began in earnest now, bathing Jenny's face in a fine, cool mist. Her damp, auburn hair fell loose from its bindings, and the hood of her cloak fell away, whipping about in the wind and obscuring her view. Great drops of moisture gathered on her woolen cloak, then ran onto the flanks of her horse.

She reined the mare to a stop, her green eyes sweeping across the verdant and undulating slopes of the countryside. She was not certain where she was. If she could locate the River Clyde winding through the lower glens, she could get her bearings.

The mare was nervous, not accustomed to the unfamiliar terrain. Although it was springtime, the intemperate climate could turn harsh and unforgiving. She must find shelter soon. But where? In the distance, she could see some buildings huddled against a gently sloping hillside, perhaps a crofter's home. Urging her mount into a gallop, Jenny headed toward the buildings in the glen, praying that the Crofters who lived there would be sympathetic to her plight.

* * *

Through the mist of the cold spring rain, Peter saw the rider approaching on a Galloway pony. His heart pounded with excitement. Surely, it must be Katherine. Long months had passed since she had received the young king's summons to court. She had not returned, not even to say goodbye. At the very thought, a dull ache formed a knot in his stomach.

Suddenly, the approaching horse stepped sideways, frightened by a large badger leaping from the low brush. The mare reared, pawing the air in fear and throwing the rider to the ground. Peter waited for the rider to appear again, but the figure did not rise from the wet upland.

Swinging swiftly onto the bare back of the sorrel gelding he was leading, Peter rode quickly to where the inert figure lay nearly buried in the heather. Leaping from his mount, Peter approached the figure with some trepidation. A young lass lay motionless in the long grass, her auburn hair spreading across her face like a veil. Her eyes were closed, and she was perfectly still.

Kneeling beside the young rider, a trickle of fear raced through Peter's heart. Who was this girl flying across the moor as though she were pursued by the devil? What if the lass were dead?

With a steady hand, he gently lifted the bright chestnut tresses away from her face and neck. Then laying a finger against the small hollow of her throat, Peter searched for a pulse. Though a wee bit fast, her heartbeat was strong and steady.

Peter studied the face of the unconscious girl, blew out a deep breath, and sighed with relief. The lass looked vaguely familiar, but he could not put a name with the face. Even in her disheveled state, the lass was heart-stoppingly beautiful. Her face was streaked with tears and smudged with mud. Tiny freckles sprinkled the bridge of her nose and complemented her fair complexion and burnished auburn hair. A purple and yellow bruise darkened one cheek. This was not a wound from her fall in the heather, since the bruise was beginning to lighten and heal.

Suddenly, as though she knew he was watching, the eyes of the lass fluttered open, revealing expressive green eyes flecked with gold, eyes that gave Peter the impression of shaded pools in the summertime, deep and fathomless, holding secrets.

Seeing Peter kneeling above her, his dark hair falling across his broad forehead, his blue eyes questioning, she startled, looking around with some alarm, then struggled to rise.

"Easy, lass," Peter said evenly. "You had a bad fall from your horse, and you need to gain your feet slowly and carefully. You may have hurt yourself, and it would be unwise to move too quickly."

Gingerly, the girl rose to a sitting position and stretched her legs, moving them about, flexing her arms and torso.

"I don't think anything is broken," she said in a soft, melodious voice. "Had the wind knocked out of me, I believe." She looked around in the field for her horse. "A badger darted from the underbrush and frightened my horse. She threw me and . . . "

"And here you are," Peter said when she left off speaking. He stood, offering his hand. Without hesitation, she took it, her eyes fastening on his. He lifted her gently to her feet. The lass scraped at her tousled hair, pulling it away from her face and tucking it behind her ears.

If she had worn a bonnet, it was lost in her mad dash across the heather. Looking down at her gown, a tiny frown creased her brow, wrinkling her slightly upturned nose. The once lovely blue dress was torn and wet, splattered with mud and plastered to her body like a wet rag.

Peter smiled. He could not help it. She looked so funny with that cute little frown wrinkling her nose. Instantly, her eyes sparked fire, and she glared at him, daring him to comment on her outlandish appearance. Then, just as quickly, the frown faded, turning to a smile, then a laugh that sounded like water trickling over stones in the burn.

"Well, no point in being angry with you! After all, my present condition is not your fault." The lass threw back her head and laughed that musical laugh.

"It's my hair, which is outrageous at best; but now, I'm afraid it appears like an ancient bird nest, and I've chosen clothes from the rag picker's barrel."

She cocked her head to one side, looking curiously at Peter, then shifted her weight from one foot to the other, testing her ability to walk.

"I think I know you," she said, a question in her voice. "At least, you have that look about you . . . a Carmichael, perhaps?"

"Aye, a Carmichael . . . son of William, nephew to Sir John and presently . . . " he answered with a grin, "'chief stable mucker' for King James and his many blooded horses."

Again, that rippling laugh. "And do you have a name besides Chief Stable Mucker?" she queried. The rain had stopped, and she scanned the fields for her horse.

"Aye, lass, I am called Peter . . . Peter Carmichael."

He shook the bridle of his horse. The gelding was growing quickly impatient for his supper. "Whoa, Major! The lass will think you are ill-behaved."

She smiled. "I am Genevieve Lynn Chancellor from Quothquan . . . near Biggar. Everyone calls me Jenny, though. Do you remember Shieldhill Castle?"

She waited for Peter to respond, then moved to stroke the neck of the prancing gelding. "I believe we met some time ago . . . when we were much younger—mere children—but I remember. You were with your father and cousins at my father's birthday celebration at Shieldhill."

Recognition registered on Peter's face. "Oh, aye, lass, now I remember." He chuckled softly at the memory. "You wore your hair in two braids and darted among the guests like a wee fairy."

"Well, I don't look much like a wee fairy now," she said, looking down at her ruined dress and disheveled appearance. "I would like to find my horse, Peter Carmichael."

He glanced at her wet and soiled attire. "I imagine your mount has joined the other horses in the pasture near the stables. Shall I take you to your destination? I need only to turn Major into the pasture and locate your mare, and I am free to see you safely on your way."

Jenny hesitated, her eyes fastening on the distant hills. "Could you tell me exactly where I am and how to . . . to . . . " Suddenly, tears welled in her green eyes, and she turned her head away, but not before Peter saw her distress.

"Perhaps," he said gently, "you would like to go to Carmichael House and . . . and allow Sir John's maid servants to . . . to assist you . . . uh . . . repair your clothing?"

Peter's discomfiture at suggesting such a notion was apparent, but then, he was not quite certain how to approach this delicate subject without offending the lass. Genevieve Lynn Chancellor, lass of the misty morning, was obviously in need of attention. Keeping her head averted, she did not answer. Peter saw her shoulders begin to tremble.

"Hop onto Major if you can manage, lass, and we will locate your mare."

This suggestion seemed to calm Jenny. Major was not saddled, so Peter formed a makeshift stirrup by interlocking his long fingers. Placing her boot in his strong hands, she easily mounted the gelding. Peter swung effortlessly up behind her, positioned the bridle to fit around Jenny's slender form, and turned Major in the direction of the stable.

He had often ridden pillion with Katherine, but never with another lass, and certainly not with a virtual stranger. As they cantered across the rain-drenched field, Jenny's auburn tresses blew free in the wind and clung to his face and lips. Her hair smelled of wet heather and lavender. Peter scraped the fine strands of hair from his face, only to have it blow back and cling there, as though it belonged.

Sensing Peter's movement, Jenny turned, trying to see his face, but he was hidden behind her. His arms were strong and secure, and he felt warm to her chilled body. She understood then that her wildly streaming hair was nearly blinding him.

Jenny laughed, her mood changing as abruptly as the churning skies of the early morning. She gathered the long wavy hair together, tucking it beneath her woolen cloak, then faced forward again.

The strange events of the morning left Peter somewhat unsettled. He wondered if somehow, the lass knew of the telling tragedy that had fairly jerked him into manhood. He thought of Patrick, of the far-reaching effects of that terrible day, and of the ensuing unrest in Scotland. Where would he fit into this unfolding drama, and what would this red-haired Jenny think if she knew his story?

chapter 9

And ye shall seek me, and find me,
when ye shall search for me with all your heart.

Jeremiah 29:13

WHEN PETER AND JENNY ARRIVED at the stable, they dismounted and found Jenny's mare grazing contentedly with the other horses. Peter brought the reluctant mare into the stable, gave her some oats, then brushed and groomed her muddied coat.

"Here you are, lass," he said handing her the reins. "She seems to be unharmed by your wild ride across the moor. Will you follow me to Carmichael House, or would you rather . . . "

"Please," Jenny said interrupting him, "I don't wish for anyone to see me in this . . . in this condition. If I must, I will return to Shieldhill Castle . . . if you will give me directions from here, that is."

"If you must?" Have you run away then?" he asked with a humorous lilt to his voice.

"Actually," she answered with a measure of defiance, "I have. But for all my trouble, I seem to have a problem. I'm not sure I know where I'm going from here."

Peter sucked in a breath and furrowed his brow. "May I inquire why you are running away from your home?"

"Because of this," Jenny said in an uncertain voice. From the pocket of her gown, she carefully drew a small leather-bound book and opened the volume for Peter to see. Dark ink stains smeared the printed text, and some words appeared to be unreadable. The book, dampened by rain, was damaged by her fall into the heather.

"Oh, no!" she wailed. "It is ruined." Her eyes widened, and tears pooled, ready to spill over. She held up the smeared pages for Peter to see. Then suddenly, as if remembering the book was outlawed, she snatched it back, hastily replacing it in the pocket of her gown.

Peter held out his hand, palm upward, a silent plea to understand her grief over the damaged book.

"Let me see, lass. Dinna fash yourself. Perhaps it can be repaired or rewritten where it has been spoiled."

"Nay," she answered hopelessly and sat down heavily on the oat straw scattered on the stable floor. "I am being punished. I just know it!"

"Punished?"

"My father said I am a terribly wicked lass." She hesitated for a moment, then said, "If I tell you, Peter, can I trust you to keep a confidence?"

"Aye, lass, you can trust me." Peter's strong jaw tightened, his face an expression of resolute determination.

Jenny lowered her head and began to weep in earnest. She cradled it in her hands, and her silky red tresses fell forward, covering her face.

"You see, Peter," she said between sobs, "I disobeyed my father and accepted money from my governess to buy the book. Then . . . then she was dismissed, discharged from her position, because of it . . . because of me!"

A torrent of unrestrained sobs surged from Jenny's throat, her grief over the incident quite apparent. "And now . . . since father has discovered my deceit, he will make me confess to the parish priest . . . do countless hours of penance for my disobedience, perhaps spend hundreds of years in purgatory, and . . . and, Peter . . . I have no one to pray me out of that terrible place, no one to buy masses for my undying soul. I have a brother who is a monk in France, so perhaps he will pray for God to have mercy on me."

Heat rose in Peter's breast on hearing the shameful confession of the bruised and disconsolate young lass. He knelt by her side in the straw, gently drawing her trembling hands away from her face. "Jenny, Jenny lass, look at me." Hesitantly, she looked up, her eyes still streaming with tears.

"Don't take on so, lass. You have nothing to fear from me. I am not a papist and do not hold to such false teachings that have you quaking with fear. Surely, ye canna believe such tales!"

"My governess said the words of this book are God's own Holy Word . . . that I could read it for myself . . . could avoid the terrors of Hell, if I could only understand . . . and . . . and . . . " A fresh torrent of tears spilled from her eyes. "I haven't even read it through yet! I only know that our parish priest forbids us to read it . . . under penalty of the council."

"Your governess has told you the truth, Jenny. If you read God's Word for yourself, you will soon understand God's will for your life. It is not complicated but has only been hidden away so that the common people remain ignorant of what God is saying to all of mankind. And it is for everyone."

"But, Peter, you don't understand. Father may bring me before the parish priest because of this very book."

Peter looked incredulous. "Surely, your own father would not betray you for having the Holy Scriptures in your possession! You are his own lass!

"Aye, Peter, he would. He is a strong supporter of Rome and has much influence and values his political connections with the archbishops and cardinals of the Holy Mother Church. Aye, tis true, Peter. He would have me confess my disobedience to him and beg our priest for mercy. If I agreed to that, I think he would forgive me."

Peter's face grew unusually severe, and his wide mouth stretched in a hard line. "God's Word is for everyone to read, not just the hierarchy of papal Rome," he said through clenched teeth. "Until recently, it has been hidden from the Scottish people; but since it was translated into our own English language, it is our right and privilege to read it for ourselves. The chains that bound it to the altars of the local parishes have been broken."

"But, Peter, what should I do? I heard much from my governess about the coming Reformation and wanted to understand for myself, but there is father . . . "

"Have you any sympathy among your relatives?" Peter asked.

"Nay, they are of the same mind as Father. I can trust no one."

"But you were going somewhere when you fell from your mount," Peter reasoned. "Where did you plan to go?"

"Oh, I don't know where I was going, just getting away from Shieldhill Castle, from my father. He is so angry with me, and . . . and I am afraid of him, Peter, especially when he is angry. He . . . he . . . "

Her voice grew soft and trailed off into silence. Jenny turned away from Peter's intense gaze, frightened of the anger she saw in his face.

"Jenny, answer me this; did he strike you? I notice the bruise on your face, and it is not from a recent fall from your horse. Did your father dare to . . . " Peter could hardly ask the question. "Did he cause that bruise?"

Jenny looked down; shame written on her features. "Aye, he struck me . . . many times over . . . for having the book. And I suppose I deserved it . . . I am such a disobedient lass, he says. But Peter . . . I just had to know; I had to understand for myself. I didn't mean to be defiant or to deceive him, but there was no other way!" She lowered her head again, cradling it in her arms.

Peter's body tensed with anger at her confession. He rose to his feet, so angry he could not speak. After a few moments, he said, "Come, Jenny, let me take you to Carmichael House and see that you are cared for. It is only a short ride from here."

Jenny rose from her seat, grabbing hold of Peter's shirt to detain him. "Please, Peter," she implored, "wait. This may not be wise. Perhaps your father . . . your uncle . . . will they go to my father, maybe give my name for an inquest?"

Endeavoring valiantly to hide his anger that necessitated such a question, Peter spoke to the lass in a reassuring tone.

"Nay, lass. No inquest . . . there will be no inquiry. Do you understand? Sir John is the soul of caution. He will not betray your confidence. Fear not."

"My Scripture book," Jenny said fishing it from her pocket. "Will you keep it for me?"

Without hesitation, Peter opened his hand, palm upward, and Jenny placed the small book in his outstretched hand.

"I told you," Peter said, "you have nothing to fear. But if it makes you feel better, I will keep the outlawed missive for you." He shook his head, a slight grin curving his lips.

"Tis not funny, Peter. I hear they are searching the parish for any who may have this book. I am afraid, and I don't want to lose it so if you will keep it for me."

Peter sighed. "Vera well. I will hide it for you in a safe place at Carmichael. Aye, lass, I will take the fall for you if I'm caught." He laughed then and placed the book in the pocket of his tunic.

"You are very chivalrous, sir," Jenny said wiping away the last vestige of tears. "Let us go then."

They mounted their horses and trotted leisurely down the widening glen to where Carmichael House lay hidden among the towering trees. Peter had chosen a shorter path through several acres of woodland now carpeted with a profusion of colorful bluebells. After the morning rain, the sun streamed through the trees, dazzling the mist-soaked bluebells in brilliant shades of blues and greens.

A slight breeze blew from the west, and the forest floor seemed to sway in an ancient woodland dance, appearing as though the earth itself was breathing.

Jenny reined her mare to a stop, observing the blue-tinged meadow swaying in rhythm to the gently blowing breeze. She dropped the reins and threw her arms wide, laughing her pleasure at the floral display so delightful to watch. Peter smiled, holding back his horse to wonder at the auburn-haired lass.

How could this disheveled tear-stained lass of the misty morning feel such joy, sorrow, pleasure and despair . . . all in the same hour? He would remember this day, the mystery of changeable womanhood that baffles even the strongest of men.

When the two young people arrived at Carmichael House, Peter took Jenny to the kitchen entrance and asked Auntie Coira, the pleasant and amiable housekeeper, to look after Jenny's needs. If the housekeeper were surprised, she hid it well; and with a few clucks of comforting and nonsensical words she used for the wee folk, she took Jenny off to Katherine's old room to bathe and find some suitable clothing.

Peter found Sir John in the east wing, looking over some documents that were spread haphazardly across the expansive mahogany desk. When Peter knocked quietly on the half-open door, Sir John looked up in surprise. Customarily, he did not consult with Peter during the weekday—unless, of course, there was a problem at the stables—and William usually dealt with issues concerning the horses.

"Morning, lad," Sir John said in way of greeting. He leaned back in his chair, folding his arms behind his head and entwining his fingers, giving Peter an appraising look. "If ye are looking for your da', he rode with his clansmen to the southern borders of Carmichael early this morning. He'll be back by evening."

"Well, Uncle, I would see both of you, but it is yourself I wish to speak to. Everything is fine in the stables," he assured his uncle. "I have another matter."

Sir John leaned forward in his chair, resting his brawny arms on the polished surface of the desk. "Say on, Peter, and will ye please have a seat, lad? Ye make me nervous twitching about like that."

Chapter 10

Misty fogs so long concealing, all the hills of mingled night.

Evening Light Songs

SEATING HIMSELF ON A CHAIR near his uncle, Peter began his story. "It is like this, Uncle. While tending the horses this morning, a lass came riding rapidly through the heather, lost her seat, and took quite a tumble. When she didn't rise, I went to help her." Peter ran his fingers through his dark hair, pausing in his narrative.

"Go on, Peter," Sir John prompted.

"In brief, Uncle, the lass has run away . . . run from her father's house at Shieldhill Castle. You know the place—the hamlet of Quothquan, just northwest of Biggar."

Sir John raised his bushy eyebrows. "Och, well, the lass must be a Chancellor then."

"Aye, Uncle, she is Edward Chancellor's lass."

"So, what does the lass say to this?" queried Sir John. "She must have a good reason to run away from her father, from her home. Aye?"

"Let me explain, Uncle. Her name is Jenny, short for Genevieve. She secretly managed to obtain a copy of Tyndale's translation of the New Testament from her governess, desiring to read and understand God's Word for herself. She did this without her father's knowledge. One day, he discovered Jenny reading the Testament. When Jenny confessed to obtaining the Testament from her governess, he was furious. He forbade Jenny to read or even have the Testament in her possession."

Sir John slowly shook his head at Peter's account. "Did Chancellor report the governess?"

"From what I understand, he sacked her, and she left. Jenny begged him not to report the incident." The air in the study seemed to grow warm with tension. Peter rose from his chair, too agitated to sit still.

"When Jenny refused to give the Testament to her father," Peter continued, "he struck her, Uncle, many times over—his own daughter! Then he threatened her with excommunication from the Holy Mother Church. Rather than be chastened further, Jenny hid in some outbuildings for several days and then fled from Shieldhill Castle with her horse."

Sir John's features remained impassive; but his eyes gathered sadness, and he spoke with a measure of chagrin in his husky voice.

"Fortunately for the governess, Chancellor didn't report this." He propped his head wearily on both hands and spoke in a tired voice. "I know the Chancellors—not well, but they do have strong political ties to Rome; royalists they be."

Peter nodded. "Aye, tis true, according to the lass. Her governess sent a message saying she would go to England since she has family there."

"And where is this troubled lass now, Peter?"

"I brought her here, Uncle. Auntie Coira is looking after her. She was quite . . . well, not at all presentable after her fall. I encouraged her to speak with you, and perhaps you could give her some direction."

A long pause ensued before Sir John spoke again. "Ye know, Peter, she canna stay here at Carmichael. If we are found to harbor a runaway—especially one who has broken the law—buying a copy of the forbidden English Bible, well, lad, our good name can only go so far."

"But we have influence, Uncle, and the king—"

"Stop, lad. Listen to me now," interrupted Sir John, raising a hand, gesturing for his nephew to hold his tongue.

"King James will only be lenient as long as Katherine . . . as long as . . . as she is with him." The pain over losing Katherine to the young King James as one of his mistresses was still too raw, like an open wound to the old war chief, too painful to hear.

"But, Uncle, must we send her away? Where would she go? She left Shieldhill Castle with nothing but the clothes on her back!" Peter's agitation was palpable. How could Sir John send the lass, so young, frightened, and alone, away from the protection of Carmichael House to fend for herself?

Understanding Peter's distress all too well, Sir John said, "Let me speak with the lass first; then we shall see what must be done."

Peter turned to leave, his displeasure filling the tense and silent space between uncle and nephew.

"Aye, lad," Sir John said to Peter's retreating figure, "do not think me harsh and unfeeling. Foremost in my duties as chief of our clan is to protect our people, to insure a future for the lands of Carmichael . . . for our clan. I dare not jeopardize our own safety by offering a safe haven for a 'rebellious papist,' as this lass would surely be considered."

Peter turned to face his uncle. "But you are in sympathy with those who are calling for reformation, Uncle. You and Da', you both have studied the Scriptures many times over. You understand the corruption of power, the many abuses of the papal system."

Sir John studied his nephew's face, seeing the passion of youth written across the broad slope of his brow and reflected in the strong set of his jaw. He understood Peter's desire to right the wrong, knowing that his nephew had seen firsthand what happens to those who spoke against Rome.

"It is not yet time, Peter. But be assured, the time will come. Until then, we must wait on God, be 'wise as serpents and harmless as doves.' That is what the Scripture teaches us, and that is what I am endeavoring to do. If we allow our passions to rule us, we can lose all that we have—our homes, our lands, our way of life. We must exercise great caution when dealing with such complex matters."

"That philosophy did not save Patrick, did it, Uncle?" A burning heat rose in Peter's chest, and his tone was harsh and unforgiving. Memories of Patrick, painful and vivid, flashed before his eyes to mock him once again.

Sir John rose from the old tapestry chair and placed both hands on his hips. His very presence was commanding, strong and war-like, and he would not allow a rebuke from his inexperienced nephew to go unchallenged. He glared at Peter with penetrating eyes, a sharp reprimand at the ready. From his years as a clan chief and veteran soldier, he fixed his attention on Peter.

"That is exactly why age makes a better advisor, Peter. Your attitude is impatient and misguided, and ye judge the matter on one bad experience. Cool heads are needed, Peter, not impulsive and inexperienced youth. Passion is indeed necessary to move us forward, but it does not always think and act responsibly. I have fought many battles in my life, many wars, but never have they been won by passion alone."

The old clan chief softened, removing his hands from his hips. "Remember this, my son, ye must maintain your wits at all times. How do you think our clan has survived these many centuries?"

The warning was unmistakable, and Peter felt the rebuke to the bottom of his boots. He slowly sucked in a deep breath, not answering his uncle's query.

Furrowing his brows, Sir John said, "I will tell ye then, although I believe ye have heard it many times before from your da'. Ye know already, from the earliest times when this valley was only a raw wilderness, that we kept our homes and lands by feudal conquest. It was not simply by swinging a sword, but by understanding the difference between hasty and thoughtless action and choosing rather to act with carefulness and discretion and not allowing greed for power and reputation to become more important than what is best for our people. Do you understand what I am saying, lad?"

Peter nodded, thoroughly chastened for his emotional outburst a few moments earlier. He knew his uncle to be a strong leader, wise and prudent in all matters, but even so, he did not want to see this young lass forced to return to her father, who would beat her into submission.

"I . . . I'm sorry, Uncle," Peter said with a measure of remorse. "I have spoken unwisely, as you assume, and have spoken in haste. I meant no disrespect to you or your counsel. Truly. I merely wished for the lass to avoid any further abuse at the hands of her father."

Sir John nodded, acknowledging Peter's apology and his concern for the welfare of the thoughtless young lass. Then, Sir John posed another question.

"Do ye know this lass?"

Turning to face his uncle again, Peter said, "I believe I met her at Shieldhill Castle when we were only bairns; but nay, I do not know her. Just came upon her this morning when she fell from her mount, but, Uncle . . . "

Sir John raised one hand as he often did when he wished for silence. He came near to Peter then, and laying a weighty hand on Peter's shoulder, he said, "Dinna fash yourself over the lass. It is not for ye to take this upon yourself to resolve. We shall see about it. Send the lass to me when she is ready to speak."

Peter felt the genuine warmth in his uncle's voice and nodded, smiling slightly. He left the study to search for Jenny in the west wing of Carmichael House. After Coira had seen to Jenny's needs, she seated her in the ladies' parlor to wait for Peter's return. Jenny wore one of Katherine's gowns and looked quite presentable with her wild, reddish hair neatly brushed into place.

Coira swept through the doorway, passing Peter as she went. She leaned close to Peter's ear, whispering her parting comment. "The child has been beaten, Peter." Her eyes filled with tears. "Bruises all over her body. None of my business, but I dinna kin . . . who would beat the bairn so harshly."

"I know, Coira," Peter said, pressing her hand. The housekeeper returned to her work, wiping her eyes.

When Jenny saw Peter enter the room, she jumped to her feet, twisting her hands together in a nervous gesture.

"Peter," she breathed, "I am ready now . . . to speak with Sir John . . . if you will go with me. Auntie Coira gave me this lovely gown to wear . . . said it was your cousins . . . and . . . "

Suddenly, she left off speaking to look at Peter, his head slightly cocked as though to listen.

"I'm babbling," Jenny admitted. "I do that when I'm nervous or frightened. I must confess, I am rather afraid to meet your uncle. I hear that he is rather austere and quite intimidating."

Peter made a sweeping motion with his hand toward the wide hallway, ushering Jenny from the room. "Not so, lass. He is not as austere as his countenance suggests, nor is he as gruff as he is made out to be. In fact, Sir John is a kind and caring laird to his people, a just and honorable man. You have nothing to fear."

They traversed the hallway to the east wing, and Peter knocked softly on the solid oak door of Sir John's study.

"Enter," came the voice from within.

Gently pushing Jenny in front of him, the two companions entered the ancient room. It was clearly a man's domain, smelling of beeswax, old leather, and lingering wood smoke. Books, parchments, letters, and an assortment of old maps were scattered about on two large tables.

Mounted on the walls were leather-covered targes, swords, and armor, all manner of weaponry. This was a soldier's study, if it could be called that. It silently spoke of battles won and lost, a memorial to a lifetime of struggle and conflict.

Sir John rose to his feet in deference to the young lady, then moved around his desk to stand before Jenny, his large frame and erect bearing causing Jenny's knees to weaken. How could she explain to this clan chieftain and laird that she was rebelling against her father's wishes? He would think she was young and foolish. She felt like bolting from the room.

"Uncle . . . Sir John," Peter said hesitatingly, "this is Jenny Chancellor of Shieldhill Castle, at Quothquan, near Biggar. She will speak with you now." Peter sent his uncle a pleading look as though to say, *Be gentle.*

Taking Jenny's hand in his own, Sir John felt the lass tremble at his touch. He understood—the lass feared him beyond reason. He would be careful of her tattered emotions. Bowing, he kissed the top of her fingers. The youth and bearing of the lass reminded him of his own daughter, and memories of her happy childhood days tugged at his heart. How he missed his fair-haired Katherine!

Turning to Peter, Sir John said, "Thank you, Peter. Ye may leave us now. I will speak with . . . your friend." He motioned Jenny to a chair and seated himself behind the desk, propping his elbows and steepling his strong fingers.

"Peter tells me ye have run away from your father's house at Shieldhill Castle," Sir John began, "and brought ye here to Carmichael House after ye fell from your mount. I am pleased to see ye appear unharmed."

"Yes, sir, I am quite uninjured, just a little bruised."

Unconsciously, Jenny touched the slightly swollen place on her face where the bruise had discolored her lightly freckled cheek. The injury had not gone unnoticed by Sir John, and he inwardly seethed with anger. For a father to strike his own lass in the face seemed to Sir John a heinous crime. He hid his burning outrage from the lass so not to frighten her.

"I have met your father on occasion over the years—socially, not as a soldier, but as another landowner with a voice. And in our troubled times, landowners wield some influence in the Clyde

Valley." He paused for a long moment, watching the trembling lass seated before him. With a note of compassion in his voice, he asked, "Have ye any plans?"

Jenny twisted her hands in her lap. "I have no plans, sir. I only wished to get away and be . . . be free. I'm sure Peter explained my reasons for leaving Shieldhill Castle and . . ."

Before the lass could continue further, Sir John wanted her to understand one thing. "Ye must return to your father's house," he said. "Although I would not mind having a lass about Carmichael House to cheer this old soldier—as did me Katherine—but nay, ye canna stay, must not stay."

Jenny's face dropped, and her lips quivered; but she gathered her strength to listen to the counsel of the clan chief.

"The clans in the valley must be cautious, ye understand—the inquest. We cannot harbor runaways and jeopardize our own safety and that of our people. Your father is a devout papist and not one who is tolerant of the Reformation. He is also a man of influence." Sir John paused. "I'm truly sorry, lass."

Jenny hung her head, then lifted it again, looking intently at Sir John, a determined light rising in her green eyes. "Then I will leave you in peace, Sir John, but I cannot return to my father's house. He . . . he punishes me when I disobey him."

Jenny's lips trembled, and tears rose to her eyes. "My crime was in obtaining a Testament without his knowledge, but it wouldn't have mattered. He would never allow me to have one. I only wish to know the truth, to read the translation of God's Word, to understand for myself. Is that so wrong? Can you explain why this is such unusual thinking, sir?"

Sir John rose from his seat and walked to a tall, stained glass window with a collage on the upper level depicting an arm clutching a broken spear. The window overlooked a central courtyard. Spring flowers and kitchen herbs bloomed in profusion, adding vibrant color and subtle fragrance to the lands at Carmichael. After a moment, he turned to Jenny, his eyes filled with an unspeakable sorrow.

"Let me tell ye a story, lass; then, perhaps, ye will understand the price for running away. Ye and others like ye must learn how to avoid the terrors that are coming to our land."

Drawing a deep breath, Sir John returned to the seat behind his desk. "Peter was a young lad when he acted as groom for Sir Patrick Hamilton's horses. He and another lad traveled with Sir Patrick, learning the trade of the horse master. One day, he hoped to work with his da' as Master of the Royal Stables, a coveted position. He often stayed with the horses the king kept at Linlithgow."

Jenny raised her eyebrows in question. She didn't know much about Peter, only that he had rescued her, had been kind and caring, was sympathetic to her plight; but as to his background, she had little knowledge.

Continuing his narrative, Sir John said. "Peter was about fifteen, the other lad sixteen, when Patrick was summoned for enquiry at St. Andrews. He was tried by Cardinal Beaton and other church leaders for heresy—for accepting false doctrine, the council said. Patrick—a noble, young Reformer—was preaching and teaching the simple principles of Scripture, taken from the original Greek and Hebrew, which cancelled many of the edicts of Rome, principles that were in direct opposition with the man-made laws used to impose fear and control." Sir John's face wore a look of infinite sadness.

"At this present time," he continued, "the papal religion is a ruling political system; and sad to say, it is filled with greed and corruption and doctrines that hold the people in ignorance and fear—definitely not the Church that Jesus built, the one we read of in Scripture."

At his words, Jenny looked distressed, her features revealing a mixture of hope and fear.

"Och, lass, I know this is too much to take in, but I want you to remember I am giving you facts, not opinions. Will you remember this? It is imperative that you do."

"Aye, sir, I will remember."

Sir John cleared his throat, finding it difficult to relate this tragic story to this young girl, but he felt she needed to know the seriousness of the situation, of her leaving Shieldhill Castle with the Testament in her possession. He sighed heavily, then continued. "Peter accompanied Patrick to St. Andrews to care for his horses and to offer assistance to Sir Patrick during the inquest. He had no idea that events would turn as they did."

"I am not afraid to hear of those events," Jenny said. "Do continue."

"Well," Sir John said rubbing his temple, "he and the other stable lad were summoned by the archbishop to swear in a written statement that Patrick was teaching that a person could gain Heaven by faith in Jesus Christ alone, not by works, nor a mediator such as a priest or the Holy Mother Mary, neither by adhering to a religious system."

A cool breeze wafted through an open window, filling the room with smells of springtime, of new life and second chances. He hesitated, hearing the bleating of the newly born lambs, remembering that another season was bringing new challenges to the Valley of the Clyde and new opportunities for the Reformation.

"The lads signed the statement," Sir John said as he turned from the window, "believing this to be truth, not realizing their statement, along with other false witnesses, would be used to condemn Patrick as a heretic. Patrick was found guilty of heresy and sentenced to death, to burn at the stake; and since Peter and the other lad were signed witnesses, they were made to watch the execution."

Jenny's eyes grew wide, and she bent forward as though she had been kicked in the stomach. "How cruel," she cried in distress. "Why would they be made to watch? They were just young lads at the time, signed papers or not."

Sir John shrugged his shoulders and looked away. "Perhaps to bring fear upon the people of the border regions. And to make an example of those who resist the authority of Rome and teach against the corruption of the papal system."

"What a wretched torment for Peter, and so unfair, to be tricked by the papists, then made to watch the execution."

"Aye, it was that," agreed Sir John. "The lad does still have nightmares, and it has been several years. No marvel. Even a seasoned warrior has recurring dreams about those he kills in battle, even in a fair contest."

A quiet gasp escaped Jenny's lips, and she kept her eyes averted, not wanting Sir John to see the tears that gathered there.

"It took six hours for Patrick to die," said Sir John. He poured a tumbler of water from a pitcher on a side table and offered it to Jenny, but she waved it away. She would not be able to swallow as much as a sip of water. Her throat had tightened, and she felt a heaviness in her chest on hearing the description of Peter's involvement in Sir Patrick's death sentence.

"Those in charge of the fires couldn't keep the flames burning . . . so cold and damp was the wood . . . had to be stoked . . . over and over again," continued Sir John. "But in spite of it all, Patrick was brave unto the end—never wavered, never lost his faith as his tormentors had hoped."

Once again, Sir John urged Jenny to take the tumbler of water, noticing how pale her countenance had grown. She took it this time and drank the cool liquid slowly, trying to grasp the magnitude of Sir John's account. "Were you present at the execution?"

"Aye, I was there, lass." He drew in a gravelly breath, his voice growing low and raspy. "After it was over, many were challenged by Patrick's bravery and his faith, and believed that truly 'the just shall live by faith,' not by works, nor the teachings and traditions of man. Still, the actual execution is what I see when thinking of this innocent young man."

Sir John raised his head, fixing his gaze on the green-eyed lass seated before him—so young and naïve she was, yet so daring and courageous in her own stubborn way. A flame burned in her spirit, a desire strong enough to drive her from her home in search of truth. He could not help but admire her tenacity. A faint smile curved his lips, and his blue eyes reflected understanding.

"Of course, the execution of Patrick Hamilton gave rise to further inquests and more burnings," Sir John explained.

"I understand, Sir John. It would be difficult for anyone to assist me without inviting suspicion. I have been sheltered from news of . . . of these executions and burnings. And, of course, my father is a devout papist, as you have said, and a strong advocate of the Holy

Mother Church. I have a brother who is a monk at Mont Saint Michel's Abbey, and my father is very proud of that."

"I see," said Sir John, "your father has more to consider than a runaway daughter. However, if ye wish to read the Testament—to understand the Scriptures—we must think of a way to accomplish this, a way that will enable ye to read the translation without disobeying your father's wishes."

"But, Sir John, I have already disobeyed, fled from my father; and no doubt he has formed a search to bring me back."

"Aye," Sir John agreed, "no doubt he has. I have thought of that since ye arrived at Carmichael House."

"Then, what shall I do?"

Clearing his throat, Sir John said, "I will take ye to Shieldhill Castle meself and give the Testament back to your father. Ye must apologize for your rash behavior and submit yourself to your father again."

"What!" Astonishment was written on Jenny's face. "How can this accomplish anything? Indeed, it will only make matters worse. How will I ever discover the truth of the Scripture? No disrespect, Sir John, but this is not a good plan for me."

From deep inside of Sir John's broad chest, what seemed like a low growl rolled up from his throat. His steely blue eyes were bright with concern for this impetuous young girl. He studied her countenance for a brief moment, mindful of her sincerity, but knowing all too well that she was ignorant of the danger she had put herself in. He wanted this lass of the misty morning to trust him. He decided to put a question to her.

"Do ye think ye can trust me, lass?"

"I . . . I want to, Sir John. My heart is always seeking for someone who will listen to me, who will believe that I am sincere in my pursuit of the truth."

"Och, lass, being a father of a spirited lass meself, I know there be a soft corner in a father's heart . . . aye, tis so, and a tearful apology will always find the tender place a man has for his wee lass, for she will always be that to him. Dinna kin that wee lassies hold the wand that charms our lives?"

"I'm afraid, Sir John, that I, his defiant daughter, will certainly hold no charms for him. You do not know my father well. He is not easily influenced by what I have to say, neither does he listen to me, nor is he not opposed to physical punishment for disobedience."

Like a fleeting shadow, Sir John's smile appeared for a moment, then slipped away. "We shall see, lass. We shall see."

Chapter 11

*For there is one God, and one mediator between God and men,
the man Christ Jesus.*

1 Timothy 2:5

FROM WHERE HE STOOD ON the terraced entrance to Shieldhill Castle, Edward Chancellor watched the party approaching on horseback, trotting easily up the gentle rise. He strained his eyes to see what was forthcoming, wondering if the riders brought news of his daughter's whereabouts.

After he had chastened the foolish lass for secretly obtaining a Bible Testament without his permission, Jenny had vanished. Not that he would have allowed her to keep the forbidden book, but even so, his heart felt heavy over Jenny's disappearance, knowing his harsh action was the cause of her sudden flight.

His anger had boiled over, and he had thrashed her soundly. Now he was sorry and felt remorse for his unbridled temper. Nevertheless, he would not apologize. After all, he was the ultimate authority over his daughter. To repent over his actions would make him appear weak and irresolute. He would not do that.

* * *

A little distance from the keep, Sir John Carmichael, third of Carmichael, reined his mount to a stop. He raised a hand for Jenny to wait behind him. His keen eyes swept over the immediate area, noting every place where an enemy might hide, any hindrance to a speedy retreat, all the time counting the number of servants milling about the grounds. From his years as a soldier, this caution was second nature to him.

As Sir John approached the keep, chickens and geese scattered before the thundering hoofs of Sebastian, squawking loudly and complaining their annoyance at being disturbed. The dogs of Shieldhill Castle came running, whining and yipping at the approaching rider. They were all too eager to greet the stranger, hoping their frantic efforts of alerting the guard would bring a reward.

Sir John was in full regalia, his war sword slung across his shoulder, his dirk in his belt. Now in his late forties, he was a striking figure, his age only complementing his formidable character, a demeanor that spoke of unwavering courage, of legendary skill in battle. He emulated wisdom and authority, a sagacity that comes from years of experience.

He fully intended to face Edward Chancellor as an ambassador, ready to plead the cause for peace, for the safe return of his willful daughter. Sensing all was well, he signaled to Jenny and moved forward, appraising the imposing edifice silhouetted against the blue-gray sky. Early morning had been wrapped in mist, a cloak of gray obscuring the road, but the sun had broken through the dense fog, bringing to light the dew-drenched earth and outlining Shieldhill Castle in bright relief.

Sebastian, Sir John's war horse, named for his strength and prowess, made his own impressive entry. Whinnying loudly, the mount shook his massive head, his thick mane flying, prancing in place as though to announce his arrival. He ignored the dogs nipping at his hoofs, too proud to give them consideration. The huge gelding was a dappled white and gray with a white mane and long, flowing tail. Sebastian rather resembled Sir John himself—large, graying, magnificent, and formidable in appearance.

Since the end of the tenth century, Shieldhill Castle was the Chancellor family seat. The three-story fortified structure was situated on a gentle rise and was constructed of native sandstone with an expansive square tower that served as the main entrance to the keep. Above the door, a large engraved stone lintel with the Chancellor coat of arms was boldly displayed, and to the left was a shield with the family crest and engraved initials of former Chancellor ancestors. Thus, the name Shieldhill Castle became the Chancellor family seat.

The family emigrated from France during the Norman Conquests and were influential papists and sympathizers of the Roman decrees. Their loyalties to Rome and the papal hierarchy had granted the family favors and influence in the Clyde Valley.

Reining his mount to a stop several yards from where Edward Chancellor waited, Sir John held up one hand as a sign of peace. He remained in the saddle, gesturing for Jenny to come forward.

"Good day to ye, Chancellor," Sir John began without waiting for acknowledgment. "As ye can see, I have escorted your daughter safely home to Shieldhill Castle. I request an audience with ye concerning the lass."

"So . . . Chief Carmichael," Chancellor answered with obvious interest, "is it ye who shelters my defiant lass, and me not knowing her whereabouts?" He crossed his arms across his chest, waiting for Sir John to respond.

Dismounting, Sir John handed the reins of his horse to a servant and approached Edward Chancellor, his eyes dark with determination. "Before ye draw conclusions and assign blame to anyone, ye need to hear me out. If me intentions were to shelter the lass indefinitely, why would I bring her back to ye now?"

Chancellor dropped his arms, relaxing his posture. He was a tall man, slender-boned and wiry with dark eyes and a swarthy, olive complexion. His nose bore a prominent bridge, but he was considered to be handsome with regular aquiline features. Unlike Chancellor, his deceased wife, however, had been fair-haired and blue-eyed.

He looked past Sir John to where Jenny sat astride her horse a few paces behind him, trembling with fear, her green eyes pleading. Seeing her apparent anxiety and distress, her father spoke more gently. Since the death of his wife, he had little consideration for the babe who had taken her life.

"Jenny . . . lass . . . " His eyes grew bright, revealing some inner emotion. "Ye did wrong, aye, but ye have done right to come home." His voice softened. "I was too harsh with ye, I'll admit that. I am your da'. I canna bear for ye to leave your home, your family."

Sir John studied the man standing before him, observing Jenny's father with keen eyes, testing the sincerity of his words. He knew the Chancellors were long-standing papists and royalists, seated in the shires of the Clyde Valley near Biggar, but his dealings with the family were limited to community occasions when their paths crossed with other neighboring clans. But never had he known Edward Chancellor on a personal level. The Chancellors claimed no clan alliance and remained aloof from clan gatherings or political meetings. Their only known loyalties were to the Holy Mother Church and the local parish.

"Go on inside and find the new governess, lass," Chancellor said, speaking to Jenny. "She is a Sassenach, but better an English governess than a Scottish deceiver like the last one. Go on now."

Jenny cast a doubtful look at Sir John, then dismounted her mare; and handing the reins to a waiting stable lad, she disappeared inside the castle.

"Come, Carmichael. We can talk in the library and be done with this," Chancellor said in a frigid tone. A servant swung open the heavy doors, and they passed into the ornately carved double doorway.

The two men entered the large central hall, their boots echoing on the flagstones. Near the end of the hallway, a rather small, medieval, arched doorway opened into a well-appointed library with a heavily beamed ceiling and massive stone fireplace. Sir John had to duck his head as he entered the room. A small fire burned on the stone hearth.

Two ornately carved wooden chairs with high backs stood on either side of the fireplace. Chancellor motioned for Sir John to be seated. Removing his war sword, Sir John sat in the chair opposite Chancellor, his eyes meeting those of the unsmiling man before him.

"So," Chancellor began, "would ye like a drink—some ale, perhaps?" Despite disputes or disagreements among inhabitants of the Clyde Valley, it was a well-known fact of the resident Scots that hospitality was always offered, even if a duel followed.

"Nay, I must be on my way shortly and only wish to speak with ye concerning your daughter, Genevieve."

Pouring himself a drink from a decanter on a nearby table, Chancellor said, "Proceed then; say on."

"It seems that Jenny was riding her horse across Carmichael lands, evidently unaware of where she was going. Her horse threw her into the heather. My nephew found the lass and brought her to Carmichael House. We cared for Jenny until we decided what to do . . . about her circumstance."

"Circumstance? And what circumstance might that be? She is just a disobedient child with foolish notions. Since Jenny is my lass, there is nothing to suggest any other option than to bring her home—where she belongs, I might add." He curled his fingers tightly around the tankard.

"Let us be honest, Chancellor." Sir John looked directly into his unblinking eyes. His hand rested lightly on the dirk attached to his belt. "Your lass was punished beyond reason for merely desiring to understand God's will for herself."

"What I do with me own lass is none of your affair," Chancellor said with contempt. He poured another drink, then gulped down a hefty portion of the strong brew. To emphasize his words, he pointed his cup at Sir John, daring him to object to his reasoning or his authority over his daughter.

"Physical abuse of an innocent lass such as your Genevieve is my concern—any father's concern," Sir John insisted.

"I thank ye to mind your own business and stay out of mine," he said glaringly. "I have long connections with the great Mother Church, and ye know yourself that anyone found with that heretical Testament in their possession will be brought before the Privy Council. Of course," he added, fixing a steely eye on Sir John with a measure of chagrin, "I would not betray me own daughter. I am merely protecting her. She doesn't realize what she is doing."

"You protect your daughter by beating her?" Sir John leaned forward in his chair. "Let me say this, Chancellor: if ye beat Jenny again and she leaves Shieldhill Castle, I will do all in me power to keep her from your *fatherly* protection, as ye suggest. Furthermore, if ye report the lass to the parish for reading the English Bible, ye will lose her to a greater punishment than ye can imagine. I warn ye now," Sir John said in a commanding voice fitting his fierce, soldierly manner, "let the lass alone and permit her to find her own way to God."

"Find her own way? Ha!" Chancellor gazed at Sir John for a long moment and then stared into his tankard. "Man cannot find his own way except the holy Mother Mary and her priests intercedes for us. Ye know this . . . or perhaps ye are one of those who defy the decrees of Rome and the Pope?"

Sir John's steely blue eyes bore into Chancellor's determined face, daring him to present an accusation.

"It has been rumored among the clans of the lowlands that ye are sympathetic with those who subvert the doctrines of the Church and that your brother is hiding those who are summoned for inquest. Is this true, Chief Carmichael?"

"I am not here to dispute those allegations," said Sir John. "But as your neighbor and fellow Scot, I will say this: when people have been ill-taught about God's Divine Word, God, in His mercy, will not allow them to gaze too long upon Moloch, the god men have set up to represent Him. Indeed, His Spirit will endeavor to turn their minds from that image, which men call God, and guide them into the right way—that of true religion—so they might have a correct vision of Who the Father truly is."

"That is heresy talk!" Chancellor bellowed. His face grew red with anger, and he shook his head as though to shake off Sir John's words.

"If ye studied the Scriptures for yourself," Sir John reasoned, "ye would know that what I say is the truth. I would venture to say that ye have never read an English translation of the Bible or even the approved Vulgate, since it is chained to the desk of your priest. So, how can ye know what is certain?"

"And would you dare to compare the Holy Mother Church, who guides our souls, to your own understanding? And how dare ye compare my religious views to a false god? Never heard of any Moloch. Your boldness to speak such sacrilege will find you on a heretic's pyre," Chancellor thundered.

"Do ye think I shall find meself on trial?" queried Sir John. "If ye withhold the right for Jenny to seek truth, ye are sacrificing her to a false god, a crime punishable by death, according to Leviticus. Anyone who gives any of his children to Moloch shall surely be put to death. It would appear, Chancellor, ye might find yourself on a pyre, too."

"How dare ye suggest I would sacrifice me own daughter!"

"What are ye afraid of, Chancellor? Are your beliefs so steeped in tradition that ye have never inquired into God's Word for yourself? Are ye totally dependent upon a religious system to get your one and only soul to Heaven? Stop gazing at Moloch, Chancellor, and open your eyes."

"Ye are a traitor to the Church and to Scotland, and furthermore, ye have no right to lecture me about me lass or me beliefs. Just who do ye think ye are to dare question me about anything?"

"Have a care, Chancellor. Ye may have influence with Rome, but there is a higher Authority over us all," said Sir John pointing upward.

"A father who will beat his lass until she is black with bruises cannot be respected of anyone, papist or Scot. See that ye remember that."

"I will do as I please with me own lass and keep me own counsel," bellowed the offended father.

"It is only natural and right for the lass to seek the truth for herself," said Sir John. "How can you refuse this simple request? What is there to fear? Are your beliefs so weak, your convictions so feeble, that ye fear she will discover the truth, that the Romish Church needs radical reforms?"

"Ye may leave now," Chancellor said in a fury. He pointed toward the door, his meaning unmistakable. Rising from his seat, he knocked the chair over backward, then slammed his cup on the table, sloshing the contents from the tankard. Deep creases lined his forehead, and he spoke through his teeth in barely concealed anger.

"I said, *go*!" Chancellor thundered.

Sir John rose slowly and slung his war sword over his shoulder. "Aye, Chancellor, I will take me leave. I am a believer in radical reform of the Church; but even so, as ye are a devout papist, I wish ye no ill. Ye are a neighbor and fellow Scot, but let me warn ye. Notify the council of Jenny's intention, and ye will bring a world of hurt on yourself and lose your lass in the process."

"Och! Who are ye to proclaim what will happen in my own dooryard, Chief Carmichael?"

Sir John paused; his demeanor untroubled. "Know this, then: those of us living in the Clyde Valley must have a care for all who live here. We want peace, and we must work together for freedom of spirit and for reconciliation. If ye are honest, ye know the Church needs reform. We must work to see that happen. Let us not be enemies."

At Sir John's parting words, Chancellor appeared to soften. His rigid form relaxed, and he cleared his throat. "Aye," he said grudgingly, "let us not be enemies. We both know the ravages of war, of conflict. And in most cases, there are no real victors."

"Just so, Chancellor, just so. A fire may burn for the heretics, but a fiery sword awaits those who would fight the truth. Let it not be so with us."

Sir John nodded and took his leave, ducking his head through the low doorway. Edward Chancellor remained in the library, not willing to escort his uninvited guest to the castle entrance, although hospitality demanded that he do so. He was in no mood to feel neighborly, and Sir John Carmichael's words had unsettled him.

He snatched up the Testament Sir John had returned to him, gaping at the small volume as though it would bite him. The parish priest had warned his parishioners that even holding the forbidden book would burn their fingers. Turning the book over in his hands several times, he felt no burning, nor did he feel any condemnation. Of course, he must destroy the volume or give it over to the parish priest. But if he did that, he might be questioned as to how he had obtained the Testament.

He thought of his two sons, one a soldier living in Rome, and the younger son, a monk, living on the remote island monastery of Mont Saint Michel on the northern coast of France. He could not help but wonder what might happen to his sons, his family. How could he stop the widening gulf that threatened to divide those loyal to the Holy Mother Church or those who sought reform?

Jenny slipped out of the castle and into the dooryard, glancing nervously over her shoulder as Sir John mounted his war horse. She ran to detain him, clutching the bridle of his prancing mount.

"Sir John, Sir John!" Jenny called. "What will father do? I beg you—do not leave without telling me if he is still angry."

"I gave him much to think about, lass, but dinna fash yourself over much. He may be angry, but I don't believe he will betray ye. I doubt he will give ye leave to have the Scriptures in your possession again. There will be another way."

"But how will that happen? I see no way of obeying my father and having a Testament so I might study the Scriptures for myself."

Sir John leaned over the saddle and grasped the trembling hand that held so tightly onto the bridle.

"Listen to me, lass, and take heed to me words. Be kind to your father. He is a troubled man. Submit yourself to him as a daughter should. If he raises his hand to ye again, send word to me, but I don't believe he will. If ye sincerely desire to understand the Scriptures, pray and ask God to make a way for ye."

"I will try, sir, but I am so afraid."

Compassion and concern filled Sir John's heart for the young lass who looked up at him with such intense longing. "Fear not, little one, for it is the Father's good pleasure to give ye the Kingdom."

Sir John Carmichael, laird of the barony named for his family, turned his mount with easy grace and cantered down the narrow lane toward his own ancient lands near the River Clyde. He turned once at the end of the private drive leading to Shieldhill Castle, waving a hand as Sebastian reared, whinnying a goodbye; then rider and horse disappeared among the towering trees sheltering the carriage road.

Chapter 12

A good name is rather to be chosen than great riches,
and loving favour rather than silver and gold.

Proverbs 22:1

THE SMELL OF DRYING LEAVES and decaying foliage permeated the chilly air sweeping through the Southern Uplands, foretelling the end of summer and the arrival of autumn. Home-brewed cider simmered over low peat fires, the spicy aroma drifting on the morning breeze. From the chimneys of neighboring crofters, a smoky blue haze curled upward, the predictable harbinger of an approaching winter.

From the high meadows at Carmichael, shepherds herded fat, grass-fed sheep to lower pastures to shelter during the winter months. The disgruntled sheep, bells tinkling, bleated noisily while the high-pitched barking of sheepdogs echoed throughout the glens.

The Carmichael estate lands and their inhabitants were preparing for winter. In the Highlands of Scotland, winter could be harsh and unforgiving; but in the Southern Uplands, weather was milder. And due to their proximity to Glasgow and the trading merchants, residents were able to obtain necessities to carry them through the difficulties of the cold winter season.

With the arrival of winter, border raiders and frustrated clansmen relaxed their hostilities, waiting for another spring to resume their ongoing disputes. Likewise, the smoldering fires of the continuing Protestant Reformation took a back bench at the Privy Council. Everyone living in the Lowlands of Scotland waited, hoping for peace and safety.

At Linlithgow Palace, Katherine Carmichael prepared to leave the royal suite of rooms the king had so lavishly furnished for her. In a private moment during a court supper honoring her, she pleaded with James to allow her to make a short visit to her country home to see her father.

She missed him terribly and wished to surprise him for his birthday. Since agreeing to the court summons to become the mistress of young King James V of Scotland, this would be her first visit to Carmichael House. To her delight, King James had agreed.

The king strolled leisurely with Katherine to the stable yard, where the royal guard waited, ready to escort her to Carmichael. She wore a deep green velvet cloak with a hood that protected her from the wind and weather, also giving her a semblance of privacy. Her boots were of the finest leather, a gift from the king. Indeed, her entire wardrobe had been chosen by the king himself. James delighted in bestowing her with gifts and presents.

Drawing Katherine aside for a private word, King James said in a confidential tone, "Give my high regards to your father, Katherine. You know how much I esteem Sir John's loyalty to Scotland and to the royal house of Stewart."

"Aye, Jamie, I will convey your regards."

Dropping her eyes, Katherine looked away from the intense dark eyes of her intimate consort. Her compliance to the king's request had been more difficult than she had imagined. Although she was very fond of Jamie, she did not love him like a soulmate. Jamie was a kind lover; but when he called for her, she did not look forward to their meetings.

James Stewart had grown into a handsome and charismatic young man with thick auburn hair and intense, dark, heavy-lidded eyes, which gave him a drowsy appearance, a feature inherited from his Tudor ancestors. He possessed the strong aquiline features of his Tudor mother, Margaret, who was sister to Henry VIII of England.

Katherine's gentle influence encouraged a genuine concern for the welfare of the common people and for his Scottish subjects. He and Katherine often traveled disguised as simple farmers, endeavoring to see firsthand the needs of the people. Consequently, when this was made known to his subjects, he became a much-loved sovereign.

But how long would it be, Katherine wondered, until the king commanded fealty—full devotion to his reign as monarch of Scotland and a dutiful observance to the dictates of the Holy Mother Church, to which he remained faithful?

James naturally assumed that Katherine's loyalties would lie with him and his compliance to Rome. But a shadow of mistrust and speculation had fallen over the court in recent months as papal officials at St. Andrews sent messengers to the king, reminding him of his duty to the Mother Church as reigning monarch of Scotland.

As did most kingdoms of Europe, James V bowed to the authority of papal decrees. Recently, however, pressure was brought to bear on the royal house of Stewart to reaffirm their allegiance to papal hierarchy and the judgments of the Roman Church. Monarchs and kings alike were expected to bring their subjects into compliance and to forewarn the unruly who openly joined ranks with the Reformers or spoke ill against papal dictates that inquest awaited all heretics.

"And shall I tell my father all the news—that the house at Crawfordjohn will soon be finished?"

After Katherine's arrival at Linlithgow Palace, the king had ordered construction to begin on a trysting place where he and Katherine might meet unobserved by his other mistresses—and of course, from the reigning queen—whenever negotiations for an acceptable political alliance was finalized.

The plan was to remove Katherine from view of the governing queen, a tolerated practice for kings. In choosing Crawfordjohn, James considered Katherine's strong attachment to her family and clan.

"Aye, Jamie, I have no doubt he will be well-pleased."

He paused as though to reaffirm his words. "I'm certain, Katherine, having you closer to Carmichael will be a comfort for him."

The king hesitated for a brief moment, then laughed softly, his eyes narrowing, whispering into her ear, "Ye know what they say about Crawfordjohn . . . out of the world and into Crawfordjohn."

She smiled warily; his meaning unmistakable. For many years, the lands surrounding Crawfordjohn with its tiny hamlet was controlled by Clan Douglas but was now a royal domain. It was an out-of-the-way parish, situated in the upper ward of Lanarkshire, bounded on the south by the River Glengonner and on the east by the River Clyde—a perfect place for their clandestine meetings.

The king had chosen this secluded setting for this very reason, but also because it was close to Carmichael. When he chose a queen,

Katherine would reside there, close to her old home but still available as his mistress should he choose to come to her.

The arrangement sickened Katherine. She desperately hoped the king would find a love match that excluded her altogether. She kept her eyes downcast, but her thoughts spun about her head like so many autumn leaves, whirling and twirling to the earth.

"You will see Peter during your stay, I assume," Jamie said. "Let him know that I am pleased with his work with the royal mounts. He has managed admirably in his father's absence, has prospered under his excellent supervision."

The king idly played with the tassels on Katherine's cloak.

"Aye, indeed." She lifted her eyes to the king, her lips curving into a smile. "My uncle William is a good instructor. He taught me to ride when I was just a wee lass."

"If Peter remains faithful . . . " the young monarch said, pausing in his narrative, a wisp of doubt hovering over his words. Then the moment quickly vanished. "If he remains loyal to the house of Stewart, that is, well, his ascendency to a higher position is certain."

The remark contained a subtle message, and the gentle reminder was not lost on Katherine. Weighing her words carefully, she said, "You know, Jamie, Peter does not wish to ascend in the royal household. He is content in his present situation. He loves everything to do with horses, loves caring for them, training them. He is a natural equestrian. That's what he aspires to, not to gain opportunity or favor."

The king shrugged his shoulders, then rested a gentle hand against Katherine's soft cheek. "Perhaps not now, sweet love, but there will come a time . . . a time when royal privilege has its advantage. Don't discount the blessing of the king's favor."

Smiling shyly, Katherine made no further comment but held out her hand to her intimate companion, a signal that she was ready to go. He brushed a light kiss on her slender fingers, his eyes studying her intently.

Although he had known Katherine before he had summoned her as his mistress, James V of Scotland wondered if he could fully trust her. He was aware of her family's sympathetic views toward the expanding Reformation; but at the end of the day, he was positive Sir John Carmichael would not decamp to join the Reformers in their fatal cause.

Climbing onto the carriage block, Katherine mounted her chestnut mare, a gift from the king. The steed pranced in place, eager to be off. Katherine tugged on her riding gloves and gathered up the reins.

"Farewell, dear Jamie," she said pleasantly. "I shall return before the snow flies."

"See that ye do, sweet lass." He reached for her gloved hand, pressing it gently.

"Farewell for now, Katherine, and be safe. I eagerly await your return to Linlithgow. Perhaps when you return, we will spend some weeks at Stirling. It is so beautiful there in winter."

Stepping back a few paces and lifting his hand, he said, "The court will miss you."

"And I, the court," replied Katherine. The king's court had been welcoming to her from the very beginning, and she had made friends she felt understood her dilemma. It was no easy task to please court and king; but God had favored her, and she was now a favorite at court.

The captain of the royal guard gave the signal, then turned his horse toward the south, heading the procession with Katherine in the midst of the company. As the mounted horsemen journeyed through the lingering mist of early morning, Katherine puzzled over the king's words of farewell—*the court will miss you*. He had not said that he would miss her, only that the royal courtiers residing at Linlithgow Palace would miss her presence. No doubt he would seek out another mistress in her absence.

If the young king truly knew her heart—her desire to spare family and her own cherished clansmen from papal retribution—how would he respond? What would he do if she refused to confirm her loyalty to his authority, to his administration, and the Holy Mother Church? Even more frightening, what would he do if he discovered that her real purpose in agreeing to become his mistress was to influence him to spare her people?

The royal guard escorting Katherine traveled along the narrow country road leading to the picturesque river valley that stretched from the Southern Uplands to the west coast, where the great meandering river emptied into the Firth of Clyde.

For Katherine, the ride to Carmichael was always so enjoyable, especially in autumn. She loved the changing colors, the sights and smells that greeted her along the roadside. The crisp autumn air was pungent with the spicy aroma of wild crab apples, the tiny fruit still clinging to the branches as if afraid to let go.

And today, the sky wore a garment of downy clouds, like so many long gray feathers moving about, dusting the sky clean. Wild geese flew over the heads of the company, squawking and honking directions to their fellows. How Katherine wished she could fly away with them to some warm, quiet loch, undisturbed by human disparities.

She had missed the lush, green glens of home during the summer season, the small lochs where she fished for trout on lazy summer days.

She missed her father and her home and longed for her own rooms in the familiar old house resting quietly in the glen. And how she longed to climb to the moss-covered stone kirk that seemed to beckon for her return. The Church stood on a high hill, silhouetted against a magnificent skyline overlooking the ancient lands of Carmichael.

Living at Linlithgow Palace was an experience of monumental change for the daughter of a celebrated country soldier. After spending months surrounded by the majesty of King James V and his courtiers, Katherine was weary of the showiness, the ceremony, and customs of courtly life.

Although only a mistress to the king, Katherine was held in high regard by the court. This adoration would continue until the king chose a queen; and sometimes, if well-favored by the king and court, a mistress often continued a romantic relationship with the king, even after he chose a queen. The politics of the day dictated the choice of a queen, and the queen must be of the royal bloodline. Marriages between the royals were typically a political alliance to further peace and ensure the financial welfare of the kingdom. Some of these diplomatically arranged marriages were in name only, the bride and groom total strangers until the wedding day. Their sole duty was to produce an heir of the royal bloodline. At least, Katherine often thought, she knew Jamie Stewart and was at least as fond of the young king as he was of her.

When at length they arrived at Carmichael House, Katherine's eyes filled with hot, stinging tears. Joy and sadness welled up in her heart, and she searched for her father's dear, familiar face in the gardens surrounding the keep. Her decision to accept the coveted role as mistress to the present king had hurt him deeply, leaving a gaping hole at Carmichael and in the lives of the people she loved most.

Her one idealistic love, John Robert Somerville, had been devastated when Katherine had told him of her decision. For years, Robbie had waited, laughingly telling her that when she grew up, he would marry her. He was ten years her senior; and true to his word, he had waited, only to see Katherine give herself as mistress to the king. Now, she must tell him her secret—news he would not want to hear.

As the party approached the keep, stable lads ran quickly to assist in the arrival. Katherine had not told her father of her plans, so their sudden arrival was unexpected. Sir John's birthday was only a week away, and Katherine hoped to surprise him.

Sir John's great wolfhound, Zebulon, greeted her with slobbery kisses and joyful barking that brought the servants running. Katherine ran nimbly into the central hall, excitement coursing through every muscle. Coira, the housekeeper, threw up her hands in surprise and said, "Well, now, is it my own sweet Katherine, or am I a'dreamin'?"

She opened her sturdy arms wide, and Katherine ran into the comforting warmth of her embrace.

"Aye, Coira, indeed, it's me!" said Katherine throwing her arms around the dear old housekeeper. "I've come home, home for a wee visit! I am so happy to see your dear face once again."

Coira returned the affectionate greeting, kissing Katherine's flushed cheeks. "Your da' didn't say a word—bless me soul—or I would have prepared all your favorite dishes—indeed, lassie, I would—and made up your room, fresh and tidy-like. But now, you have gone and surprised me and me not being prepared!"

"Nay, Coira, not to worry over such trivialities. I am just so thrilled to be here again . . . at Carmichael. I wanted to surprise my dear old da'. You know his birthday is next week, and I wished to spend it with him."

"Well, now, lassie, he will be surprised, that's certain. Your da' is in his study, I believe, so go right on in and surprise him," she said, laughing merrily. "I just hope he doesn't keel over at your sudden appearance! Now, sweet bairnie, I must get back to the kitchen. We will visit later, aye?"

"Aye, indeed. I can always find him in his war room." She smiled warmly at the housekeeper. "I will go right now, so be off to your kitchen, Coira."

Carmichael's housekeeper turned to leave, then hesitated a moment longer, a troubled look crossing her soft round features. She was Irish and spoke in the melodic lilt of the Irish tongue.

"Wait a wee bit, Katherine. I just recalled that Sir John has a visitor with him; unless, of course, he has left already. Visitors come and go, and I never know. Perhaps ye might want to come to the kitchen for a wee bite first. Aye, lassie; catch up on all the goings-on at Carmichael House."

"I will only peek in to say hello, Coira. I promise not to disturb him for long. Most of Papa's visitors are known to me. I simply can't wait another minute. Oh, Coira, I have been so lonesome for him."

"I know, I know, dear lassie." The housekeeper's eyes reflected the deep sympathy she felt for the motherless girl. When Katherine left for Linlithgow to become consort for the young king, the entire household of Carmichael had felt the loss.

Without another word, Katherine skipped down the hall to her father's study on the east wing of the house. She knocked softly. A moment later, her father's deep gravelly voice answered, "Enter."

Opening the door, Katherine saw her father standing by the fireplace. She ran to him, throwing her arms around him and laughing with delight. Sir John's face wore a look of utter surprise; then he drew her into his strong arms, encircling her trembling form.

"Katherine! Where on earth did ye come from?" Sir John said, folding her in a strong embrace that left her barely able to breathe.

"Where do you think, Papa? I didn't pop out from under a toadstool! Just now arrived from Linlithgow Palace! Aren't you happy to see me?"

"Of course, of course, lass," Sir John said, releasing her from the embrace. He glanced across the room to where his guest was slowly rising to his feet.

The visitor turned to face Katherine. His expression registered shock; then his face reddened.

"Hello, Katherine. This is quite a surprise," he offered in way of greeting. There was a slight tremor in his voice as he spoke; then the visitor bowed slightly from his shoulders in deference to the presence of a lady.

Astonishment showed on Katherine's delicate features. Her father's visitor was John Robert Somerville—Robbie to his friends— the man she had loved, the man who had waited for her to grow up, the man who had said he would marry her. Katherine felt her face grow warm as their eyes met in mutual surprise.

Of all the men who often visited her father, the caller would have to be Robbie! Robbie, her own dear Robbie Somerville of Cambustian. How should she manage to escape this uncomfortable chance meeting? What must he think of her?

Sir John cleared his throat, searching for some way to ease the mounting tension in the room. Glancing from one to the other, he said, "Well, this is quite a surprise, Katherine."

He scratched his forehead, and a smile was tugging at the corners of his mouth. "Would ye like for me to send for tea, perhaps some cider? The cider apples were newly pressed this week, and I be certain that Coira has some shortbread or tea cakes at the ready."

"Oh, no, Papa. I'm sorry. I didn't mean to intrude." Katherine hesitated, looking confused. She glanced hurriedly around the room as though she were looking for a place to escape.

"Nothing for me, Sir John," Robbie said with a discernible strain in his voice. "I must take me leave now." He gathered up his riding gloves and hat laying on a table beside the chair he had vacated.

Katherine walked the few paces to where Somerville stood. Courtesy and hospitality demanded that she greet her father's guest. Robbie's hazel eyes were cool, his face inscrutable. She offered her hand, and he kissed the top of her fingers with an air of indifference.

"Aye, Robbie . . . I . . . I didn't realize . . . know that you were visiting . . . that you would be here . . . at Carmichael House, I mean." She knew she was babbling, but she couldn't get her thoughts together.

"Forgive me, Katherine. I wasn't aware that ye would be arriving from Linlithgow this day." He spoke with cool control, but a pained look touched his even features, then quickly vanished. "I will take my leave now." The uncomfortable feeling in the room was almost palpable.

Sir John raised his hand in protest. "Nay, John Robert, ye need not trouble yourself to leave. I am quite surprised as ye are. The lass never let me know she was coming. Och, lass," he said turning to Katherine, "ye should have sent word."

"I'm so sorry, Papa . . . to interrupt, that is. I simply couldn't wait to see you, and I . . . I . . . "

"No matter, Katherine," interrupted Sir John. "Robbie and I were only discussing horse breeding, a never-ending subject here at Carmichael, to be certain, and not one the ladies usually prefer. Perhaps ye and Robbie might take a turn in the gardens. No doubt, ye have much to talk about . . . and I know Robbie has much to say to ye, lassie."

Katherine understood her father perfectly; and in that moment, she wanted to be anywhere but here in her father's study. He had urged her to be plain and honest with Robbie, but she had put it off, hoping for the right time, thinking somehow that it would become easier. But that had not happened.

Chapter 13

Many waters cannot quench love,
neither can the floods drown it.

Song of Solomon 8:7

WHEN KATHERINE LEFT FOR LINLITHGOW Palace to join King James, she left without any explanation to Robbie. It was an utterly wretched, terrible thing to do, but courage had failed her. She knew Robbie would be sickened at the arrangement, that he would not understand her reasoning. Now, Sir John was forcing the issue, and there was no place to hide, no avoiding this unexpected meeting.

After the awkward, tension-filled moment, Katherine prayed desperately for the floor to open up and swallow her. If she could somehow become invisible, turn herself into a toad, anything but face Robbie without a moment's notice. She dare not defy her father in front of Robbie, and Robbie would comply as well.

Somerville glanced around the room as though to find an escape, then gathered up his gloves and hat, and breathing deeply, held out his arm to Katherine. Reluctantly, she took it, almost feeling the acute painfulness through his sleeve. His manner was polite but cool. With an accusing look at Sir John, Robbie bade him farewell.

Katherine cast a smoldering look at her father, who was doing his best to hide a smile while intently studying some papers on his desk. Her hand barely touched Robbie's woolen waistcoat, but still, she felt the familiar tenderness rise in her bosom, a tenderness born of years of watching Robbie grow into manhood, then patiently wait for her.

She had loved him but knew he could never love her again. He would despise her, wonder why she had not chosen exile, feel she had betrayed him; and truth be told, it was so. Now, she must tell him the truth and pray that he would understand and not condemn her completely.

They left the study without further discussion, continuing down the length of the hallway to exit the house through the rear double doors. The orchard gardens lay a little distance from the keep, and they walked in silence, uncomfortable with each other, with the circumstance that had created an impossible gulf that lay between them.

Once they had spent many pleasant hours in this quaint garden hidden from view of the keep, tucked away near a sheepfold. Amid the natural beauty of the landscape and the bleating of spring lambs, they had shared their dreams, planned a future.

But then, the Reformation had swept northward to Scotland like a rushing mighty wind, upsetting the long-held traditions of papal Rome. Everything had changed. Life would never be the same for those living in the Clyde Valley or in all of Scotland.

In the orchard, apples and pears weighed heavily on the trees, permeating the air with a fruity fragrance, a telling sign of harvest. Reaching for a pear on a low-hanging branch, Robbie dropped Katherine's arm as though it hurt him.

He rubbed the ripe fruit against his coat, and looking at Katherine with eyes full of pain, he posed the simple question, "Why, Katherine? How many times have I urged you to marry me quickly? The king has watched you for years. It was inevitable. He will never be loyal to one woman."

Seating herself on a stone bench underneath a gnarled old apple tree, Katherine sighed wearily. She gazed up to the heavens, now dark and ominous, and felt her heart sink lower than the gathering clouds. She prayed for words to explain, words to restore, if only in a measure, this broken relationship with the man she still loved.

Robbie deserved an answer. She must tell him everything. She had not been fair, not been honest. Her unwillingness to share her heart with him and her decision to comply with the king's summons, had cost her in many ways, but it had cost Robbie more. Now, as he posed that simple question—*Why, Katherine*—she would understand just how much she had hurt him.

Chapter 14

This poor man cried, and the Lord heard him,
and saved him out of all his troubles.

Psalm 34:6

IN THE VALLEY OF THE River Clyde, evening was approaching, stealing across the glen like a shy maiden. The gloaming settled softly over the green fields, bringing with it a mystic sense of something ethereal, as though a curtain were dropping from heaven, telling the end of another day.

The imposing edifice of Carmichael House, surrounded by tall trees and century-old stone walls, cast long purple shadows across the gardens bordering the keep.

Still, Katherine lingered in the orchard, summoning the courage to face her father, to tell him of her brief visit with Somerville. The unexpected meeting—this unplanned, tension-filled meeting prompted by her untimely appearance at Carmichael—had not gone well, to say the least.

At length, Sir John sent a servant in search of her. Some time had passed since he caught a glimpse of Robbie riding speedily away from Carmichael on his blooded horse as though pursued by devils.

Reluctantly, Katherine returned to the great hall, where the household was preparing for supper. Her face was somber, her eyes swollen, and her demeanor subdued. No one said a word, however, and supper passed agreeably enough; but tension was present as well, an unseen guest lurking about, hoping to spread depression and gloom. Alistair MacDougal, captain of the royal guard, was a guest at the table of Sir John, and the captain's amiable manner helped to ease the tension.

At length, the supper hour ended, and Sir John and Captain MacDougal excused themselves. MacDougal was a pleasant man with a deep, robust voice and a body to match. His service for the king was to lead the royal guard through all kinds of weather to various events, keeping watch over the royal household and escorting the king and his entourage throughout Scotland. The company would be returning to Linlithgow Palace at first light, and Sir John wished to learn of the young king's plans for the coming winter.

MacDougal would know if the military portion of the guard would halt activities during the coming season or perhaps be sent to other regions of Scotland to gather pertinent information on the whereabouts of supposed dissenters of the Holy Mother Church. To his great relief, Sir John learned that MacDougal had heard of no plans for the guard to leave Linlithgow, except to escort the court to their various events. He assured Sir John that any aggressive activities would cease during the winter months and that all was well at present.

When Sir John returned to the house from the long, stone guest quarters near the stables, Katherine had gone to her room with an unusually severe headache, saying the long journey from Linlithgow had worn her out. She would speak with her father in the morning.

Early the next day, Sir John rose to see the royal guard off to Linlithgow, then saddled his own mount and rode to the highest point on Kirk Hill. A heavy mist shrouded the glens below in milky white, hiding Carmichael lands from view and filling the empty spaces with ghostly like haze.

He rode Sebastian to the old stone kirk that beckoned him from an ancient time. For centuries, his people gathered in this quaint, old parish, well-hidden from the passersby or aimless wanderer.

Behind the ancient kirk, a small stone cottage stood, almost lost from view. The cottage appeared as lonely as a monk's tomb; and except for the smoke curling from the chimney, no one would think anyone was about. Father Leonardo, the old parish priest, lived there, directing his flock from this high, heavenly place.

He was growing old and knew little about the present Reformation sweeping across Europe, and for that matter, cared little when his parishioners tried to inform him of the changing times. He would smile and nod his head and go on as he always had. He was, as always, a common man.

Dismounting his steed, Sir John entered the graveyard through the wooden gate and walked to where the graves of his ancestors rested beneath the moss. A four-foot stone wall enclosed the burial ground, keeping out the red deer and other forest creatures.

The door of the cottage opened, and seeing Sir John, the old priest waved a gnarled hand and closed the door again, leaving Sir John to his solitary visit.

Finding the graves of his wife and infant sons, Sir John sat on an old stone bench, wet with dew and covered with moss and lichen. He rested his elbows on his knees, cradling his head in his hands.

"Guid day ta ye, Gwendolyn, me love," he said to the foremost stone marker that bore his wife's name. "I need to talk to ye, about many things . . . about our sweet daughter." He knew she could not hear him, but somehow, it comforted him to sit by her grave, unburdening his heart when life became too heavy for even the strongest man.

"I be a soldier—ye know that, Gwennie," he whispered huskily. "This be me life. Now, Katherine has come home, and . . . "

His voice trailed off into soundless words, words that only God or angels could hear. At length, he felt a gentle hand pressing against his shoulder. He looked up to see the old parish priest standing quietly by, his old eyes filled with compassion.

"Aye, lad," the old priest offered, "He hears ye—'tis certain He does, me son. Bottles up tears, that's certain—remembers everyone, Sir John. Dinna fash ye heart over much."

Sir John rose, knowing his old friend was not intruding on his privacy, only offering what he had to give—kind-hearted compassion. Sir John embraced the old priest of Carmichael parish, thankful that he seemed to have escaped the confusion and chaos of the present religious turmoil. This high, secluded mountain and lichen-covered cottage afforded the gentle old man a peaceful existence far from Romish dictates.

The light above the low-hanging clouds grew brighter, and Sir John bade the old priest farewell and left the quiet refuge of the ancient kirk yard, where the weathered stones glistened with dew drops, like so many tears.

Descending the crest of the hill, horse and rider were enveloped in the dense low-hanging clouds hovering just above the tree line.

Sebastian whinnied, not liking the loose footing. Sir John halted as they neared a precarious area near a steep ravine. He paused, knowing the danger of continuing without seeing the trail clearly.

As he waited, his mind reeled with a thousand thoughts of what the future days might hold for his people. Blowing and snorting his displeasure, Sebastian chafed at the delay. He tossed his head repeatedly, pawing at the rough trail beneath his hoofs. Sir John patted the muscled neck of his steed, speaking softly to calm his mount. "Aye, laddie," he said quietly, "we be home soon."

Sir John, Man of the Broken Spear, felt hot stinging tears gather in his steely blue eyes. He was unaccustomed to the strong emotion now filling his heart. After all, he taught men to persevere through battle, to refuse the rising passions that could deter them from their duty.

Yet, in this moment of vulnerability, tears spilled over his own eyes, running down his cheeks onto his beard, reminding him that he, too, was only a man and could not always obey his own stern instruction. He felt weak and powerless to stop this sudden flow of tears. Lifting his trembling arms toward the heavens, he raised a halting voice to God in a desperate prayer.

"Aye, Lord, ye know what I be hearing—Your voice ever calling—speaking to me from the clouds, from the mist . . . but I . . . I be only a whisper in the wind, Lord, a feeble candle in the mist . . . and I canna see me way."

His voice faltered, and he strained to see through the blur of salt tears. A muffled groan escaped from his throat, and his arms dropped, too weary with grief to hold them up any longer. In all the battles he faced down through the years, this was the most complicated.

There was no clear battle strategy, no secure footing in this invisible spiritual warfare. How must he proceed?

"It be dark, Lord, so vera dark in the land of me fathers." His body shook as though to shake off the disturbing thought. "I dinna kin how to guide me people—to help Katherine, me own bonny lass. We be in a quagmire of confusion, deception. I ask Ye, what can be done? Ye brought me to this place, but this be a place a soldier canna go, a war I canna fight." A vision of past battles, of swords clashing, of men falling, blood and death all around, tormented his mind.

"I have raised me sword in battle, defeated me enemies, but, Father, I canna understand this war. When I read the Holy Scriptures, I am baffled, perplexed. Unless ye lead me, O God, I will be only a trembling candle in the mist, a vera wee light in a world of darkness."

Sir John waited expectantly, but no answering Voice spoke to him out of the mist. The only sound was the soft, nickering of his war horse and the cooing of a morning dove in the distance. He felt no sense of assurance that somehow, someway, God would step down from the heavens and fix the wrongs of the world.

Mankind chose long ago to do things his own way, to disregard God's simple instruction, and the result of this disobedience had plunged the whole world into sin. But most difficult to understand was that sinful mankind seemed to prefer this willful life, so why would God listen to his desperate prayer for help?

Chapter 15

So, teach us to number our days,
that we may apply our hearts unto wisdom.

Psalm 90:12

SIR JOHN TURNED HIS MOUNT toward home, descending the steep slant with caution. Sebastian picked his way over rocky areas, where recent rains had washed away the soil, exposing the rocks beneath.

Studying the wall, Sir John halted, remembering his grandfather and father—men who had begun this wall so many years ago. The dry, stone fence stood two feet high on either side of the trail. It would continue to grow taller as the years passed, each generation adding more stone. The bothersome stone was part of the natural landscape of Scotland; but until the stone was cleared away, it was almost impossible to raise crops or navigate the countryside.

Skilled wall builders would remove the stones from the roads, creating the stone walls that dotted the countryside. The walls kept sheep and cattle from wandering and marked the boundaries of neighboring clans. *Now,* Sir John thought, *Scotland is building invisible walls, dividing our countrymen and threatening our way of life.*

When he reached Carmichael House, Katherine was in the dooryard, a basket of flowers in her hand. She looked up when she heard him approach and waved. Sir John dismounted and threw the reins to a stable lad, who took Sebastian to be groomed.

"Well, lass, ye are up early this morning," Sir John commented. He bent to kiss her cheek.

"Aye, I am that, Papa," Katherine said, using her English title for him. "Gathering the last of the flowers before frost comes. And you are up early as well. And where have you been?"

"On Kirk Hill," Sir John answered with a casual sweep of his hand. He shifted his eyes away, hoping she didn't notice his red-rimmed eyes.

"Visiting Mama and the wee lads?"

"Aye, among other things. Shall we take some breakfast?" Sir John did not want to continue this conversation.

He held out his arm, and together they passed through the double doors into the main hall and entered the dining room. Breakfast was laid out on a small hunting buffet placed against one wall. Katherine set her flower basket at one end of the buffet, then filled their trenchers with eggs, ham, fruit, and bread. Father and daughter sat facing each other at one end of the long oak table.

A fire burned brightly on the hearth in the center of the adjacent wall, dispelling the early morning chill. Katherine, who usually ate breakfast with a good appetite, toyed with her food, sneaking choice tidbits to Zebulon, Sir John's great wolfhound, who was a favorite with Katherine. The great dog, sniffing the odors of the freshly made breakfast, had followed them into the hall, hoping for some castoffs.

"I have something to tell you, Papa, and I don't think my news will please you."

Showing no concern over Katherine's statement, Sir John said, "Say on, lass." He pointed a long finger toward her trencher. "Perhaps then, ye can finish your breakfast—if ye haven't sneaked it to Zebulon first, that is." He smiled warmly, enjoying this unforeseen time together.

"Papa, I . . . I am carrying a child . . . to be born in early spring." Katherine waited for what seemed like hours for her father to respond. She worried her bottom lip and leaned forward slightly, dreading to hear any censure of her news. Long moments passed as Sir John tried to absorb the extent of what she had said.

His face remained impassive, schooled into an expressionless mask through years of self-discipline. Silence hung heavy in the room, like the unexplainable calm before the storm. The only sounds were the muffled hums and clangs of the workings in the kitchen and the swish, swish, swish of Zebulon's tail against the wood plank floor.

Placing his knife judiciously on the tabletop, Sir John breathed deeply, allowing his breath to escape in a long sigh. He had hoped this would not happen, even prayed it would not. His hopes for Katherine had not been as consort for the young king, bearing him bastard children who would forever be included with the growing number of the king's illegitimate offspring.

Words came at last, but they were tinged with disappointment and displeasure.

"I believe the king has already sired a number of bastards by his mistresses, Katherine. I suppose I shouldn't be surprised. After all, it is an inevitable part of your role as his courtesan, is it not, lass?"

Katherine's face blanched, pale as a dove's wing, and her sorrowful blue eyes filled with tears. "I'm sorry, Papa. I hoped that you would—"

"What!" Sir John interjected, not waiting for Katherine to finish. "Did ye suppose I would be pleased at the prospect of a bastard grandchild?" he asked indignantly. "Think again, Katherine. Ye are in league—or might I say in bed—with a papist and will now bear his child. Do ye truly expect me to be pleased?"

"First of all," Katherine said defensively, "I am not in league with a papist! You are speaking from your own sadness, Papa, from your solitary ride to Kirk Hill this morning, from distressing memories that disturb your thoughts. Say it is so, Papa! Say you don't blame me or wish to shame me, to make me feel undeserving of your love."

A sob broke from somewhere deep inside, and Katherine rose awkwardly from the table, sending the bench tumbling over backward.

Sir John stood as well, facing his distraught daughter now weeping in earnest. The long table was between them like an invisible wall. He knew his words had stung her. Aye, he had meant for them to sting. But on reflection, perhaps the lass was right.

For years, she had witnessed his visits to the quiet resting place where Gwendolyn lay on Kirk Hill, returning home in melancholy silence. Did the lass blame herself for her mother's death? Surely not!

He ran his fingers through his silver-black hair, then raised one hand in appeal. "Aye, lass, don't weep. Perhaps ye are right after all. I did speak from my sorrowing heart. When I ride to Kirk Hill, memories linger—but only for a time—then the sorrow passes. It be so."

"I know, Papa," Katherine said between sobs, "I was a poor substitute, an unwelcome exchange for the woman you truly loved. How I wish she had lived . . . for your sake."

Shock registered on Sir John's strong features, and he shook his head in denial. "Katherine, me own sweet lass, never, ever have I at any time thought that. Nay, lass, ye were me consolation, the joy and wonder of me old age. The news of a bairn to come by Jamie Stewart is not welcome news to me, although I know it is acceptable with the king and his court. But, Katherine, ye have not been raised so. I fear it will end any future relationship with Robbie Somerville, the one you truly love. This is what I fear. And, Katherine, I know the value of true love."

"Perhaps that is so, Papa. Since my only option was exile, I have chosen to answer the summons, and I will accept the consequence."

"Ye know, Katherine, your choice to be the king's consort will have far-reaching effects."

"But, Papa, your judgment is too harsh. It is not the fault of the babe to come. If someone is to blame, I am the one. Have you not said to me many times all events in life, good and bad, are blessings in disguise, given to us to learn from?"

"Aye, I have said that, and believe it, too. Be patient with your old da', Katherine. I be speaking from me own perspective, not from the sound ruling of a clan chief. Come to the war room with me where we can speak privately."

Katherine nodded and gathered up the remains of their breakfast on a tray, and the two walked down the hall to Sir John's private study. Placing the tray on a round table near the window, father and daughter looked long into each other's eyes, and Katherine began to weep. She went to her father, and he folded her in his arms, like he had so many times in the past.

"Oh, Papa, don't forsake me now, now when I need you so much." The tears on her cheeks were hot and bitter, and Sir John wiped them away with a brawny hand.

"There, there, lass, forgive me. I spoke in frustration, from a thousand devilish emotions I canna understand meself. Aye, your da' will love and support ye always, dinna fear."

"Papa," Katherine said, wiping her eyes, "did you speak to Robbie?"

"Nay, lass, he rode away quickly without saying a fare-thee-well. He . . . he left in haste, not speaking to the groom or to anyone. Did ye tell him about the bairn?"

"I could not tell him, Papa. I lost my courage and . . . and . . . I had not planned to see him, you know." Katherine lowered her eyes. "He asked me why . . . why I complied with the summons to court. I suppose he felt I should leave Scotland, go into exile. I tried to explain, but I don't believe he understood. And even if he did, my reasons were not acceptable with him. They never will be, Papa."

"I will be the first to admit, the situation be hard to understand," agreed Sir John, "especially when ye and Robbie were . . . were so close. Our people felt ye would marry someday soon, as did the Somervilles."

"I know, oh, I know. I hear rumors among the servants at Linlithgow about the Somervilles, that they may be in danger, that they are sympathizers with the Reformation movement. Have you heard of this, Papa? Is Robbie in danger?"

Sir John sat down in his accustomed chair near the hearth, where a blazing fire crackled on the stones. Katherine sat across from him, twisting her hands in her lap, her eyes expectant.

"The Somervilles are in no more danger than we are at this point. I spoke with Lady Somerville not long ago. She . . . well, lass, she is greatly disappointed in your decision, and she says Robbie is saddened and perplexed. Ye have been like a daughter to her, so often were ye under her protection when at Camwath."

"I feel so wretched, Papa, about what the Somervilles think of me. I hear talk at court of their name connected with heresy, and my heart fails me for fear."

"Scotland is not as rigorous in their search for heretics as are other countries of influence," Sir John said, "countries that have revolted against the edicts of Rome."

"How so, Papa?"

"Since our country seems so insignificant and our landscape undesirable by many, the Scottish clergy have cultivated a spirit of independence and, so far, pay only requisite honor to papal bulls and their war against heretics. Patrick Hamilton was the exception because he was so well-known, but this lull in aggressive action against the Reformation will not last. It is just slower in coming."

"But, Papa, it is already in progress."

"Aye, but our inaccessible landscape, our powerful clan chiefs and nobles, even our Scottish cultural boundaries all make it far more difficult to hunt protestors. But indeed, the pursuit for heretics will become more vigorous. Even now, James Beaton, our Glasgow bishop, is pushing for stronger measures against dissenters."

"But the Douglas was acquitted."

"Aye, he was, but for the reasons I just mentioned. As ye know, Clan Douglas be a powerful clan, have considerable influence in the Southern Uplands. The Scottish clergy have limited power. The charge against the Douglas would not serve to further better relations between clergy of Scotland and our people.

"Do you feel the papal clergy fear a clan uprising?" Katherine queried.

"Aye, they do. Most have kin among the clans, and they do not soon forget the peasant uprising in England that devastated the hierarchy of that time. The chiefs, the nobles—well, lass, they be unwilling to surrender their people for a papal tribunal, nor will they stand still while their people are burned at the stake. Nay, they will not! They will resist."

"I believe, Papa, I have convinced Jamie to listen to our clan chiefs, to allow them a voice in this coming spiritual awakening. He is under great pressure from Rome to root out all heretics, and he is loath to go against the Pope; but I urged him to let his inquest rest for the winter, and he readily agreed. I cannot accept that my choice has been in vain. I *must* not believe that."

Sir John's eyes gathered sadness. Reaching for Katherine's hand, he looked into her child-like face, so grief-stricken, and said, "The young king knows how strong the feudal ties between clan chiefs and their vassals be, Katherine. Those ancient ties, those blood-soaked 'life and death' bonds that have bound us together for centuries. That kind of bond—well lassie—it be not easily broken."

"Oh, aye, and our ties, Papa, as father and daughter, they are not easily broken either. Is it not so, dear Papa?" Her eyes filled with sudden tears, and her chin quivered with some deep emotion. "I am so sorry. I have disappointed you."

Sir John walked leisurely to the table where Katherine had placed the breakfast tray. Pouring a tall decanter of newly pressed cider, he said, "It is done, lass. Aye . . . it is done." He sighed deeply. "We must move forward and pray God will have mercy and will keep us safe—our family and our home— and, of course, we must maintain a respectable relationship with the Somervilles . . . with Robbie."

"It makes me unhappy to think I have hurt the ones I love, Papa." Katherine rose to her feet and rested a small hand on her father's sword arm. "I feel my choice was right . . . even though it has brought grief and suffering to those I love."

"Aye, the way we live our life is a choice, lass. This is your life, and indeed, this has been your decision." He took a long drink of his cider. "I have cautioned ye to choose wisely, conscientiously, to choose honestly. Whatever ye do, Katherine, be satisfied with your decision. Dinna fash yourself for what ye have willingly chosen."

"I wish I'd had the courage to live the life others expected of me, but dear Papa, I must be true to myself, true to the way I feel God is leading me. I must be free to choose. Please understand, Papa."

Sir John nodded. "Oh, aye. I do understand ye, to be sure, lass. In these troubled times, it takes more courage to go against what others assume is the best way, meself included. This be true enough, but remember this, God does not send us into a compromising situation to accomplish His will, even though we may feel we are doing the right thing. Aye, ye are free to choose, but you must also face the consequences of your decision."

Katherine lifted her head, her voice strong and resolute. "I know, Papa, but the only choice I had was to leave my homeland as an exile; but believe this—I have considered the consequence for my decision. I suppose some will react with scorn when they learn about the bairn, but, Papa, if you cannot love me wee one soon to come, it will break my heart."

Laying his tankard aside, Sir John closed the space between them, encircling Katherine with his strong arms. He leaned his chin on the top of her golden head, rocking her gently as he did when she was a wee lass. The sweet perfume of lavender was about her person, and at this very moment, she seemed so like his own Gwendolyn, Katherine's sweet mother.

"I was vera angry when ye first told me of your plan to go with the young king, but your da' will love ye always. And, Katherine, we canna govern the reactions of others, nay, we cannot. 'Tis futile—a useless and tiresome endeavor." Sir John glanced at the weapons hanging across the paneled wall, then looked at his only daughter with serious intent.

"At the end of the day," Sir John continued, waving his hand in a circle, "when ye lay a'dyin', what others think is a long way from your mind. I've seen many men die—aye, lassies, too—they be not thinking of what others thought of them, what others did. They be thinking, did I live true to me purpose in this life; did I do all to honor God and me fellowman? That is what they be thinking, Katherine."

"And I may come home whenever I wish, Papa?"

"Aye, lass, of course ye may. Ye kin, Katherine, the king will soon choose a queen, and most likely, he will not keep all his mistresses—except for his favorites, shameful as it is." Sir John's hands tightened into fists. "I will speak to King James V meself, ask for a release for you . . . from his service, that is."

Katherine's face heated, and she turned her head away, considering how it would feel to be returned to Carmichael, turned out by the king, the man who once loved her. If she remained at Linlithgow, she would do what she could to persuade the king until the day he chose a queen.

Sir John released Katherine from his grasp and strode purposely to the window, pulling back the drapery to peer onto the approach to the keep. Glancing at Katherine, he said, "I wish for ye and the bairn to return to Carmichael. Perhaps, Somerville will soften in his opinion of the matter; perhaps, he will wait. He loves ye more than ye can know."

"I cannot feel he still loves me after all this time, Papa. Not only that, my babe will only be with me until an age when he is called to court to live with all the other . . . " Katherine swallowed the lump rising in her throat, the words sounding so harsh to her own ears. " . . . children fathered by the king."

"It is the way the royal bastards have been brought up, Katherine. The king will give them some position of authority when they are of age, bastards though they be. They can never inherit the throne, as ye well know."

"I understand that, Papa. I was praying that I would remain barren, so I would never have to face that part of this . . . agreement with the king, but it is not to be so. If I return to Carmichael, you will learn to love my babe; then he will go to court. It is too much to even think about."

The sound of horse's hoofs beat a rapid cadence on the hard-packed earthen road, approaching the western side of the keep. Katherine joined her father at the window, straining her eyes to see who was coming.

"Someone comes, Papa; but before you leave, I want you to know, you are wrong about Robbie waiting for me, redeeming me from the king's service. He is too hurt to even speak reason to me. Please, Papa, do not speak to Robbie of me. I would not wish for him to feel, well, because of our long family relationship, that he owes our family— clan loyalties, you know. He will not have me—after the king, that is." Katherine dropped her head, waiting for her father's response.

Sir John studied his trembling daughter for a long moment, his heart melting with fatherly compassion. "Vera well, lass, it will be as ye wish. I will say naught to Robbie, but I will speak to the king to release ye when the time comes."

Katherine nodded an assent, and Sir John turned to the window again to see two riders dismounting their horses in the dooryard. It was Peter and Jenny Chancellor, the lass who came to Carmichael to study Scriptures. Their horses were weary and lathered from the long ride, but the faces of the two young people standing in the dooryard were bright with the joy and energy of youth.

"Ah . . . " Sir John said with a twinkle in his eye, "that appears to be Peter and Jenny." He laughed softly as he pulled aside the drapery. "And if I be seeing things correctly with me auld eyes, I be a'sayin' they be studying more than the sacred Scriptures!"

Chapter 16

Crawfordjohn, Scotland

1532-1538

Be not wise in thine own eyes:
Fear the LORD, and depart from evil.

Proverbs 3:7

YOUNG KING JAMES V OF Scotland took a great interest in Crawfordjohn, spending much time at Boghouse, his manor house which he made comfortable for Katherine, his childhood friend and consort. James V loved the fine hunting the area afforded in which he took great pleasure pursuing. But uppermost in his interest was the gold and silver mines he claimed as royal properties. On occasion, James served his guests sweets containing newly minted coins made from the profitable mines in the area. The sweets were served on golden chargers designed by local craftsmen that used the same high-quality gold taken from area mines.

Young James V, his father's only legitimate living son, was crowned king while still an infant. He grew up guided and governed by the regents of Scotland acting in his stead. James enjoyed every royal privilege, except for those years he was held prisoner by his stepfather, Archibald Douglas, sixth Earl of Angus.

For this dangerous region of Scotland, James garrisoned Crawford Castle, located on the north bank of the River Clyde in South Lanarkshire. It stood as guardian to the southernmost part of the barony of Carmichael. A captain was appointed to watch the approach of travelers and Border Reivers from the south, a necessary security for the upper Clyde Valley.

And, as with so many kings, both Scottish and English, having a mistress or keeping many mistresses had, for centuries, been a royal prerogative. Many of these consorts produced a number of illegitimate children; and if the mother was of the nobility, the offspring were given royal privilege.

At age sixteen, the young king took the throne and began to reign as monarch of Scotland. His father, James IV, had several mistresses and seven bastard children; thus, James V came by this excess honestly. Although many of his mistresses were the daughters of Scottish nobles, the bastard children were not able to inherit the throne because of their ignoble birth. In 1529, at age seventeen, James V produced his first illegitimate son, another James Stewart, by his mistress, Elizabeth Shaw.

While Katherine was in confinement at Crawfordjohn, the place James had chosen for her confinement, Margaret Erskine, second mistress to James, gave birth to a son, another James Stewart. On hearing this news, Katherine felt a deep sense of regret over her present agreement with Jamie Stewart, King of Scots. She longed for the comfort of her old home and those familiar, loving arms of her dear old housekeeper, Coira, a servant who had been like a mother to her. And there was Lady Somerville, graciously offering her guidance and protecting Katherine from the advances of the sixteen-year-old king of Scotland.

Now at Crawfordjohn, awaiting the birth of Katherine's first child, King James was summoned to Katherine's bed chamber. He turned to the midwife, his eyes questioning.

"The lass is vera young," the midwife said. She schooled her face, endeavoring to wipe out any hint of disapproval, although she felt a great deal of anger toward the king while assisting Katherine during the long night of intense struggle. No smile accompanied her words.

"Aye, me lord," said the midwife with a sympathetic glance toward Katherine, who lay still as death in the great bed chosen for her confinement. "The lassie be barely eighteen, ye know, and . . . she be a slight one for her years, not guid for bearing hefty-like bairns."

During the early morning, when dawn was creeping across the horizon, Katherine gave birth to a healthy son with broad shoulders and fair hair. Before Katherine could see her son, the infant was promptly whisked away to be bathed and fed by a waiting wet nurse.

"Aye, she is young," James affirmed. "Will she recover?"

His face grew pale as he glimpsed his latest consort lying in the great bed, looking for all the world as though she were dead. He swallowed a great lump rising in his throat. His other two sons had been born with relative ease, but he could see that Katherine had endured a terrible struggle to birth this son. He had been waiting all night for news of the birth of his third child by his young mistress, a favorite at court and with him.

This experienced and skilled midwife now preparing to exit the room had assisted in the birth of his first two sons by Elizabeth Shaw and Margaret Erskine. She did not answer his question at once but shrugged her shoulders as she gathered a bundle of sheets to be taken to the laundry, a frown creasing her broad forehead. She kept her eyes averted, plumping the pillows around Katherine's head.

"I dinna kin, me lord. In God's hands now. Were a hard birthing, and the lass lost considerable blood. I suggest," she said casting a sidelong look at the young father, "that ye stay wi' the lassie but a wee minute. It was a terrible birthing. She needs rest."

Bobbing a slight curtsy and pressing her lips together in a hard, straight line lest she say more and incur the king's disapproval, she exited Katherine's bed chamber, closing the door quietly behind her.

James approached the ornately carved mahogany bed where Katherine lay pale and still. Her eyes were closed as though she slept, and her golden hair streamed across the pillows, damp with perspiration.

A thousand unwelcome thoughts crossed the young king's mind. What if Katherine died? He recalled Sir John's accusing finger pointing at him like the tip of a dagger when he had insisted on Katherine's presence at court as his mistress. With stinging words, Sir John had reminded him that His Royal Highness had no need of his Katherine, since he already had two mistresses and two bastard sons by said women, and that should be sufficient for any king.

Sir John showed no fear of the king whom he had known since a bairn. He didn't seem to realize that he, the king of Scotland, could grant favor to the families of his mistresses; or perhaps Sir John didn't care for such special treatment. After all, he was a war-hardened, old soldier who needed nothing from the king.

The king approached the bed where Katherine lay against the pillows, pale as a winter morning. He took her hand, cool to the touch, and sat next to her in a soft, velvet chair brought in for his comfort. Katherine slowly turned her head to look at him, tears rising in her troubled blue eyes.

"Katherine, me love, we have a son . . . a healthy son." She opened her eyes but did not respond. "Does this not please you?" he continued with a measure of irritation.

She turned her head away, not wanting the king to see her distress. James did not wait for an answer. He wanted to rid this chamber of the melancholy he felt hovering over his young mistress. Although weakened by her long ordeal, she should show some feeling of pleasure at the birth of a son.

"What shall we name the lad? The midwife tells me he is robust and bonny, bound to be a king's son."

"A king's son? Aye, Jamie," she answered weakly, "a bastard son—not an heir—a son who will spend his life with the knowledge of his ignoble birth. Does this please you, Jamie?"

"Is that what these tears are all about? Ye know, Katherine, the lad will be well provided for and have favors and positions above all common lads, bastard though he may be. And Katherine, ye knew what complying with my summons would be expected. Do not fret, my love. It is common enough among kings. Now, what shall we name the lad?"

Katherine's eyes searched his. According to the days of her birthing, Jamie had been with Margaret at the same time he had called for her. She felt too weak to even think. Her free hand fluttered nervously on the comforter. "Common enough among kings? So then, did Margaret Erskine name your son born to her this week?"

The king appeared uncomfortable with the question and shifted in his chair, a look of annoyance crossing his aquiline features. "She named him James—for me, of course—but what does that matter? This is our son, yours and mine. We shall name him as we wish."

Katherine sighed, but tried to appear more cheerful. She was so weakened from the birthing that it was difficult to think coherently. "I would like to name him John."

"John?" The king frowned. "Surely ye are not thinking of John Robert of Cambusnethan, your, ah, neighbor in North Lanarkshire."

At his words, a faint smile tugged at the corners of Katherine's mouth. Referring to their neighbors to the north made her want to laugh, but the effort would be too great. Jamie spent most of his fifteenth year at the Somerville estate, hunting with Robbie and pursuing her and other willing lasses, so he knew very well of her affection for Robbie. The young king's rise to power at age sixteen seemed to make him conveniently forget his days as a youth who took pleasure in his own peers.

"You mean Robbie of Cowthally Castle, don't you, Jamie? Nay, not John Robert, but for my father, Sir John."

"Oh, aye." He seemed relieved, then added, "I don't suppose Sir John will welcome the idea of his grandson, his bastard grandson, being named after the ancient and noble name of Carmichael."

"Perhaps not, but I wish to name him John just the same . . . if you have no objection."

"I have no objection. There are already two lads named for me. It does get a bit confusing with both mothers wishing to name their sons after their father. I understand, of course. John it shall be then.

Now, I must go. Your midwife warned me not to linger. But he shall be John Stewart, not John Carmichael."

He bent to kiss her forehead, noting the paleness of her skin and the dark circles beneath her eyes. He softened, his eyes reflecting compassion for his young mistress. "I shall come again tomorrow. Be well, my Katherine."

"Wait, Jamie. I wish to know of Henry Forest. I heard the servants talking. They were saying he was brought from prison and will be burned for heresy. Is this true?"

"Why do you think of such dark thoughts at such a time? You have a wee bairn to think of, so don't trouble your mind with what is happening at St. Andrews."

"But, Jamie, you promised to speak to the Privy Council, to beg for clemency."

"I did try to speak to the head churchmen, but Rome says Forest has been detained in prison long enough. He will be tried and executed, Katherine. I cannot overrule their decision. Now, I must go. Do not speak to me of this again. I forbid it."

Regardless of the king's warning, Katherine continued. "But his only crime was having the Word of God in his possession," Katherine persisted. "How can he be executed for that? It is wrong, Jamie. You know it is. He is from Linlithgow, a neighbor, and a man of God!"

"Beware, Katherine. See that you speak of your sympathies to no one else. My protection goes only so far when it comes to Church matters. I cannot interfere. Besides, it was the heretic Tyndale's translation in his possession, the English one, that which was forbidden."

She reached feebly for his hand and said in a quiet voice, "It is a sad day when a king cannot rule his own country. Cardinal Beaton is more powerful than his own king. Indeed, that is a sorry state of affairs."

"Ye assume too much, Katherine. Do not take advantage of my affection for you. I am still the king, but I am also a devout supporter of the Holy Mother Church, who is over us all."

"I know you are in a difficult place, dear Jamie. I am pleading for humanity in general, simply a matter of right and wrong for all mankind. It is wrong to execute a man for stating what you have said yourself—that the Church needs reforms. What I say is not treasonous to king and country."

"That will do, Katherine!" His anger was apparent.

She sighed in resignation. "When will the execution take place?"

"In a week or so, I am sure. Now, think of your sweet babe and be happy, me love."

Katherine turned away, her eyes filling with tears.

With a heavy sigh of frustration, the weary young king left the bed chamber, his heart heavy with the weight of the past few days resting solidly on his shoulders. Pressure from his council was urging him to take a wife, a political alliance that would benefit his country. If it weren't for Katherine, he would have complied with the council's request, but he cared deeply for the lass, loved her; and if she were only of royal blood, he would have taken her to wife long ago.

Then there were the endless missives sent from the Pope and his bishops, urging him to declare all in Scotland who opposed the Holy Mother Church in word and deed be brought to trial as heretics. *The Church certainly needed reforms*, James thought. He had said so himself but at what cost to his kingdom? To deny the clerical corruption was no longer possible, as by this point in time, the

Catholic Church in Scotland had become infamous across Europe for corruption and immorality.

If he did not comply with the papal dictates constantly urging him to take more aggressive action on the heretics, he would surely incur the anger of the Pope; but if he hesitated in submitting to the wishes of Rome, then he would certainly please his uncle, King Henry VIII of England, who had broken away from the Holy Mother Church to establish the Church of England. Henry sent his ambassadors to Scotland to talk with James, hoping to find an ally in his nephew for his bold move to break from the rule of Rome.

As he left Katherine's bed chamber for his own quarters, he knew he must continue firm in his decision to oppose the Reformation movement in Scotland. He recently wrote to Pope Clement VII reassuring him that he remained a devout follower of the Church of Rome. This meant hunting down the heretics who were gaining a foothold in Scotland.

James V of Scotland remembered the words of his sweet Katherine, always encouraging him to look to God as his guide, to trust in Him for Divine help. He knew her advice was honest and sincere, but he could never admit to it. Perhaps the execution of Henry Forrest would put enough fear in the heretics to cause them to cease in their preaching against the papal abuses in Scotland.

The young King James V of Scotland realized that those who were accused of possessing the Bible in English would face arrest and inquest. If found guilty, which they always were, they would be burned at the stake at the town center, a sentence too harsh for any man.

The man hunt had begun in earnest with the arrest and burning of Patrick Hamilton, an eager young Reformer of spotless character.

This one execution of a noble young man caused James to appear as a ruthless leader in the eyes of his people.

This thought tormented him, plagued his mind in the night hours, leaving him sleepless and disheartened. He sought the comfort of his mistresses and the relief from the pressures of his reign as monarch of Scotland.

If only he were not a king! In the beginning of his reign as a sixteen-year-old sovereign, everything seemed glamorous and powerful. Reflecting on those early days, he realized now that he had been arrogant, a novice, and truth be told, not ready to guide a nation.

If only he could return to those carefree days of his childhood when life was simple, when he and Katherine rode their mounts through the heather-strewn meadows on a misty morning in May. But those days were gone forever. He could never go back.

Chapter 17

From the mountains and hills let us gather the few
Who will stand for the right and dare to be true.

Evening Light Songs

RAPID HOOF BEATS SIGNALED AN approaching rider near to the stables where Peter was leading the horses into an adjoining pasture. Whirling quickly, he saw his father pounding down the roadway on his black stallion, Shadow, a cloud of dust rising in the morning mist. The horse was in a dead heat, lathered with the effort of his master's unrelenting urging.

William reined in his weary mount next to where Peter stood beside the pasture gate. He dismounted, wiping dust and grime from his face with the back of his coat sleeve.

"Peter, lad, has anyone come by the stables this morning?"

"Nay, father," Peter replied with some alarm. "What is happening? Your horse is lathered and quite overheated." It was not like William to be careless with his stallion, unless he were being trailed by border raiders.

The border regions were periodically raided without regard to their victims' country or nationality. Normally, the Border Reivers, as they were called, did not follow him this far north; but on occasion, if highly provoked, they did pursue the guardians of the border as far as southern Lanarkshire.

"Are you being followed?" Peter asked, holding onto the reins of the panting horse as his father dismounted.

"Perhaps. I canna say." He bent over to pick up the hoof of his mount, inspecting it for signs of lameness.

"Well," Peter said as he began to wipe down the flanks of the horse with a cotton cloth, "I am expecting no one except for Jenny. We are riding to the wee lock to fish. You know the place, where Katherine and I used to meet for the day, the loch hidden among the trees."

"Aye, lad, I know where it be." William unsaddled his mount and turned to his son. "Now, Peter, listen to me, lad. Do ye have a Testament in your possession here at the stable?"

A frown appeared on Peter's broad forehead. "Nay, father. Sir John has mine in his keeping . . . at Carmichael House. And why do you ask?" A sudden fear chilled the morning air like a cold winter wind.

"Henry Forrest is to be executed, Peter. I am sorry to tell ye, lad. I know it will stir up sad memories in the telling of it, but I canna hold me peace." A dark mask descended over William' strong features. He paused, looking away from the face of his son, a face that stared back at him in surprise, then shock.

"Executed! Henry Forrest! The friar from Linlithgow, the one so long in prison? Was he not to be pardoned? Surely, this is not true."

"Aye, lad, it is true. He was betrayed by his confessor. Now the Privy Council has ordered magistrates to send men into the countryside to find anyone with a Testament in their possession. If found with Tyndale's translation or material exposing the corrupt practices of the papal Church, they will be arrested for heresy."

"So, it has come to this? The secret believers are in danger then?"

"Afraid so, lad. I must ride to warn anyone possessing such damning material. Must act fast, Peter. Ready the Galloway pony, and I will pick her up after I talk to Sir John."

"Is it that urgent?"

"Aye, Henry Forrest will not have a fair trial. He will surely be burned at the stake. This execution will ignite a fire storm among the clergy, a regular witch hunt for heretics. I must inform our people. Sir John will know what to do."

"Before you go, Father," Peter said running a hand through his hair, "do you believe Chancellor will reveal what he knows about Jenny . . . about discovering the Testament in her possession?"

William shook his head. "From what Sir John has told me, Chancellor himself has the Testament. He returned it to him, so it would hardly benefit him to divulge the matter to the magistrate. In fact, he would be under suspicion himself if he still has the Testament at Shieldhill. Now, Peter, I must go."

Peter readied another mount for his father, and William left for Carmichael House without further delay. Memories, unbidden, assaulted Peter's mind, filling the early morning with vivid detail of Patrick's execution. He could not bear the thought of his own countrymen, many who were covert believers, arrested and possibly executed for reading for themselves the truth of what was taught in Tyndale's translation of the New Testament.

He must urge Jenny to return to Shieldhill Castle at once and tell her father of the manhunt for any possessing a Testament or related material. He knew she would be fearful, but she would not have to say more. If Edward Chancellor still had the Testament, he would surely destroy it now.

During the long winter months, Jenny had gained permission from her father to visit Carmichael House now and again in the company of her governess or another female servant. Jenny could read Latin and French, so the Vulgate translation in Latin that Sir John had in his possession was easily understood by the eager young seeker.

With fatherly patience, Sir John directed her to the passages that would explain the will of God for those who believed. Sir John possessed a Bible, the approved fourth century Latin text known as the Vulgate translation. Most common folk did not possess such a precious text, and even if they did, the Latin language made it impossible to understand.

Even the Liturgy and Mass were spoken in Latin. Out of ignorance and fear, the people of Europe acquiesced to a form of religion they themselves could not interpret or understand. Therefore, the people of the medieval days remained ill-informed of the actual truth, depending solely on the priests and bishops to guide them to Heaven. But even the Vulgate translation contained enough truth to expose the falseness of the ruling Roman Church, if one could read Latin. But ever so slowly, the black stone of the dark ages began to crack. A tiny ray of colorful light sprang from the broken stone, like a long-awaited beacon in a world of darkness.

In the quiet of the early morning, a cloud of misgiving troubled Peter's mind. His thoughts were of Jenny, the lass he had come to love. Only now did he realize how much he cared for her. He recalled how this charming young lass had come so suddenly into his life, riding her Galloway pony through the heather in a desperate struggle to escape from her father's abusive control.

With Jenny's coming, a whirlwind of emotion had swept over him like a flood, filling his lonely days with unspeakable happiness. With his father so often away, guarding the lands of Carmichael, the two motherless young people formed a strong friendship that quickly blossomed into the sweetness of first love, alive and sparkling with the joy of innocent youth.

Chapter 18

In the awful age of night when the clouds
Of papal darkness filled the sky.

Evening Light Songs

THE MORNING SUN ROSE SLOWLY, timidly at first, climbing across
the Valley of the Clyde and bringing with it a clear azure sky. A warm
breeze swept away the mist of pre-dawn, leaving the sky scrubbed
clean of clouds. The earth was warming, preparing for the growing
season, just as it had from the beginning of time.

Arriving at Carmichael House at a full gallop, William found Sir
John immersed in the herb garden, inspecting the fragrant plants
while offering suggestions to the gardener for transplanting the
bergamot to a more favorable location. Sir John himself was an avid
gardener, enjoying the quiet pleasure of tending the herb garden
situated close to the keep.

The vegetable garden and orchard lay beyond the walled plot of
kitchen herbs. In autumn, when additional farm workers arrived,
Sir John supervised the gathering and preserving of the substantial
vegetable and fruit harvest for winter use.

Much of this bounty was distributed to the tenants of Carmichael,
who could not grow a sufficient amount of food in their own gardens

to last through the winter. A circular dovecot was meticulously maintained to help supply eggs and doves for the stew pots of the widows and infirm.

Reining his horse to a sudden stop in the dooryard where Sir John was dipping fresh rainwater from a wooden barrel, William hailed his brother with a wave of his hand, pointing to the terraced portico at the rear of the keep. He beckoned for Sir John to join him there.

Acknowledging William's arrival with a wave of his hand, Sir John removed his garden gloves and made his way through the newly planted furrows to where William waited.

William dismounted and handed the horse over to a stable lad, who led the panting and snorting horse away to be watered and fed. At this moment, William appeared much like his horse, pacing the stone terrace in an impatient attitude, waiting for Sir John who seemed to be taking his own sweet time, stopping to inspect some plant on his way to join his brother.

As Sir John approached the keep, William pondered his stalwart brother, thinking of how he enjoyed working in the herb garden nestled between the two wings of the house, an ideal spot for a kitchen garden, a warmer place where the southern sun kissed the mist away, and where tender young plants grew in profusion. Perhaps his brother felt close to Gwendolyn in this lovely aromatic nook, for this was Gwendolyn's garden, the wife lost to him shortly after Katherine was born.

"Aye, William," Sir John said in greeting, "and what brings ye to Carmichael so early this morning, riding your poor horse into a lather? I was not lookin' for ye to be up from the border this soon."

William did not answer, just slowly shook his head, impatient with Sir John's jovial outlook.

"Trust ye are not bearing ill tidings," Sir John continued with a note of apprehension. "Your face is a'tellin' me that ye have urgent news. Aye, that is what I be thinkin'. Off to the war room then, and I'll send Coira for some breakfast, aye?"

"Aye, John, but I canna stay. There is much I must tell ye, much to do before the sun sets this day. I must be leaving shortly."

Sir John raised his heavy eyebrows. "Then we must talk, William. Come, let us go inside."

He called for Coira to fetch some refreshment, and the two men strode in silence to Sir John's private study. They waited for Coira to bring the breakfast tray before speaking.

"Will ye be needin' anything else, Sir John?" Coira questioned.

"Nay, Coira, this be plenty." He waved a hand in dismissal and added, "Thank ye ever so much. I appreciate your good food . . . and," he added with a smile, "your kindness to this auld soldier."

"'Tis no bother, sir. I be going about me business since ye have need of nothing else." She bobbed a curtsy and left the room.

The brothers filled their wooden trenchers and sat at the round oak table by the long window. The cooing of a mourning dove could be heard near the window, and William could feel the melancholy in the song.

A world of frustration and unbridled anger seemed to radiate from William, but he remained silent, waiting for Sir John to eat his breakfast. He began to eat, but his agitation triggered a total lack of appetite. He pushed his food away.

"Brother," William began, "I have grievous news. Came soon as I heard to warn ye."

Sir John looked up from his trencher, concern written on his rugged features. "Now, William, what is so urgent that ye canna even eat? Are the Reivers heading north into Lanarkshire? All appears to be quiet so far this season."

"Nay, no raiders making trouble," William affirmed. "Clan men be posted at our borders, watching in shifts, and nothing amiss along our lands. The news comes from St. Andrews. The churchmen abiding there, Cardinal Beaton in particular, brought Henry Forrest from prison to stand trial, and he will surely be executed."

"What!" Sir John said in alarm.

"The trial will commence in a fortnight, perhaps sooner—I canna say for certain—but he is accused as a heretic; that has been determined. Forrest will surely burn at the stake."

Sir John set his knife on the table none too gently and pushed his trencher aside. "Nay, ye must be mistaken. Surely not! I understood at last report he would be acquitted. He has been in prison for so long now."

"Aye, I heard the same. Thought it to be true, but John, the council sent a certain priest, name of Walter Laing, to act as confessor for Forrest. Believing this priest to be a true man of God and not knowing it was a plan to trap him, Forrest told him all his heart, confessing to reading Tyndale's translation, declaring it was God's truth."

"So, Forrest himself is a Benedictine and should have an opinion that would not call for execution. The churchmen surely take care of their own."

"He also confessed to abuses he personally suffered under the thumb of the papal hierarchy, chiefly that reforms must be addressed speedily, or Scotland would deny the Pope's authority and join the Reformers. This is considered heresy."

Sir John's jaw tightened, the outline of his chin standing out in relief. "Well, the king himself has spoken of necessary reforms."

"Aye, at times, the king acknowledges the need for restructurings—that is so—but he would never admit to actual corruption at such high levels of the ruling Church. After all, King James himself must answer to the Pope, so he is careful. But, John, that is not all."

"Not all? What more then? Say on, William."

"The council has authority over the magistrates, and now, even as we speak, they be sending men to search for anyone possessing Tyndale's translation. And if the forbidden text is found in anyone's possession, the guilty person will be arrested and tried as a heretic."

"I feared it would come to this," Sir John said.

William glanced around the room, careful that no one was listening. "Aye, it is even unto our doorstep."

"I canna imagine," Sir John said with incredulity, "after all his time in that wretched prison with no substantial charge against him, that Forrest will finally be executed, burned at the stake. God have mercy!"

"Not only that," William continued, "any person found with pamphlets or material suggesting corruption in the papal church system will be excommunicated or worse. I want to ride through the Southern Uplands to warn Reformation sympathizers to beware, to hide any such material; then, if possible, I'll ride on to St. Andrews to be present at the execution."

Sir John rose from the table and gazed out the window for a long moment. His appetite had suddenly left him, and he began to methodically pace the wooden floor, his brow furrowing into deep irregular lines.

"Forrest was an honest man, who trusted that so-called confessor of the faith. But he was deceived. What an abysmal way to exact a confession from a man. Was there any other charge, William?"

"His only crime was reading Tyndale's translation of the New Testament and believing what it said, which, of course, denies the absolute authority of the Pope."

Sir John ran his fingers through his silver-black hair. "I fear, William," he said, pausing in mid-pace and turning to face his brother standing near the door as though to leave, "there will be dark days ahead for believers. We must find a way to survive, to protect our people, our children."

"Listen to me, John," he said with a warning tone in his deep voice. "Hide any English translations of the Reformation writings. They will turn Carmichael upside down to find any shred of evidence against us. We are not above suspicion, and those heretic hunters will be sure to stop at Carmichael."

"If Katherine knows of this, surely she will speak to the king on our behalf. He thinks highly of Katherine and wants to please her. But," Sir John said, pausing in his thought, "perhaps it is too late for that now. The upcoming execution of Forrest says the king has given consent. So, there ye have it."

"Only a matter of time, John. Katherine herself may be in great danger. Jamie will protect her if he can, but he can only go so far. He will never deny the absolute authority of the Pope or the Church, not even to save Katherine. He fears papal retribution, and he is making that clear by executing Henry Forrest."

Sir John said no more. He shook his head in silence, watching speculatively as William turned toward the door, preparing to leave. Sir John grabbed his arm, detaining him. "Wait, William, not so quickly. We must talk, plan."

"What is there to plan, John? I am certain of me course."

"Ye have a son to think of, William. Do not act on passion alone. Nay! That is a dangerous course. When we are wounded through injustice, when our loved ones suffer hurt or abuse, we become vulnerable to error. Be careful of your course, me brother. If ye would be part of something larger than yourself—this Reformation—ye must believe in the things ye canna always see with your eyes."

William turned to his brother, grabbing his forearms in a tight grip. "What are we to do, John? Sit idly by, do nothing while believers are executed, hunted down like common criminals?" Frustration stung his eyes. "What is it ye can say to me that will change me mind?"

He held firmly to John's arms—not in anger, but in a deep aching feeling of dread, of what might tear them apart—two brothers whose ancestral ties bound them together from birth, binding them firmly into one solid cord.

"William . . . William, I know ye strive to right what is wrong," Sir John said, his blue eyes intense with feeling. "Your heart is guid and brave, but we canna do this ourselves. Be patient, me brother. Ye know what the cost will be to us, to our people, and we canna see what lies ahead. We must keep faith, believe in the things we canna see. It is God's way."

Slowly, William shook his head, not caring that tears welled in his green eyes. "Nay, John, I canna agree. We must fight for the right, for the truth. Aye, there will be a rising in Scotland; and if it means taking up arms, I will stand with the Reformers."

"I want ye to promise me this, William," said Sir John, his own eyes growing misty. "Promise me that nothing will divide us from one another. Nothing must drive us to betray or deny our family, our clan. We are brothers, William. Promise me!"

For a long moment, William held his brother close, his love and affection for his older brother—the one who had taught him to be a man—intensely apparent, even though they seemed to be at cross purposes in this present distress.

"I promise, ye, John."

"Offenses will come—ye know that William—and it seems sooner than we believed, but know this: if ye understand the Gospel, never think the spread of this Truth, that Truth revealed when the papal stone of offense was broken, can move forward without great opposition. God has not deserted us if this happens. The Word is a sword, and it will cut. And William, let it not cut us apart."

"Aye, John, let it be so. But as I see it," William said with conviction, "warfare may come as a result of this oppression; and ye know, this means ruin for many, perhaps even death. As it stands now, if this inquisition is not stopped, aye, all of Scotland must drink of the deadly poison."

"Not so, William, not all. There will always be people who will not bow the knee to the dictates of men. The problem is we do not understand this kind of spiritual warfare, but I know ye canna take hold of the serpent with your own hands and not be bitten. To stand firm against the enemy, we must use the Sword of the Spirit, the Word of God. It be an able weapon, and we must learn how to use it."

"Henry Forrest understood Tyndale's work and personally experienced the brutality of the papal Church, and he, a monk, one of their own; but it dinna save him, John. Do ye think any of the believers expressing the same sympathies will be spared? Nay! I go to warn our clansmen, who even at this moment may be under suspicion."

Sir John slowly shook his head, a great sadness settling over him. He said no more. How could the believers wage a war with the spirits of darkness? In Scriptural accounts written in the Old Testament, the priests and prophets told of the inhumaneness of war, of death and destruction, of slavery and bondage. Biblical text told of the advancement of kingdoms through carnal warfare.

Even so, Sir John could not comprehend the impact that such a war would bring to his family, to his clan, and to his country. "Perhaps if we listen for the still, small voice in the silence of our heart," Sir John said, "then perchance we can make sense of the chaos and confusion about us."

A soldier himself, Sir John had experienced the ravages and brutalities of war. The terrible disaster at Flodden Field had impacted the people of Scotland forever. At the end of the day, everyone lost something or someone. All wars, it seemed, were the result of greed and lust for power, for land, for domination and control. Surely, there must be another way to obtain freedom from spiritual tyranny.

On the other hand, William was in favor of taking up arms to defeat the injustices of papal Rome. The more Sir John studied Tyndale's translation of the New Testament, the more convinced he was that a physical retaliation was not the way to right the wrongs of the papal system of religion.

For that is what it had become, a politically organized system that dominated the world and persecuted those who sought freedom from oppression. Reforms must be sanctioned by the Church, and soon, or bloodshed would surely follow.

Sir John raised his arms in a futile gesture. "If ye are determined to go, William, then leave straight away. And for heaven's sake, leave your own cloak and borrow one of the crofters. Don't ride Shadow, or ye will surely be recognized. Ye kin these things, aye, but ye will be in much danger. Stay clear of the main roads from Edinburgh if ye can."

William nodded. "Our clansmen will guard our southern borders while I be away, so not to worry on that count. After warning those I feel are in danger, I will ride to St. Andrews—disguised, of course—and learn what I can, aye?"

Sir John nodded, a bit reluctantly. His concern for his brother's safety was quite obvious.

Laying a hand on his younger brother's shoulder, Sir John said, "Send word if ye go north to St. Andrews, William, but let me warn ye—make yourself invisible, or ye will bring the magistrates to our doorstep."

"Aye, John, I promise I will be careful."

"Ye are possibly already under suspicion. I know ye be careful when warning the secret believers of a raid on their meetings, but your efforts to spare the so-called heretics by helping them escape to England has not gone unnoticed, even though ye be disguised. Ye worry me, William."

"Trust me, John. I must do this."

William left Carmichael House, stopping at the stables to ready the Galloway pony with provisions and exchange his cloak for a dark serviceable garment of thickly woven wool. His mission was to warn the secret followers of the upcoming inquiry of any suspect sympathizers.

And in the rugged and misty shires of the southern borders, so long oppressed by the impenetrable stone of darkness and deception, the New Testament truth written in English had broken open this formidable religious system, igniting the fires of the Protestant Reformation in the blood-soaked land of bonny Scotland.

Chapter 19

The fear of the LORD is the instruction of wisdom;
and before honor is humility.

Proverbs 15:33

THE MORNING MIST LAY IN the dips and bends of the undulating countryside. The ghostly-like vapor stretched thin, then slowly melted away as the sun climbed higher, warming the cool earth.

Through the mist-drenched Valley of the Clyde, Peter rode his sorrel gelding, intent on his quest to intercept Jenny, who might already be on the road to Carmichael, and to warn Edward Chancellor, Laired of Shieldhill Castle, that if he still held the English translation of the New Testament in his possession, he could very well be questioned and even arrested.

As Peter rode his gelding toward the village of Biggar, he remembered the bitter quarrel between Jenny and her father, an argument that had driven Jenny from her home. He prayed Chancellor would not be so hostile today and that he would grant him an audience. He would be completely honest with the man.

Perhaps, Peter thought as he contemplated meeting Edward Chancellor for the first time, Chancellor had thought better of the methods he used in handling his determined young daughter and, rather than lose her altogether, had decided that finding some middle ground was a better option. After all, she had proved brave enough to strike out on her own, not knowing how she would survive. Then again, because of his strong loyalties to the Church of Rome, the likelihood of Chancellor still having the forbidden book in his possession was not probable, but Peter must warn him and Jenny just the same.

* * *

At Shieldhill Castle, Edward Chancellor sat in a leather-bound chair in his private study, idly thumbing through the Testament that Sir John Carmichael had insisted Jenny return to him. That very morning, his Factor had informed him that Henry Forrest, a priest of the Benedictine order at St. Andrews, had been brought from the sea tower to face trial for heresy. If found guilty, he would be executed in a fortnight and all because of believing what was written in this missive.

Chancellor could not help but wonder why a man would risk his life just to read this outlawed and insignificant manuscript. Perhaps he should read it himself to see what all the blather was about. The volume itself was small and unimpressive. The cover was plain, cheaply bound, and not worth the money it took to purchase it. On the first few pages, someone had carefully penned in a portion of the missing text, where it had been spoiled by some mishap.

A sharp knock sounded on the heavy oak door of his study, and Chancellor quickly placed the prohibited Testament inside a leather-bound replica of an actual book, especially crafted for the express purpose of hiding important documents and other valuables. He then placed it among the other volumes on the shelf against the stone wall of the study.

"Enter," he said, then resumed his former position in his favorite chair. He schooled his face, endeavoring to appear nonchalant and relaxed. But in reality, unwelcome thoughts pierced his mind, visions of the magistrates coming to search Shieldhill Manor for any material promoting the Protestant doctrine.

The Testament was well-hidden, but still, he felt uneasy. Why was he feeling so troubled? After all, he was a loyal subject of the king and Crown, and a passionate supporter of the Holy Mother Church. The only reason he even had the Testament was because of Jenny and Sir John's insistence that she return it to him. He should burn it, but for some reason, he felt reluctant to destroy it.

He had not made known Jenny's duplicity in obtaining the copy, nor had he given the Testament over to the parish priest. After Sir John Carmichael's stern warning, he thought better of sharing this information, grudgingly reconsidering the esteemed war chief's advice.

Misguided lass Jenny might be, still, he did not wish to bring a papal inquiry to his only daughter—and in truth, to his own doorstep. He had been too harsh with the lass, and now, because of his quick temper, the Carmichaels were unwittingly involved.

This ancient clan, the Clan of the Broken Spear, had kept their land holdings by feudal rights, but now they held a registered deed to that same land. Carmichael House maintained close ties with the neighboring clans of the border regions, supporting and protecting the interests of the other. Chancellor did not want to provoke the already compromised relationships. He understood that clan alliances were a powerful force in Scotland, a force to be reckoned with.

The heavy timbered door swung open, and Jenny approached her father with a confident air. She had made a concerted effort to be sympathetic and gentle with her father, despite his harsh and overbearing ways. In response to her overtures, Chancellor had softened in his manner, warming to the charm and affection of his only daughter.

"So, Jenny, I thought you were riding out this morning. Have ye changed your mind?"

"Aye, Papa, I have. Someone has come to see you," Jenny announced with a smile. "It is Peter Carmichael, son of William and nephew of Sir John, whom you have met on several occasions. Shall I show him in?"

Chancellor's eyebrows raised in surprise, and he straightened in his chair, a slight frown forming across his brow. "Is this the lad you say cares for the horses at Carmichael? If so, what is it he wants?"

"I have no idea, Papa. He said he would speak with you first. I am certain it must be of some importance. Perhaps Sir John has sent a message for you."

"A message? Aye, knowing Chief Carmichael, he would have come himself if he wished to see me." He rose from his chair and rubbed his chin, carefully searching Jenny's face. She went to him and laid a hand on his arm.

"Papa, you can trust Peter. He harbors no ill will toward you, I am certain, so please allow me to show him in."

"Vera well, lass," he said with resignation, "we will see what the lad wants; but rest assured, the word of the Laird of Shieldhill Castle is not to be misrepresented. Ye shall stay as witness to his complaint, if he has any."

A merry laugh bubbled up from Jenny's throat, and she put her arms around her father's angular form, gently hugging him, a gesture she had practiced at Sir John's prompting. Amazingly, it had helped to heal the breach between them, and Chancellor had warmed to Jenny's affectionate embraces.

"Oh, Papa, you suspect everyone is out to get you. Ever since your sons left home to follow their own dreams, you have been far too bothersome about insignificant matters. After all, I am still here," she said smiling.

"Aye, that ye are, lass, and glad I am of it, too. We are good now, are we not, lass?" he said returning her embrace.

"Indeed, we are, Papa," she agreed. Crossing the cool flagstone floor, she opened the door and ushered Peter into the study.

The two men eyed each other for a long moment, then Peter bowed slightly, acknowledging the older man.

"Good day to you, sir," Peter began. "I am pleased that you have received me on such short notice, but I was sent in haste to speak with you about a matter of importance."

"Aye, then, say on," Chancellor said abruptly. "I have matters to attend to meself, so best be on with it."

Peter shifted his weight uneasily, glancing at Jenny, who was frowning at her father's less-than-cordial manner.

"My father, William Carmichael, sent me to warn you of the upcoming trial and impending execution of a Benedictine priest who will be tried for heresy in that he read and believed an English translation of the New Testament Bible."

"And what has that to do with me?" Chancellor said. He resumed his chair behind his desk and tapped the polished mahogany surface with the tips of his fingers. "From my understanding, the priest, who has been in prison for years, is indeed a heretic."

"It has nothing to do with you directly, sir," Peter said. He knew he must be careful with Jenny's father if he were to ever win favor with this austere man.

"Those at Carmichael know that Jenny returned a Testament to you, the one she obtained without your knowledge. Since Henry Forrest, this priest, will be tried as a heretic and most certainly be executed for having this same Testament in his keeping, the church council has ordered the magistrates to search out any Scotsmen who may have one in their possession."

Chancellor said nothing, but his eyes smoldered, boring holes into Peter's pronouncement.

"Of course," Peter continued, "we have no way of knowing what you did with Jenny's copy, but I only assume that you have destroyed it. If, for some reason, you still have the copy here at the manor, it would be in your best interest to burn it immediately."

Chancellor continued to stare at Peter, assessing the young man standing before him, wondering if this tall, dark-haired lad was trying to trick him into admitting he still had the Testament. He was not certain where the Carmichaels stood on the matter; but since the acquittal of their Douglas kinsman over a year ago, he assumed they were sympathetic toward the Reformation movement.

But then, the Douglas in question had voiced only offensive statements of a political nature, nothing against the Holy Mother Church—or so he had been told. Perhaps, there was no more to know about the incident.

"I would say to ye, lad, in the presence of my own Genevieve, who was punished for the same by me own hand, that your warning has been taken. However, mark my words, Peter Carmichael: I have no need of your warning."

The lie set uneasily on his tongue, but he would give no occasion to this bold young man to doubt his loyalty to the Holy Mother Church. The burning of Henry Forrest for the same crime did not bode well for him either. Must he confess this deliberate lie to his parish priest? If so, would the priest betray him just as Henry Forrest's confessor had? He must burn the forbidden book as soon as the young man left Shieldhill Castle.

"Very well, sir, I will take my leave. I—we, that is—knowing the Testament was returned to you, gave us concern, for Jenny's sake . . . and for yours, of course, since you still may have the copy in your possession." Peter knew he was babbling and was certain Chancellor would notice his more-than-usual care for his daughter's welfare.

Rising from his chair behind the desk, Chancellor did not offer the usual hospitality of food and drink. The resemblance of the young man to his father was noticeable, but his features were softer, less warlike than that of William Carmichael. Over the years, he had occasion to observe the ruggedly handsome William at neighborhood meetings, where area clans exchanged ideas concerning problems with the Border Reivers. William Carmichael, second son of old Archibald Carmichael, was an austere but principled man.

"Ye understand, young Peter," said Chancellor, "that Genevieve has been carefully brought up by the best governesses and teachers I could afford. Likewise, my two sons. All are baptized members of the Holy Mother Church. My youngest son is a dedicated monk at Mont St. Michel, serving the Church in prayers and solitude." He paused in his narrative, studying the young man's countenance.

"I understand that Genevieve is your friend," Chancellor continued, "but keep in mind what I say. There is no chance whatsoever that she will ever be anything but a loyal follower of the Holy Mother Church and of the Pope, all he has instituted as the Vicar of Christ. Is that understood?"

Peter understood perfectly. What the Laird of Shieldhill Castle had not said was quite obvious. Peter was not to pursue a relationship with his daughter based on Chancellor's own convictions. Perhaps, the laird had reasoned, Peter was sympathetic to the Protestant Reformation, or maybe even a believer, and for that reason alone, he was not an acceptable suitor for his daughter.

"Aye," Peter said, meeting Jenny's eyes. Understanding passed between them. "I realize what you are saying, Laird Chancellor. I will bid you farewell for now. It is a great relief that you need not take this warning for yourself and for those under your protection." Peter bowed his head and exited the study, closing the door behind him.

"Papa!" Jenny protested. "You did not offer him a drink of water or any provisions for his journey. That is not like you to treat visitors in such a manner, especially when he came purposely to warn you of possible danger. I will go to the kitchen myself and ask the cook to prepare some refreshment." Disappointment narrowed Jenny's eyes, and she shook her head slightly, her incredulity apparent.

"Aye, I did not offer him hospitality," Chancellor admitted, somewhat discomfited, "but if ye wish, see that he has some refreshment for the journey back to Carmichael. It is none of me concern, since he came unannounced."

"He came out of neighborly concern, and we should show our gratitude and hospitality for his good intentions."

The spark in Jenny's eyes gave rise to Chancellor's suspicions that his daughter and young Peter harbored more than just a neighborly friendship. Perhaps the two young people had formed an attachment that was more than casual. He would address this at once.

"Aye, lass, before ye go, let me say straight away . . . do not think on this Carmichael lad as a possible suitor." He hesitated, not sure how much he should reveal to his impressionable young daughter. "It has been rumored among us that Chief Carmichael is a secret believer of the Reformation dogma, and if that be so, he has no part in your life."

"He is a loyal patriot, Papa, and I know he is fond of his parish priest on Kirk Hill." Jenny felt the sharp edge of worry prick her, and her spine tingled with apprehension.

Jenny knew that the Carmichaels were, indeed, undeclared Reformationists and that Peter's father acted as an undercover informant. If William knew a raid by local magistrates was imminent, he would ride through the countryside to warn the believers who met in secret.

"Patriot he may be," Chancellor agreed, "and loyal to king and country. But devoted to the Holy Mother Church? Now, that is debatable."

Jenny said nothing. She must be extremely careful with her words and actions. How she hated hiding the truth from her father, but there was no other way without implicating herself. In her search for truth, she had spent hours studying the Scriptures with Peter. She was convinced that all she had been taught, all she had known, was simply a deadly deception and perversion of the true Gospel.

She exited the room, hurrying to find Peter before he left Shieldhill Castle. He was mounting his gelding, preparing to leave. She called to him, and he turned his mount around to face her.

"Peter! Peter! Wait a wee moment. I am sorry that my father did not offer the customary hospitality to you. I have sent to the kitchen for some provisions for you to take with you."

Dismounting his gelding, Peter gazed into Jenny's troubled eyes. "Dinna fash yourself on my account. I have no need of your father's hospitality. I am quite certain of his feelings regarding me and my family. He made that quite plain." He sighed and mindlessly twisted the leather reins in his hands. "Your father does not like me, Jenny."

"He does not like anyone he feels is not wholly devoted to the Holy Mother Church and all the Roman bulls that come across the water. There is nothing personal he can fault you with, Peter, just his blind ignorance of what is true." She rested one hand on the sleeve of Peter's jerkin.

"Jenny, you know . . . you know how I feel about you. This last year has been the happiest of my life . . . because of you, because of our friendship." Reaching his hand to touch a wispy, wayward curl away from her face, he continued. "I bless the day I watched you riding your pony through the heather."

She smiled, her eyes filling with sudden tears. "You mean the day you found me lying flat on my back with my dress muddied and my hair looking like a scarecrow? You mean that day?"

"Aye, lass," he said with infinite tenderness, "that day."

"Oh, Peter," she said hopelessly. One lone tear rolled down her cheek. "What are we going to do? Father will never consent to allowing us to be together. Never!"

With his thumb, Peter brushed the tear from her cheek and smiled into her woe-begone face. "There will be a way, Jenny. Just be strong and don't lose courage."

"I will try, Peter. I am so frightened for . . . for all of us.

Stepping back a few paces from the prancing horse, Jenny waited while Peter mounted his gelding. She handed Peter the provisions from the kitchen and looked up, her eyes filling with tears.

"I am sorry, Peter. I will try to be brave."

Peter patted the neck of his gelding and said, "I will try to get word to you if there is trouble. I feel confident that all will be well. Let's pray that God will soften your father's heart and give me favor in his eyes."

"Aye, Peter, let us pray, and God be with you and your family."

"And God's blessings to you, sweet Jenny." With one last look at the girl who had so miraculously come into his life, the girl he had come to love, Peter turned his mount toward home.

In the laird's study at Shieldhill Castle, Edward Chancellor swept the heavy drapes back from the window, watching as Peter Carmichael rode his gelding down the narrow lane to the main wagon road. After Peter had vanished from sight, he retrieved the outlawed book from the shelf. He locked the door, then returned to his desk, lifting the Testament from the leather-bound box.

He added more logs to the glowing coals smoldering and hissing on the hearth. Sparks flew upward, igniting a flame that snapped and crackled as it ate into a vein of pitch. He stood next to the blazing fire, the heretical Testament in his hand. He must burn this provocative, outlawed book before it was discovered in his possession.

Even now, he could almost feel the deadly fires of execution, the papal retribution for any who were found in possession of this very same Testament. There was no question. It must be destroyed.

Chapter 20

Fear not to rely on the word of thy God,
Step out on the promise, get under the blood.

Evening Light Songs

THROUGHOUT THE SOUTHERN UPLANDS OF Lanarkshire, William Carmichael rode a steady mount, warning those sympathetic with the Protestant Reformation of impending papal retribution. He dressed as a simple crofter, wearing a dark woolen cloak over his crofter's attire, a common disguise not easily recognized by the casual observer.

When alerting believers of a possible raid on their secret meetings, Peter readied a sturdy Galloway pony for William to ride, an endurance mount that could go through the countryside for hours at a time.

Pub owners and tavern keepers, in collaboration with William, alerted him if the gossip they heard over mugs of strong ale, especially prepared by the tavern keepers, included an impending raid by local magistrates. When a warning alert was in progress, William's black stallion, Shadow, easily recognized as belonging to William, remained in the stables at Carmichael. This dangerous approach to alerting the Reformers involved constant pursuit, near capture, and repeated escapes, but William was willing to take the risk if by alerting the believers, the Reformation could move forward.

The secret believers in the area became familiar with this mysterious stranger riding through the glens and hills, but they did not know from where he had come, nor did they guess his identity. They called him the Reformation Rider, since the mysterious horseman appeared only when trouble threatened their peaceful gatherings. When the warning came, the believers quietly vanished, leaving the magistrates scratching their heads, wondering if they had been misinformed.

After learning that Henry Forrest was brought from prison to stand trial and that certain punishment awaited any having a New Testament in their possession, William mounted his pony, quietly warning sympathizers to hide or destroy all materials referring to papal injustice.

William rode his Galloway pony northward, avoiding the main roads and taking a ferry across the Firth of Forth, arriving at the ancient town of St. Andrews a week later. St. Andrews was the seat and headquarters of the Roman Catholic Church in Scotland. The University of St. Andrews was a prestigious center of learning, where priests and monks were educated and ordained. In 1410, Benedict XIII issued a papal bull to a small group of Augustinian clergies who founded the several colleges that comprised the university. It remained under the auspices of the Roman Church and wielded a powerful influence on Scottish political and religious views.

On the rugged shoreline of the North Sea, a castle was built on the rock surface. The castle was a fortified structure, the chief residence of the bishops and archbishops of St. Andrews. It was fashioned from stone, built to defend the churchmen and their exalted status. The castle also protected the town from any invaders brave enough to face the ravages of the cold North Sea.

A moat and drawbridge surrounded the entrance to the fortress with an impregnable sea wall of solid granite bordering the northeast side. Besides serving as a defensive stronghold, the castle was also an episcopal palace where guests were richly housed and lavishly entertained within its walls. Many of the castle's common rooms were resplendent with the expensive trappings of the papal churchmen.

The castle was also an appalling state prison. On its northwest side, a moss-covered sea tower loomed high above the walls, complete with a dungeon hollowed out of the stone. The dark and dreary dungeon housed papal prisoners awaiting trial. In winter, the sea relentlessly pounded the wall, shooting sprays of icy water to the top of the keep. Many a prisoner was sent to an untimely death from his miserable existence in the despicable dungeon beneath the sea tower.

Less than a hundred meters east of St. Andrew's Castle, a magnificent abbey stood silhouetted against the impregnable shoreline of the North Sea. This outstanding edifice was the pride of the Scottish Church, a glorious gathering place where Roman priests, bishops, and monks prayed, worshiped, and said masses. Along with the archbishop, David Beaton, and his subordinates, these churchmen maintained absolute authority over political and Church affairs in Scotland.

In the damp and despicable dungeon of this impregnable tower, Henry Forrest spent several wretched years under suspicion of heresy; but in 1533, he was brought from the tower to stand trial for his crimes.

He was accused of being in sympathy with Patrick Hamilton and having in his possession a copy of the New Testament in English, translated by William Tyndale, with texts taken from the original Greek and Hebrew.

To obtain a confession from Forrest concerning his reading and possessing this unlicensed Testament, an informant priest, Walter Laing, was sent by the church council to hear Forrest's confession.

Forrest disclosed to Laing that he, indeed, had read the outlawed Testament and that Patrick Hamilton suffered a martyr's death, that Hamilton's doctrines and teachings were true. Despite the sacred oath of the confessional, in which Forrest trusted, he was betrayed by Laing and ordered to stand trial.

A nobleman and professional soldier, Alexander Lesley, was in sympathy with the Reformers and offered William a room in his own lodgings for the duration of the trial. The two men had been in close contact since the burning of Patrick Hamilton and had purposed to be present at the trial of Henry Forrest.

Bone weary from the rough ferry passage across the Firth, William arrived at St. Andrews on horseback. He stabled his horse and found Lesley at his inconspicuous lodgings on Market Street, the doorway tucked into a private close overgrown by an ancient wisteria vine. The close was Lesley's private property, hence gated and closed to the public. Lesley was eager for William to join him at the hearing now in progress.

Lesley was a tall, wiry man with keen, black eyes and a razor-sharp wit. His hair was like his build—wiry and reddish brown. He had a habit of running his fingers through his hair, so for the most part, the wiry locks stood on end, reminding William of an agitated badger.

William smiled at the thought, greeting his friend warmly. He threw his travel pack in the corner by the hearth and sat down at the table where Lesley was setting out bread and cheese.

"Ye look . . . rough, Carmichael," said Lesley assessing William' disguise. "Except for the boots."

"Och, that's the idea, me friend. I just be common folk, living and working on the edge of the laird's estate. That be me, aye?" He gave Lesley a knowing smile, then glanced down at his travel-stained clothing.

He wore a rough, woolen cloak with an attached hood and a coarse linen shirt with a leather tunic that fell to his knees. The tunic was laced to the neck and held in place at the waist with a simple hemp cord. His only concession to this costume were his leather boots reaching to his knees and lacing at the instep, an item he could not abandon for the simple footwear the crofters wore.

"I dinna kin if I be o' the same mind, aye, that's so. Everybody is suspect. Best be careful during a papal hearing. Get rid of the boots, William."

"Nay, ye are over-worried. Who will notice except someone like yourself?"

"Lots of folks come just to observe the outcome of this absolute farce, friend and foe alike. Spies be there too, aye." Lesley shoved the plate of cheese and cold meat toward William.

"Not to worry, Lesley. Tell me . . . what is happening thus far?" William broke off a chunk of the warm bread, savoring the yeasty aroma.

"Not much, just a bunch of blather by the council confirming the position and authority of the Holy Mother Church and the Pope's

Divine right to judge heretics." He poured a tankard of ale from a pitcher and set it before William.

"What do ye know of Forrest?" Lesley asked, running long fingers through his wiry locks. "He's from your neck of the woods, after all."

"Aye, dinna kin the man personally, but the family be from Linlithgow, neighbors in the Southern Uplands. Operate an armory—crafting weapons, swords, and such. Also, do work as silversmiths. I understand that Forrest joined the Benedictine monastery there as a very young man."

"The council cited the charges against Forrest yesterday," Lesley said. "Named him as a follower of Patrick Hamilton. Said he believed Hamilton to be a martyr at the hands of Archbishop Beaton."

"Och! That must have caused an uproar in the clergy!"

Lesley let out a whoop. "I'll say it did! Forrest had a smuggled copy of the forbidden New Testament in English. On hearing this, the archbishop ripped apart his ecclesiastical royal robes, had him arrested and held in the sea tower at St. Andrews Castle, imprisoned, away from contact with the Lowland Christian Reformers, I expect."

"Aye, we heard. Held him in that miserable sea tower until that wicked Friar Laing betrayed his confidence." William shook his head. "We hoped he would be acquitted on lack of evidence."

"Aye, 'tis so. Laing supplied the needed evidence at yesterday's hearing, testifying that he knew Forrest had the forbidden Testament in his possession."

"And strange as it be," William added, "Forrest is one of their own, a well-respected Benedictine friar. Seems they are not above putting their own to the fire if they can stop the truth from getting into the hands of the common people."

"Afraid that's the way of it, me friend. On the morrow, they will bring Forrest himself before the council. Ye kin, it is already decided. Forrest dinna have justice. He will be condemned for heresy and set for execution. Och, William, he is ruined."

"I must be there, Lesley—disguised, of course. Pray for some way to rescue him, smuggle him away to England. King Henry is trying to persuade our young King James, his own nephew, to join the Reformation, but Jamie fears retribution from the Pope. Wants to do right but doesn't have the backbone to stand against the ecclesiastical powers that line his pockets.

"We canna overpower this mob, William! They be calling for blood, eager to see the heretic put to the flames. Forcibly taking Forrest before he is burned would take a miracle. Och, William, ye canna do it. Far too risky. Best pray for Divine intervention. That be how I see it."

While the two men talked long into the night, darkness fell like a sinister shadow, creeping over the misty Kingdom of Fife, waiting for dawn to break and the fate of Henry Forrest to be determined.

Later, William lay awake, restless and edgy. He was desperate to come up with a feasible plan to rescue Forrest from the fiery stake. Thoughts of Patrick Hamilton and his tragic death plagued his thoughts. He remembered with hot anger the outrageous summons by the archbishop requesting that Peter and his stable mate be present at the execution. The memory tormented his weary mind, driving away the last vestige of sleep.

He sat up and stretched, then swung his feet over the side of the bed, resting them on the cold floor. He held his head in his hands, wondering what he could do to save the doomed man.

Chapter 21

There's rest weary one in the bosom of God,
Step out on the promise of God.

Evening Light Songs

DAWN BROKE OVER THE KINGDOM of Fife, cold and silent—that uncommon time when Earth holds its breath, quietly waiting, anticipating the birth of another day. At length, light burst forth, lighting up the rugged cliffs along the shore and bringing with it the joys and troubles of time and chance.

William Carmichael and Alexander Lesley slipped quietly from their obscure lodgings on Market Street and walked the two-mile distance to a high, green place at the edge of the town. Archbishop David Beaton, nephew of Cardinal James Beaton of Glasgow, was to preside over the trial and was coming from his Monimail Palace. A crowd had already gathered, eager to hear the outcome of the accused heretic, Henry Forrest.

On the advice of his council, the archbishop had moved the hearings from place to place, fearing the crowd would raise a tumult. Perhaps they would not be so willing to walk the distance to the outskirts of town in the cold, windy dawn. The hearings were public;

and after the public outcry when Patrick Hamilton was burned at the stake, Beaton feared some resistance to his verdict—a verdict he had already decided. He had schooled his council well. They already knew which way to vote.

Monimail, the palatial home of the archbishop, lay to the west of the majestic cathedral, a little distance from St. Andrews Castle. David Beaton had ordered the tower house built as a personal residence, accommodating the elite and their entourages. He imported elaborately crafted furnishings for the manor and fruit trees, flowers, and fauna from France to beautify his gardens with all manner of edible fruit and exotic plants.

Today, however, he would have the advantage by holding the hearings at the high hill overlooking the town. He had chosen this place for the final day of trial when Forrest himself would testify. Favor was in his court, and this day he would end these tiresome proceedings, be done with Henry Forrest and others like him. Fear and panic would squash the efforts of the Reformers and their followers, making an example of those who dared to defy the Pope and his edicts.

A full two hours passed without a sign of the church councilmen, the archbishop, or Henry Forrest. Hearing rumors that the trial had been moved to St. Leonard's College on the University grounds, several bystanders and drama-seekers left.

But at length, the archbishop and his council arrived from Monimail, and the trial opened. The council convened with the usual protocol and preliminaries, calling the hearing to order. They seated themselves on a high platform with a long table that faced the crowd. Archbishop Beaton sat in the center of the council, seated on an ornately carved chair, resplendent in the sacred robe of his ecclesiastical office.

At the rear of the crowd, William and Lesley, disguised in rough hooded cloaks, waited with other onlookers. Among the diverse crowd was a considerable number of Scottish nobles and clan chieftains, already nonplussed by the execution of Patrick Hamilton. Clan Hamilton representatives were present, awaiting the outcome of another papal trial. All listened carefully to the charges as read in a droning monotone by the head councilman.

Bound in heavy chains, Forrest was prodded roughly onto the makeshift platform situated on a high, stone terrace. The crowd was able to see and hear from this vantage point, and the indisputable verdict would strike fear into any who dared to defy the Pope and his churchmen.

Remarkably, Forrest was scrubbed and clean, dressed in the familiar habit of the Benedictine monk. His tunic was embroidered with the symbols of his ordination and reached just below his knees. This was worn over a great pleated habit of undyed gray wool with long, wide sleeves. The entire costume was fastened at the waist with a leather cord, the robe reaching to the ground. On his head was the ecclesiastical hood of a vowed monk. A silver chain holding a large cross lay prominently displayed across his breast.

"Why do ye suppose the council has him dressed in his Benedictine habit?" William whispered to Lesley. The two men had worked their way through the crowd toward the outer edge of the front to hear all that was said and still be somewhat unobserved.

"So, they can remove them—civilly degrade him—I'll wager," Lesley hissed. "The excommunication and damnation procedures are quite impressive, especially for the spiritually ignorant." He shook his head before remembering to remain passive and quiet.

"Hush, Lesley! Do not speak until this day's treachery is over," William warned. "Been recognized by Hamilton, but he is no threat. Saw him lookin' at me boots." William smiled ruefully. "He caught me eye, nodded, smiled, then melted away into the crowd. Didn't want to betray our presence here. Nay, he is no threat."

Lesley whispered, disgust apparent in his tone. "Told ye to get rid of those blasted boots! They be a dead giveaway." Giving William a scornful look, he pressed his lips into a straight, hard line, a signal to remain quiet.

The diverse throng of onlookers inched forward, the damp air filling their lungs with various degrees of body odor mixed with smells of both human and horse sweat. The weather was mild and cool, but the people were packed so tightly together that they were like a heated furnace, radiating an odor of human fear. But their morbid curiosity kept them moving forward, eagerly awaiting the outcome of this day's trial.

The preliminary questioning began in earnest, and the crowd grew quiet, straining to hear every word, hushing their fellows to silence.

The head councilman was a square-built, black-bearded man who rose to his feet with an air of supreme authority. He cleared his throat and read the charges to Forrest once again. "Ye have heard the reading of the charges of heresy, Friar Forrest—treason against His Holiness, the Pope, and the Holy Mother Church. How do ye answer these charges, Friar Forrest?"

Although a young man, Forrest was normally strong and active, aristocratic and noble in his bearing; but now, he appeared painfully thin. During his three-year imprisonment in the grim, bottle-shaped sea tower—a rough, hollowed-out rock dungeon—Forrest was deprived of food and warmth and the usual necessities of life.

Despite his pitiful condition, he had prepared for this moment, knowing the outcome would not be in his favor. He held his back straight, showing no fear, and his courage was evident. Looking determinedly at the council, he addressed them with strong conviction.

"How is it that ye say I have committed treason?" Forrest inquired of the council, his eyes blazing with indignation. "Never have I at any time dishonored my country by word or deed."

The council, in one accord, looked at Forrest in disgust, shaking their heads in consternation; then the head councilman stood to address the statement, releasing a heavy sigh, bored with having to answer the question.

"Did ye not hear the accusations read this day, Friar Forrest? The treason we speak of is against His Holiness, the Pope, and against the Holy Mother Church, its Holy Ordinances and the Sacred Sacraments. Nay, it is not against Scotland that ye are accused, and well ye know it."

"Canna reading the New Testament, aye, and believing it be treason? Whom am I betraying? Are we not all scholars of God's Holy Word? Why do ye fear the Word of God and declare that believing it is treason? This same Word, the Testament of Jesus Christ, shall judge me in that day—not the Pope, nor yet this wicked council. Ye, the same who send a betrayer to hear me confession, which is, above all, sacred. But it is ye who offer money, as did another wicked council, promising silver to Judas to betray the Innocent!"

Disgruntled mutterings erupted from the spectators in hearing distance of the proceedings, but whether in protest of the accusations from the council or from Forrest's bold words, it was difficult to tell. The head councilman called for quiet, and guards on horseback were quickly dispatched to remove any unruly person disturbing the trial.

William shifted uneasily, turning slightly to observe the reactions on the faces of the onlookers. Lesley had slipped away, keeping a careful distance from William. Their eyes met, and an imperceptible nod noted their position in the throng of people. It appeared that a great deal of sympathy was on the side of Forrest.

Eager, young zealots boiled over in anger and resentment, raising a loud protest for the ludicrous accusations brought by the council, but a mounted royal guardsman silenced them with a threatening swing of his sword.

"How dare ye, Friar Forrest," thundered the bulky balding councilman. "Ye hold in treasonous contempt His Holiness, the Pope, and his Divine authority! How dare ye to discount the Holy Virgin, the sinless Mother of God, and the Holy Mother Church! This is treason of the highest order."

But Forrest was not finished. "Aye, ye who judge me this day," Forrest responded with calm resolution, "know this: The Holy Mother Church is corrupted, enfeebled by abuses and false teaching. Ye have departed from the teaching of the Bible, the teachings of Christ, which ye hide from the common people of Scotland, keeping them ignorant and dependent on the Church and its priest for salvation."

"Enough! Enough! End this treasonous talk at once!" thundered the chief councilman, his bloated eyes blazing with outrage. "Cease this heretical harangue against our Holy Father and the Church!" His voice echoed over the restless crowd, carried on waves of malevolent energy.

"Enough, ye say?" Forrest challenged. "Is this not a public trial in which I may defend myself? I adjure thee by God to allow me—one of your own priests, a Benedictine of spotless reputation—to speak."

"Cease, I say!" ordered the councilman, desperate to stop any further talk. Immediately, Cardinal Beaton pointed a long forefinger in the direction of the head councilman, and the man resumed his seat, a deep scowl creasing his angry features. Then Cardinal Beaton himself rose to his feet, motioning for the guard to drag Forrest directly before the council bench.

A foul cry erupted from the crowd, making further speech impossible. They moved and shifted on their feet, like the restless troubled waves on the North Sea, churning about, raising their fists, shouting mixed messages to the councilmen.

A stout, round-faced man shouted, "Burn him, burn him! Burn the heretic!" The incensed throng joined in the chant, eager to be entertained by the burning of another heretic.

Others in the crowd protested, shouting above the tumult. "Spare him; spare him! Save the innocent!"

Slowly and deliberately, Cardinal Beaton walked from around the long table, accompanied by several of his council. He was an extraordinarily clever and unscrupulous man, given to his own pleasure. He maintained a mistress, who bore him a number of bastard children; but since he was considered celibate by not marrying his mistress, the immoral union was considered allowable under the edicts of the Roman Church.

He stood before Forrest, a triumphant smirk spreading across his insipid countenance. His shrewd, narrow eyes swept over the crowd, seeking out those placed among the people to support his judgment.

With a devious and perverse pleasure, Cardinal Beaton began to divest Forrest of his friar's habit.

He forcefully ripped the head covering from Forrest's head, waving it aloft for the crowd to see. A cheer went up from the agitators and a groan of despair from those in sympathy. Next, he removed the silver chain with the ornately carved cross, and then the tunic of the Benedictine Order of Friars. He handed them to the waiting councilmen as cheers rose from the crowd.

"I strip from ye this day, Friar Forrest, the emblems of the Order of the Benedictines of whom ye have made your sacred vows and have dishonored the Holy Sacraments in possessing and reading the heretical and forbidden English Testament, banned and condemned by His Holiness, the Pope, the Vicar of Christ on Earth. Thereby, we renounce ye as a priest and a friar of the Benedictines and judge thee a heretic of the Holy Mother Church of Rome." Beaton's rigorous and brutal manner was intended to intimidate the onlookers.

Forrest, having been stripped of all his priestly habit, even to his shoes, replied with dignity, "The Word of God says in the first book of Corinthians, 'Let a man so account of us, as of the ministers of Christ, and stewards of the mysteries of God . . . that a man be found faithful.' I fear, O' Cardinal, that ye indeed keep all things a mystery, for ye do not understand yourself, or ye would not be upon this platform acting in God's stead. I adjure thee to also remove my baptism—the salt, the spittle, and exorcisms—all my priestly vows."

The bold words brought a gasp from the crowd. They looked upward, expecting to see fire falling from Heaven to devour Forrest where he stood.

"How dare ye thus speak to the cardinal of the Holy Mother Church with such blatant disregard for God's wrath on your defiant and disobedient soul," the head churchman shrieked, his face turning purple with outrage and disgust. "Repent at once and beg for mercy ere ye shall surely be damned in the fires of Hell for eternity!"

Forrest turned to the table of councilmen and high-ranking churchmen—Walter Lang, his confessor and betrayer, sitting among them, his countenance a study of shame and confusion.

"Fie on false betrayers," said Forrest, addressing his hired confessor, Walter Lang. "Fie on deniers of truth and justice! Fie on those who betray the innocent, who will face an eternal righteous judgment by God Himself."

Chapter 22

(Of whom the world was not worthy:)
they wandered in deserts, and in mountains,
and in dens and caves of the earth.

Hebrews 11:38

FROM THE OUTER FRINGES OF the diverse crowd of onlookers, William and Lesley observed the proceedings, knowing the outcome of the trial would not be in Forrest's favor.

Weakened by months of deprivation and abuse, Forrest trembled with fatigue, his body a mere shadow of his former self. William silently prayed that Forrest would not collapse before the crowd and, by some miracle, would manage to stay calm and collected when the sentence was pronounced. The physically weakened Forrest looked around at the crowd, his own countrymen, searching the faces in the crush of people and horses, drinking in the sight of humankind after his long and lonely separation from his own kind while he languished in solitary confinement.

His blue eyes filled with tears and again he spoke, his abused body trembling, but his voice remaining calm and confident. "It is with no disrepute that I say it is a very small thing that I should be judged of ye, or of man's judgment. Aye, I judge not mine own self, for I know nothing by myself; yet am I not hereby justified, but He that will judge me is the Lord."

Archbishop Beaton grew livid with anger, his face reflecting a profane and blasphemous contempt. He returned to his council seat and stood in front of his chair. Then he requested that the entire assembled council stand with him in a show of solidarity, and he pronounced sentence.

"By the power invested in me," said Beaton in an utterly uncompromising tone, "by the authority of His Holiness, the Pope, the Vicar of Christ on Earth, I declare thee, Henry Forrest, a heretic, an enemy and adversary of truth, of the Holy Mother Church of Rome, and sentence thee to die the death of a confessed heretic by burning with fire until dead."

A score of onlookers cheered, a fiendish glee erupting from the declaration, hoping to witness the burning of the confessed heretic, Henry Forrest, former Benedictine friar, like it was a great entertainment. But a definite element of the crowd dropped their heads as if shamed at the verdict. Forrest's honest and forthright words rang clear with what many already believed—that the Church of Rome was indeed a disguise for immorality and abuse of its ignorant parishioners.

The archbishop and his council debated among themselves for a few moments; then the head councilman spoke. "Henry Forrest, judged this day as a heretic, being divested of all his Benedictine vows and his loyalty and commitment to the Holy Mother Church, the only means by which he may enter Heaven, has been sentenced by His Holiness, Archbishop David Beaton, to be burned at the stake on the highest point of this city."

This place the councilman spoke of was a high prominence near the north end of the Abbey Church. By burning Forrest on this high position, the execution fire could be seen from across the River Tay and visible in Forfarshire and Angus. Beaton hoped to bring fear and compliance to all who would see the fires of judgment from all vantage points of the city.

Barely able to stand, Forrest was led away by the guards, who roughly threw him into a waiting wagon that would drive him to the place of execution. William and Lesley made their way through the crowd to the High Street and Lesley's discreet dwelling. William made ready to leave, wrapping his belongings in his saddle pack and gathering his horse tack.

"And just what are ye doing, Carmichael?" Lesley questioned, his face a study of consternation.

"I be saddling me pony and attending the execution, me friend. Perhaps, I will be able to grab Forrest and whisk him away from the guards before they know what's happening, aye?"

Lesley grabbed William's arm, turning him around to face him. "Och, William," he said, "ye be mad! Dinna think ye can rescue the man with so many guards and this blood-thirsty throng who would burn ye with him if ye be caught! Nay, William, dinna think it! This be a foolish plan."

William paused in his preparations, considering Lesley's words. "Ye are me true friend, Lesley, but I must try. If it looks like I canna pull it off, I will abandon the rescue; but if I can save him from a terrible, unjust death, then I must try."

Lesley shook his head, unconvinced that William himself would not end up a prisoner. The idea of rescuing Forrest at this point was far too risky. What was William thinking?

"Och, me friend," William said, laying one hand on Lesley's shoulder, "dinna fash yourself on me account. Me mount is fast and steady, will go miles without tiring. If I canna do this, then I will abandon the effort; but Lesley, be thinkin' I must try. Have me son to think of, me kin, and dare not be careless. Canna risk being caught for Peter's sake, so I be the soul of caution."

"Then by all means, take your weapons and dinna spare to use them if ye must. But William, ye must be knowing, if ye be caught, I canna help ye."

Seeing deep worry lines etching Lesley's forehead, William softened. "Aye, there be great danger; I am not daft, Lesley. What ye say is true, but dinna worry over me and pray for me safety, aye?"

Turning toward the rising noise of the boisterous crowd, William said, "Appears they are taking Forrest directly to the place of execution, so must make haste, try to get close before the execution mob arrives."

"God be with ye, William, and remember, dinna return here if ye escape with Forrest. Take the long way around the firth and be off to home. Send a message when ye can, but use a sign, aye?"

"Aye, Lesley. Farewell and Godspeed." The two men embraced, knowing they would not see each other for some time. Each knew the hazards of their dangerous roles in the ongoing Reformation movement. Yet some men would rise, daring to risk life and liberty for freedom from tyranny and oppression.

The Galloway pony was quickly made ready, and William was mounted and riding toward the high hill at the north end of the Abbey. Before the prisoner had arrived at the site of execution, a pyre of wood and faggots already surrounded the stake set in the center. It was obvious that the death sentence had been previously decided.

Forrest was taken from the wagon and made to walk the remaining steps to the site of execution, but he was so weak that he stumbled and fell until the well-armed guards held him upright, lifting him over the rocky ground. An entourage of councilmen, along with the archbishop, accompanied the prisoner to witness the conclusion of the death sentence. They seemed to be in a jovial mood, and the followers and drama-seekers were equally expectant, eager for this day's entertainment.

Several witnesses and guardsmen were on horseback, sticking close to the prisoner as William edged his way toward the riders, endeavoring to blend in with the mounted horsemen. He was armed, his broadsword across his back beneath his cloak, his dirk and battle axe at his side. Others in the mob rode horses, and still others had small carts laden with children, pulled along by donkeys.

To rescue Forrest, William must dash toward the prisoner, dispatch the guards surrounding Forrest, and lift him onto his pony, then ride to safety before he was caught. It must be the perfect moment, coupled with the element of surprise, or the rescue would fail. He had done this before, but not with so many people and guards jamming the way. But try as he might, William could not maneuver his pony through the tightly packed throng surrounding the prisoner. The guards were shoving onlookers aside, endeavoring to work their way uphill to the place of execution. The crowd moved away from the swinging swords of the guardsmen, who were losing patience with the unruly and jostling swarm of people.

The surging crowd shifted, moving to one side. The eye of the needle appeared for a moment amid the sweating, odorous mob. William spurred his pony through the opening and, in seconds, was in arm's length of Forrest. Their eyes met, and Forrest understood that a rescue attempt was nearby. He smiled resignedly, shaking his head.

Two stalwart guards eyed William suspiciously, noting his close proximity to the prisoner. William moved his mount forward, drawing his dirk, ready to grab Forrest from the guards who were holding him up. Immediately, the mounted royal guard raised their swords, slashing their way toward William, cutting off his advance.

William withdrew, abandoning his position, jerking his mount away from the slashing swords of the guardsmen. He could no longer maneuver his pony close enough to grab Forrest. The moment had passed. Some of the surging throng of people grabbed hold of William's cloak, realizing that he was attempting a rescue. William kicked them off, thrusting the would-be assailants aside, then quickly retreated.

The opportunity for rescue had vanished in seconds. William guided his pony away from the crowd, groaning inwardly, his heart throbbing with keen disappointment. A sharp, stabbing pain seized his chest as the reality of failure descended over him like a wet blanket, wrapping him in anguish. The attempt to rescue Forrest was lost. The condemned man would die in the flames of tyranny.

Reigning his mount to a stop, William halted as the crowd moved around him, swelling and rushing forward, eager to have the best view of the burning. Lesley passed him at a discreet distance, and the two men nodded. William turned his pony toward the south, and Lesley responded with a fisted hand movement. He understood. The rescue attempt had failed, and William was riding south, toward safety and the familiar lands of Carmichael, toward home.

The burning took place on the high promontory already chosen for the place of execution, a place near the north end of the Abbey Church where the flames and smoke could be seen across the River Tay and visible even to the shire of Angus. All would understand that to defy papal authority would result in a cruel and shameful death at a fiery stake.

Chapter 23

The beast and his image, his mark and his name
My love and allegiance no longer can claim.

Evening Light Songs

FROM A HIGH HILL OVERLOOKING the River Tay, William watched the execution from a distance. He could see the rising flames; smell the acrid, foul-smelling smoke; and hear the waning hum and roar of the gathering crowd. They surged forward, eager to watch the heretic burn, perhaps recant and beg for mercy, or say something profound that would be worth remembering.

William prayed fervently that Forrest would die quickly, that he would resist the taunts and mocking words of the incensed mob, hold steady and strong as he gave his life for the crime of possessing and believing the English New Testament. Anger and disgust burned in his heart at the injustice of the cardinals and bishops of the papal hierarchy.

Then William turned his Galloway pony toward the south, leaving behind the brutal scene of execution. A persistent wind blew steadily off the cold North Sea, sending the acrid smoke westward, warning the inhabitants of the Highlands—those fierce, ancient clans—that any who defied the great power of papal hierarchy would suffer a similar fate.

Hot, bitter tears welled up, stinging his eyes. He halted his pony near a clump of dense, gnarled trees, waiting for this unwanted emotion to pass. Then he methodically began the task of removing his disguise; but before he even threw off his cloak, a sound from the underbrush caught his attention. He quickly removed his dirk, and turning swiftly, he saw a man crouching in the brush, hidden from passersby. No doubt, the man was a spy.

Pouncing quickly, he reached through the brush, jerking the man from his hiding place beneath the thickly woven shelter of branches. He connected with thick folds of fabric and roughly drew the man out of the brambles, his dirk sharp and ready.

A scream pierced the damp air, and a woman's voice begged for mercy. "Please, sir, I pray thee, do me no harm! I have done nothing wrong—just came to watch the execution—but the guards saw me, were coming for me, and I fled. Please, sir! Have mercy, I pray."

William lessened his grasp, then slowly slid his dirk in the sheath. "And why were the guards coming for ye, lass? Who are ye? Where do ye live?"

"Och, sir, please listen to me story. I be Friar Forrest's sister, and I see the mounted guard watching me. I fear the guards knew who I be and were thinking of bringing me to the council to be questioned or, mayhap, even held as suspicious. Aye, I dinna kin, but I left my mount where I had hidden him and ran away."

"Do ye live in the village near Linlithgow where Henry Forrest hails from?"

"Aye, I do. Me family owns a forge there, be silver smiths. We be respectable subjects, still loyal to Rome. Me da' sent me to hear me brother's confession before they took him away. They wanted to hear what answers Henry gave Archbishop Beaton for the charges of treason and heresy."

"And did ye hear your brother's words?" William asked.

"Aye, so clearly I did. Be saying them over and over to meself, so I dinna forget."

Suddenly, the pounding of rapidly ascending hoofbeats came thundering over the rise where the waiting couple stood. The two guards who drove William from the rescue of Forrest shouted a warning.

"Ye there, in the bush, halt in the name of the Privy Council of Scotland and Archbishop Beaton of St. Andrews and dinna dare move!" shouted the head guard, drawing his sword.

"Och," cried the woman now wringing her hands. "It be the two guards who were coming for me!"

"Nay, lass, they were never coming for ye, but for me! They discovered me plan, were trying to stop the rescue. Now, take me mount and be off into the woods—quickly now! Do as I say!"

The two royal guards dismounted their steeds, tying the reins to some low-lying branches. William drew his sword and battle axe, ready for what might come. The lass had quickly obeyed and was mounted and riding into the woods.

The royal guardsmen halted a few feet away, noting that William was fully armed and standing his ground, feet apart, ready to do battle. "And just who in the devil are ye?" asked the head guard. He was a churlish-looking man with thin lips that sneered easily, showing crooked, yellow teeth. He bellowed a laugh, pointing a gloved finger at William.

"Och, aye, I remember ye at the execution, indeed I do, trying to free the heretic Forrest, aye? I remember the pony too—same pony your lass is riding away on as I speak, leaving ye to fare for yourself, the ungrateful wench."

The comment did not sit well with William, but he schooled his face and voice to be calm. "Do ye have substantial charges then, or are ye just harassing bystanders present for the trial?" asked William, not answering their question of his identity.

"Anyone interfering with an execution of a condemned heretic is more than a harassment," shouted the head guard, spittle flying from his mouth. "Ye will be arrested and taken in for questioning. Hand over your weapons!"

"Ye will have to take them," said William shaking free of his cloak. He was grateful for his disguise, except for his boots. Hadn't Lesley warned him about the boots?

"Be it your way, then," said the guard and motioned with his hand for the second guard to seize William.

Casting a malignant look at his superior officer, the reluctant second moved toward William but hesitated as William stood still, positioning himself for the fight. The second man was short and paunchy with a bloated, red face, possibly not as agile and fit as the head man; but still, he must have some skill with a sword.

"Well, what, by thunder, are ye waiting for?" bellowed the lead guard. "He is just a common crofter making a bonny show with his weapons. Probably never used them, for that matter. Now, take the man down! Ye have armor on, don't ye?"

Realizing that William wore no protective armor, the royal guardsman swung his sword around, loosening his sword arm, taking courage in the lead guard's words.

William stood rooted, waiting for the man to strike the first blow. With a sudden movement, the guard thrust the sword with surprising strength; but William skillfully parried, and then swords clashed, sending sparks flying as steel met steel. Several minutes of fierce fighting followed. William waited for the right moment to employ his battle axe. The moment came, and he brought down the dreaded weapon across the man's shoulder, breaking through the armor and sending blood spurting from the wound. It was a fatal blow. The guard fell heavily to the ground without a groan, helpless and dying.

Enraged, the head guard quickly moved forward, more skilled in his ability to maneuver and fight. He moved stealthily around William, his back to the woods as William moved with him, aware of a sudden attack. The incensed man circled him like a prowling wolf, waiting to pounce. But William Carmichael was no ordinary swordsman, but a skilled fighter, fit and ready. Years of defending Carmichael lands from outlaws and Border Reivers had served him well, honing his abilities. Suddenly, he was glad for the boots that stood him solidly in position. A grin tugged at the corners of his mouth. He was the Man of the Broken Spear—always ready.

A wound on his thigh during battle with the first man suddenly began to bleed profusely, and William felt dizziness begin to blur his vision. He was fully aware of his opponent, but he felt a sense of weakness taking over. Noting this, the head guard saw his advantage and raised his sword high, ready to strike a death blow.

William could tell his momentum was off. He could feel that keen, perceptive edge slipping away. He raised his sword to parry the blow; but at that same instant, the sharp report of a Highland pistol blasted from the proximity of the surrounding trees. The guard's face took on a surprised expression, eyes widening; then his sword fell from his grasp, and he sank to the ground, his eyes staring vacantly up at the smoky, overcast sky.

From the edge of the forest, twenty feet away, William saw the lass still holding the pistol. She had crept back after tying the pony to a tree. The pistol went slack in her hand, and she moved forward to look at the two men lying on the ground. Then she looked at William, her eyes filling with tears.

"Did I tell ye," she said as tears streamed down her cheeks, "we also make Highland pistols? I test them for me da' straight from the forge, so I be a fair shot, too. I carry a pistol in me pocket . . . in times of danger. Och, I've done murder now, so I be in a heap of trouble, for certain."

"Dinna fash yourself, lass," William said, then sank to the ground, his wound still seeping blood.

The lass wiped at her tears and knelt beside William, assessing the wound. She began to rip fabric from the hem of her petticoat, applying firm pressure to the jagged wound. Next, she fetched water flasks from the horses belonging to the guards and gave William a long, cool drink. The refreshing water served to strengthen him considerably, and the dizziness faded away.

When the fog had cleared from his head, William asked, "What be your name, lass?"

"I be called Lorna Forrest, daughter of Fergus and Marjorie Forrest, sister to Henry Forrest." She began to weep then, remembering that her brother was still suffering at the stake. Sometimes, Lorna recalled, it took hours for death to come.

"Ye must not weep now, Lorna, no time. We must leave this place. The royal guards will be looking for these men. We must flee. Bring me pony, and we be off."

The tearful lass left at once, untied the pony, and was back quickly enough. "Should we take the horses?" Lorna queried.

"Nay, best to leave them. Dinna want to add horse thieving to me account."

"We could take them into the woods for a wee bit, so dinna bring attention to this place, aye?"

"Aye, we could do that," William agreed. Though it was a struggle for William to mount his pony, his mounting leg was not wounded, so he managed to mount with little difficulty.

Lorna spread brush over the bodies of the fallen guardsmen, so they would not be readily seen from the road, then mounted the head guardsman's horse and led the other. A little distance into the forest, she lightly tied the horses to low branches, so they could graze.

The two escapees rode pillion on the stalwart Galloway pony, putting distance between St. Andrews and the terrible event taking place. It was far too risky to go back for Lorna's horse near the execution site.

As they traveled southward, William threw back the hood of his cloak, exposing his burning eyes and face to the cooling dampness of the mist-laden wind. Perhaps he had failed to rescue Forrest, but he had managed to save many others, whisking them away to safety, helping them escape to England, where the disreputable King Henry VIII welcomed them, offering the believers a place of refuge.

But now, he would deliver Lorna to her village home near Linlithgow, to where her parents were anxiously awaiting her return.

If they were papists, as Lorna had said, what would they think of the dying words of their son? Undoubtedly, Henry Forrest had joined the Benedictines because he believed in their cause, but he had discovered the truth when Patrick Hamilton had so boldly declared the Gospel of Christ and was not afraid to stand by his convictions.

William had saved Lorna, and in turn, she had saved him with a well-aimed shot from her pistol forged in her father's smithy. William felt a measure of guilt over the death of the royal guardsmen, wicked men though they be; but after all, he was defending a helpless woman, or so he thought. Instead, Lorna proved to be far more than helpless. The lass possessed courage and a good aim—he would give her that. A fatal blow of the guardsman's sword could very well have taken him out, but for Lorna's skill and bravery.

The Galloway pony moved steadily southward. Lorna, now seated behind William, was weeping softly. William could feel her sadness, her slight form trembling close to his back. Now that they were riding away, the horrific events of the day were coming into focus—the ugliness, the trauma, the injustice all becoming too real. The grief of losing her brother to a horrific death by fire was too much. William had no time to study the lass in that brief meeting before the royal guardsmen had arrived on the scene, but he had noted her dark hair and tawny-colored eyes. But the lass was so distressed and covered with grime and brush that her features were lost in that intense moment when they were fighting for escape of capture.

William sighed heavily, his own grief over the failed rescue attempt as keen as Lorna's tears. Next time, he determined, he would not fail. He would never give up this dangerous and perilous calling to save the condemned New Testament Christians.

On the long trek home, they sheltered in a crofter's home or barn, sometimes under the open sky with a brush arbor for shelter, avoiding the main traveling roads. William did not reveal his identity to Lorna. She knew him as William from Lanarkshire. They shared food that William purchased from crofters with money he brought from home. He told her of his desire to save and warn the innocent believers, explaining to Lorna the words of Jesus translated from Latin, a language Lorna did not understand.

One cold evening spent around the campfire, Lorna asked, "What will happen to us, William? We have done murder."

"Murder, ye think? Well, dinna like to do it, lass, nay, but it was those wicked men or us, aye? Methinks God will not hold us guilty; but if He does, well, seems He will forgive us." A rare smile crossed his lips, and no more was said.

After delivering Lorna safely to the home of her parents near Linlithgow and briefly telling of their son's courage and bravery as he faced his accusers, William turned his mount toward home. His wound had ceased to bleed, but even after careful cleaning and bandaging at the end of the day, the wound appeared ugly and angry. William needed the skillful hands of Coira to make it well again.

Alone now and riding his pony toward home, he could hear the whispering of God and struggled to hear, to understand. Perhaps Sir John was right. It would take more than brute strength to move the Reformation forward.

"Oh, God," he prayed with burning passion, "help me understand the way. If I be wrong, give me light . . . light to see me own self! I heard it said if people have light, they will find their way. But now, we be in a cave of darkness. Send us light, O God, and we go forward to grasp it."

Chapter 24

I'll walk in the truth all the days of my life
I'll never go back again.

Evening Light Songs

DURING THE YEARS FOLLOWING THE execution of Henry Forrest in 1533, more Reformers were tried and executed. The papal clergy endeavored to close the dark stone again using terror and violence as a weapon. But during this time of persecution, many in Scotland were enlightened through the smuggled copies of the New Testament in English. These forbidden writings were distributed throughout Scotland, revealing the abuses in the papal system and among the clergy.

In Lanarkshire, the Carmichaels of Carmichael kept a low profile, enduring several searches of their property by the magistrates. The only evidence of religious zeal to be found was a copy of the Latin translation of the Vulgate Bible, kept in plain view on Sir John's desk. This translation was approved by the Church, since most commoners could not read Latin.

Sir John paced the floor in his war room, stopping periodically to gaze out the long window overlooking the stables. He watched as William thundered into the stable yard, dust flying from the hooves of his black stallion. He shook his head, amazed at the tenacity and persistence of his younger brother.

There was nothing ordinary about William. He was a risk-taker, a man driven by purpose, but loyal and trusting to his clan and family, a true Man of the Broken Spear. In a few minutes, William knocked purposefully on the heavy oak door.

"Enter," Sir John said. The door opened, and William entered, an annoyed expression crossing his features.

"Greetings, brother," William said. He proceeded to brush dust from his clothing with his hat, unconcerned that it was settling on the recently dusted oak flooring. "What is so urgent? I need to wash. I be chasing would-be pillagers from the southern borders of Carmichael lands. Your messenger caught up with me there."

Sir John raised his eyebrows, nodded, but said nothing.

"Not to worry, though," William said reassuringly, "they were just overgrown bairns looking for some fun, not dangerous, just thoughtless youth. I sent them packing to home."

"Ye can wash later, William." Sir John continued pacing the floor. He made no comment on the fun-seeking youths rollicking on the borders of Carmichael. His mind was elsewhere. Youthful escapades were irrelevant to him at present.

"It be a dangerous trail ye ride, brother," Sir John began. "Ye barely escaped from St. Andrews after the trial of Forrest and now, the Border Reivers always be raiding now that spring be here. Have a care, William."

"I told ye that they were only overgrown bairns. Dinna fash yourself, John."

"Aye, and there are the covert meetings that ye ride to warn the believers about . . . Your disguise will be discovered, and then—"

"I think I be missing something, John," interrupted William. "Surely, ye dinna call me back to Carmichael for a brotherly lecture."

"Aye," sighed Sir John, "there be other concerns; ye be right. Many of those secret meetings gather all manner of folks, even papists. We cannot expect known papists to hear a message they are not ready to receive; but at the same time, we canna underestimate the power of planting a single seed. I know this, William, but ye worry me."

Shaking his head, William said nothing. Something was not right here. He had never known Sir John to appear so agitated. He seemed to be rethinking what they already knew, the apprehensions they had discussed a hundred times over, their concerns about the recent burnings. His brother was growing older, and perhaps, the stresses of these volatile times weighed too heavily on his broad shoulders. William waited. Sir John would tell him after pacing a few more rounds.

"David never really knew Goliath's strength, and no doubt, it was formidable," Sir John continued. "But David focused entirely on God's strength alone, wee lad that he was. William, we canna do battle in our own strength; we must wait on God, allow Him to fight this battle. Look for God's will in this."

"A man often meets God's will on the road he took to avoid it," said William, smiling. Ye do remember Jonah, aye? I dinna choose this path, John. Aye, God chose it for me. I know we differ on me involvement, me way of aiding the Reformation. We have the same goals, just different methods. Now, brother, tell me why ye called me back—not for this wisdom alone, I'll wager."

Sir John sighed deeply. "Vera well then. I be troubled, William. I sent for ye . . . to ask for your help . . . for your advice on this matter.

Ye are more often with the king, or at least conferring with him concerning the horses, so I felt ye would have some insight on the mood of the young monarch, of how things be at Crawfordjohn. The king is in residence there, ye kin."

"Ha! Me brotherly advice! Aye, say on, John, and I shall give ye advice from my fathomless store of Scottish wisdom."

The jest did not amuse Sir John. He gave William a scathing look, then said, "I be serious, William. Ye have influence with the king because of your long-time acquaintance working with his horses, ye kin, so I'm a thinkin' ye might assist me in this . . . in me plan for Katherine."

William shrugged his shoulders and seated himself in a worn leather chair adjacent to Sir John's desk. He stretched his long arms above his head. "What say ye then, brother?"

"Ye understand," Sir John began, "the king and his advisors are considering a wife for him—a Catholic wife, to be sure. Me thinks he will seek a French alliance to strengthen the dictates of the Holy Mother Church. He needs protection from England . . . especially from his uncle, King Henry."

"Why does that concern us, John?" William waved his hand indifferently. "Ye kin that a marriage was forthcoming. The king will marry because his council will insist upon it; and as ye say, a French wife for his court is a predictable match."

"Aye, that's so," Sir John agreed. "I need for ye to go with me to request for the king to release Katherine, from . . . ah . . . her duties at court." His throat tightened. "To come home, William . . . home to Carmichael House. Katherine is with the king at Crawfordjohn at present, so would be a perfect time to seek her release."

The veiled features of his stalwart and determined brother could not be hidden from William. He recognized the pain behind Sir John's eyes, the urgency in his request for help. William softened his attitude, then asked in a gentler tone, "Do ye fear for her, John? Has not the king treated her well?"

"Well enough, I suppose," replied Sir John. He lifted a hand to his brow, and his mouth hardened into a straight line. "He will take a queen soon, and dinna kin what will happen when he does. The King of Scots will not only have a wife who will be queen of Scotland, he will most likely retain many of his present mistresses—and heaven knows, he certainly has enough, aye?"

Now William understood the reason of his call back to Carmichael. Sir John was worried about Katherine's welfare and thinking about his safety as well. It was almost too much for one man to bear alone.

Remembering his sweet niece acting as consort to the young king, William methodically shook his head in disgust but did not dare to voice his opinion on the subject. The young king was certainly a profligate, encouraged in his debauchery by the ungodly behavior of his councilmen. He waited in silence for Sir John to continue.

"Aye, William," Sir John explained, "I know that Katherine is unhappy. I see it in her face when we chance to visit when the king is residing at Crawfordjohn. Perchance, she has influenced the king to some extent during the heretic trials, the bonny ways of her vera hard to resist, but alas, to no avail. Jamie has no authority over the verdicts of the Roman hierarchy. Aye," he said leaning forward, fatherly concern evident on his face, "Katherine needs to come home. She *must* come home."

William studied his dust-covered boots, the same boots that Lindsey had warned him to discard. He sighed heavily. He was bone-weary of the never-ending issues with the Crown.

"Aye, John," he said with thinly veiled lassitude, "I will go to Crawfordjohn, but it would be good to take Peter with ye. The king is fond of the lad; and if Katherine is urged by her favorite cousin to resign her . . . ah, position . . . " William searched for the right words, feeling heat rising to redden his face. "And," he said, continuing his thought, "if Jamie agrees, I feel certain Katherine will comply."

"We can ride to Crawfordjohn tomorrow, first light, aye?" queried Sir John.

"Aye," William agreed, "on the morrow then. I feel certain Peter will come. The king will be wanting an update on the state of the new foals, so the timing is right. We will bring the lassie home, John."

"God willing, it will be so. Before ye go, William, have ye any news of what is happening at Holyrood Abbey in Edinburgh?"

"Aye, John, and it will grieve ye to hear it. Takes a while for word to get here. My friend Lesley sent a message last week. Ye remember the two men who were arrested and brought to Edinburgh for trial some months ago?

"Aye, names of Straiton and Gourlay? Have they been acquitted?"

"Nay, quite the contrary. They have been found guilty and will be executed." William ran his finger through his dark hair, frustration evident in the gesture. "Ye kin that I canna be there . . . so close to us here in the valley. I must be careful. And even if I were to go there, the security is far too tight to attempt a rescue."

"Aye, of course. Dinna fash yourself over what ye cannot help, William. Tell me what happened."

"Well," said William releasing a long sigh, "Straiton owns a fishing business, has a crew and boats, and does quite well in his trade. David Straiton is the youngest son of the Laird of Lauriston in Forfarshire."

"Och, aye, I have heard of them. Seated in Forfarshire for hundreds of years." Sir John leaned forward, listening intently.

"Well, he moored his fishing fleet at the mouth of the River Esk. His fishing trade did so well that the Prior at St. Andrews heard of his success."

"When it comes to gold and silver, it doesn't take long for the bishops and churchmen to hear about it," said Sir John, a note of disgust in his voice.

"After hearing of Straiton's lucrative trade," William continued, "the prior demanded a tithe of his earnings." Shaking his head, William rubbed his thumb and forefinger together, suggesting that money was the prior's motive.

"Ha! Sir John exclaimed. "That sounds about right!"

"Aye, that's so," agreed William. "Well, John, Straiton told his crew to throw back every tenth fish and tell the prior to come and get his tithe."

Both men burst into laughter.

"Of course," William said wiping his eyes, "that made the prior quite angry, so he sent a message that if Straiton didn't comply in the proper manner of giving tithe, he would be suspect for heresy; and if he disregarded the request, he would surely be in contempt."

Rising from his chair and walking to the fireside, Sir John laid one arm across the large oaken mantelpiece. "What happened next, William?"

"Ye kin, Straiton was vera much an outdoor man, loving what he did in his fishing business, but not much for books and learning. No time for God or religion either. Canna even read, had no interest, much to his family's displeasure. He didn't really understand the danger he put himself in, defying the prior's demands."

"There is always a consequence when you defy the hierarchy at St. Andrews," said Sir John with a sigh. "And men lifted up in pride and who abuse the liberty of others will make sure there is a penalty."

William began pacing the floor. Looking down, he noticed a worn path on the oak floorboards where Sir John himself had paced when thinking, seeking answers, or walking off frustration. William smiled to himself.

"Well, John, Straiton decided to educate himself on the consequences of his action—throwing the fish tithe back into the river, that is—so he enlisted a well-versed neighbor, John Erskine of Dun, to help him understand what this heresy was all about. Erskine educated Straiton in spiritual matters. It wasn't long before the young man denounced the Roman Church and converted to Christianity."

"I can see the handwriting on the wall," said Sir John.

Halting in his pacing, William whirled to face John directly, his manner filled with outrage. "That one incident, John, ignited a fire storm! The magistrates were sent out to hunt for more heretics. Suspects were summoned to appear at court. Some recanted; still others fled Scotland for the safety of England or the continent. But when Straiton and Gourlay were summoned, they refused to flee or recant. Both men stood firm. Gourlay, a young student at St. Andrews, was in priest's orders, more's the pity."

"It seems Katherine doesn't have the influence she hoped for in her position with the young king," said Sir John.

"From what I understand, Lesley says that Jamie made several attempts to get Straiton and Gourlay to recant, begged them to reconsider their stand. He seemed desperate to save them from the stake. That had to be Katherine's influence, John, but the merciless clergy boldly informed the king that it was unlawful for even a king to pardon condemned heretics since the law of the Church and the Pope exceeded the king's authority."

Returning to his chair, Sir John bowed his head in his brawny hands, his elbows on his desk. "Och! We cry for justice, but there be none. O, God, when will this end?"

"Gourlay was charged with heresy," said William. "He told his accusers that the Pope had no jurisdiction over his soul—or in Scotland, for that matter—and there was no such thing as Purgatory, if that was where the Holy Mother Church intended to send him."

"And what of Straiton?" inquired Sir John shaking his head, trying to absorb the details of this awful story.

"Well, it be that after the judgment-pronouncing Gourlay and Straiton heretics, the execution site chosen for the burnings was situated at the Cross of Greenside between Edinburgh and Leith."

William paused, remembering his own narrow escape. "Of course, this was done to strike terror in the inhabitants of Fife who could see the flames and smell the bitter smoke of the condemned heretics wafting across the valley."

"It is over, then?" queried Sir John.

Releasing a heavy sigh, William said, "Aye, John, it is over."

Silence followed the tale. The brothers could not speak for some time, both lost in thought. There were no words to express their sadness over this horrific event, so close to the once-peaceful Valley of the Clyde.

At length, William rose from the comfortable old chair to face his brother. The two men stood, clasping forearms. Sir John appeared weary. William remembered the bloody, hard-fought years that his steadfast brother had served as a soldier; the loss of his wife, his babes, and even the presence of his grown son—another John, a soldier himself, so far away in the Hebrides.

William understood loss—the loss of a wife, a mother. Aye, he vowed to do what he could to ease Sir John's mind, to help bring Katherine home. The dangers involved in aiding the Reformation were coming too close to home.

Chapter 25

Blessed is the man that trusteth in the LORD,
and whose hope the Lord is.

Jeremiah 17:7

AT FIRST LIGHT ON THE following morning, Sir John, William, and Peter mounted their horses and rode through the early morning mist southward to Crawfordjohn. They were suitably dressed for the occasion, trusting that an interview with the young James Stewart, King of Scots, would be welcomed.

The trysting place King James built for Katherine was like a large manor house secreted from the busyness and opulence of court, affording the king and his consort a place of privacy. The king was keen on hunting in South Lanarkshire near to Abington, north of the Duneaton Water, a tributary of the River Clyde.

The house built for the king at Crawfordjohn was more like a well-appointed hunting lodge, a place where the king spent many leisure hours hunting in the forests and fields where wild game was plentiful. Katherine was happiest away from court, far from the sumptuousness and opulence of the monarchy and its constant demands. She preferred the simpler life in the smaller hamlet, closer to Carmichael and her girlhood home.

The three men arrived at noon, unannounced, trusting the king would receive them without prior notice. The servants, all dressed in royal livery, ushered them into the large front hall, then hurried away to inform the king of his newly arrived guests.

In moments, Katherine came running into the hall, throwing her arms around her father and smiling a welcome.

"Oh, Papa," she breathed excitedly, "how happy I am to see you, that you have come!" Seeing William and Peter, she paused, confusion in her eyes. "And Uncle William . . . Cousin Peter," she said, hesitating, "such a . . . surprise." Katherine was obviously confused at seeing her uncle and cousin in company with her father at Crawfordjohn.

Since becoming the king's consort, Katherine felt awkward in Peter's presence, feeling his silent disapproval and knowing her decision to become part of the king's court had built an invisible wall between them. On the several occasions she had visited Carmichael, Peter had avoided her, keeping himself busy with the horses and his ongoing care of the king's valuable steeds, plus the training of Sir John's own mounts. She had learned through her father that his frequent trips to Biggar for supplies also included visits to a close friend, Jenny Chancellor.

Peter moved forward, embracing Katherine and kissing her cheek. "Hello, Kate," he said cordially. "It is good to see you again."

Katherine's eyes widened. She sensed a change in Peter's formerly cool attitude, and eager to mend the breach, she said, "Peter . . . my dear cousin."

Tears welled up in her brown eyes, and she returned his warm embrace, holding tight to his leather jerkin. She whispered close to his ear. "Let us be friends, Peter—always. I have missed our friendship, the old days."

Before Peter could respond, an inner door opened into the front hall, and the king himself entered, dressed in his riding habit. A smile of welcome crossed his youthful features.

"Welcome, welcome, me dear friends." After a slight pause, he added, "And loyal subjects of the Crown of Scotland!"

The latter comment was not lost on the three men waiting for an audience with the young king. Bowing in respect to his sovereign, Sir John rose to clasp the king's forearm with genuine warmth. As a young lad, Sir John was fond of the charismatic heir to the throne, but the once-humble youth had, as King of Scots, embraced his privilege and power beyond his ability to temper his desires, making him vulnerable to the ideas and opinions of his Privy Council and the Holy Mother Church.

William and Peter followed Sir John, bowing from the waist in deference of the king's royal position as their sovereign, then quietly waited for Sir John to announce his business. The king motioned for a footman to come forward, an air of impatience accompanying the gesture.

"And what brings ye to Crawfordjohn this fine day, me friends?" queried the king. Not waiting for an answer, the king gestured with a wide sweep of his hand. "Come, come, we shall talk in me private study and take some refreshment."

He spoke to the servant, who immediately left to prepare for the guests.

"Before we go behind closed doors, "said Sir John, "understand that I wish to speak to ye alone, privately, with only me brother present."

"Och, aye," the king said with a note of surprise and the lift of an eyebrow. "Well, then, mayhap Katherine can entertain her cousin while we talk," he suggested. The king paused momentarily, then moved to fondly embrace Peter as he would have a brother. He clasped his shoulder, turning Peter to face him.

"How goes it with the horses, Peter?" queried the king. "The last two mares foaled not so long ago, aye? I hear from one of me messengers that they are a pair of lively colts. Excellent, Peter. I shall stop by the stable to see them before they are trained and ready to be moved to Linlithgow or perhaps to Stirling."

"Aye, sire," Peter replied with a measure of equestrian pride, "they are indeed a handsome pair of colts—long-legged and well-marked, white blaze on their foreheads with white stockings and chestnut-colored coats. Fine hunters they'll be, too."

"Excellent, excellent," said the king with enthusiasm. He patted Peter on the back as though he were a small boy, a condescending gesture meant to remind his youthful friend that he, Jamie Stewart of the House of Stewart, was the King of Scots and that Peter was still a lowly horse trainer.

The three men entered the king's private library, closing the doors behind them. Katherine, aware of the king's dismissive words to Peter, motioned for him to follow her to a back entrance and through the double oak doors of the keep and into the expansive dooryard. An array of colorful spring flowers waved in the warm breeze, perfuming the air with the scent of a Scottish summertime.

The stone and timber horse stables were situated a little distance from the keep, housing several of the king's blooded riding mounts. Peter had groomed and cared for two of the horses, recently brought from Carmichael for the king's pleasure and convenience.

In the newly fenced paddock surrounding the stables, grooms were busily working with the king's latest acquisitions. They waved a hello to Peter and Katherine as the two cousins walked leisurely into the stable yard.

Once inside the stable entrance, Katherine grabbed Peter's hand and tugged him to a straw-lined pen, where a gaggle of hound puppies squirmed and whined, vying for a space at their mother's breast.

Laughing softly, Katherine said, "Aren't they adorable, Peter? There is nothing quite like the smell of a warm puppy. They were born just one week ago."

She lifted a squirming, white puppy marked with red and black patches. The pup made high pitched yelps at being dragged away from his mother, where he had been contentedly nuzzling for milk. Katherine laughed and handed the wriggling pup to Peter. "Would you like one for your own? I'm certain Jamie won't keep all of them."

"I think not, Katherine," Peter said, laughing softly, cradling the squirming pup in his arms. "We have dogs enough at Carmichael; and besides, these are hunting dogs, bred for sport. Ye know Sir John is not that fond of the hunt. Calls it the sport of kings. If I were to choose a dog for me own, I would choose a companion dog, like Sir John's wolfhound, Zebulon, a soldier's dog."

"Ah, I miss that hairy old beast," Katherine said. "But even these hounds are warm and cute when puppies and a great deal smaller. I bring wee John to see them every day, and he gets so excited, claps his hands, and tries to climb into the pen with the pups."

Peter gently placed the pup back into the pen, making room for him next to his wriggling brothers and sisters. He looked at Katherine then, remembering that his tender-eyed cousin was also his steadfast companion throughout their childhood and youth. He had felt betrayed when Katherine chose a life at court as the king's consort, but today, his heart softened toward her.

He had recently learned of Katherine's influence with the king during the hunt for heretics and that many who were arrested, awaiting trial, were released before an official papal inquiry took place, the king turning his head as they escaped to England or the Continent.

The light-hearted conversation about hound puppies had broken the awkwardness between them, and Peter said, "I hear by many that the king will soon take a wife, a queen for Scotland. I'm sure you must be aware of this. How will this affect your . . . your position?"

Peter's face grew warm, but he did not know how else to say it, to put into words such a delicate question. Perhaps he was wrong in broaching the subject at all. He was appalled at himself for doing so, but his fondness and concern for Katherine would not be silenced.

Sensing Peter's changing mood, Katherine looked away, knowing the questions on the mind of her cousin would follow. Peter's tone was solemn, a decided turn to matters more serious.

"Let's walk in the orchard gardens, Peter. It is lovely there, and we can speak freely without fear of being overheard by the servants. It vexes me that I must treat everyone as though they were a spy."

"It is a different time, Katherine—a different age—and aye, spies are about. You have changed; and truth be told, we have all changed with the times. Our beloved Scotland is no longer our childhood refuge. I feel cheated in so many ways."

"We have all been cheated in some way, Peter."

Peter shrugged his shoulders. "Sir John says we must strive to be content with the path God has marked out for us. Problem is, I'm not sure what that is. I do not like the thought of adapting to unfamiliar territory. It is hard, so very hard."

In the years following Katherine's departure from Carmichael, the cousins had grown apart, into very different people. Their youthful years were behind them, and they were challenged with events they could not control. And those events had indeed changed them forever.

They walked into the extensive gardens that surrounded the keep, alive with the fragrant wildflowers of spring. Snowdrops and Lily of the Valley bowed their tiny white heads, perfuming the grassy spaces along the walkways. Purple wood violets grew in profusion, scattered about the gardens, adding patches of bright color to the vivid green of the lawns.

At the far end of the orchard garden, they sat on a rustic bench beneath a crab apple tree in full bloom. Katherine breathed deeply, her eyes closed, inhaling the fresh spring air, secretly preparing to speak to Peter. She wanted to be honest, to hide nothing from her cousin.

Turning to face him, she said, "To answer your question, Peter, yes, I do know of the ongoing negotiations to find a queen for Jamie. Of course, she must be of royal blood, a papist, and a political alliance that will strengthen Scotland and reaffirm the king's loyalty to the Pope and his resistance to the Reformation movement. I believe an agreement with France for Madeleine of Valois will be forthcoming."

"What will you do then, Katherine?" queried Peter, his blue eyes searching hers. "Will you remain at court, secreted away from the queen?"

Katherine appeared thoughtful, her eyes downcast, studying her hands and playing with the tassels on her light spring shawl.

"If I continue . . . with Jamie," she said softly, "I will remain here at Crawfordjohn; but Peter, I am hoping I will be released and can come home to Carmichael—with wee John, of course."

Peter brightened. "Your father is discussing this with the king as we speak, pleading for him to allow you to come home. You must take courage for Jamie if permission is granted. Perhaps the king will grow to love his queen."

Katherine's eyes sparkled in amusement at Peter's suggestion and a small chuckle escaped her lips. "He has never even met her, Peter. They say she is not well, but all are hoping she will soon recover. I am praying that it will be so. Oh, Peter, I want to come home, truly I do."

She paused, looking directly at Peter, who was listening attentively. "Cousin, I want you to know . . . Jamie is kind to me; but lately, he is plagued with bad dreams, and at times, he does not seem himself. He dreams of the bloodshed, of the heretic burnings, and he grows unhappy and depressed. He fears papal retribution if he suggests reforms in the Church."

"Och, lass, Jamie was too young to shoulder the responsibilities of a kingdom. He was barely sixteen when he took the throne. Just think, Katherine, the Privy Council influences him; the Church pressures him; his mother betrays him; and his uncle, King Henry, threatens him. No marvel he is not himself at times."

Katherine sighed. "I know, Peter. Jamie leans on me for emotional support, and I fear for him. You know that King Henry was denied a divorce from the Pope. He wanted to marry Anne Boleyn, so he ordered the Archbishop of Canterbury to grant the divorce from Katherine of Aragon, which he did."

"Not surprising, coming from Henry," Peter said.

"And now," Katherine continued, "King Henry has officially broken from the Church of Rome to establish his own Church of England—no doubt to legalize his divorce from Katherine under the Church of England. Henry is trying to influence Jamie to denounce the Church of Rome and join him in his new freedom, as he calls it. Och, Peter, the whole world has gone mad, and I fear Jamie will go mad with it!"

"Is he that disturbed?"

"Och, aye, he is. Some nights, he wakes from a dream screaming, calling on God to forgive him, pacing the floor and pounding the walls. It is awful to watch, Peter. He seems fine in the daytime; but the winter was long and dark, and he suffered many nights. Now that spring is here, he seems better, quite his old self."

"I know the torment of night terrors," Peter added, "but mine are from outside sources, the burning of Patrick. But thankfully, I have not been troubled recently."

"Oh, Peter," said Katherine, laying a small hand on his, "I am so happy to hear this!"

"It appears to me," Peter suggested, "that Jamie is suffering from his own private demons—perhaps from his youthful debauchery and excess, but who can tell? His regents and his Tudor mother, King Henry's own sister, contributed to his present suffering, allowing his stepfather to hold him captive for so long."

Katherine nodded. "I cannot help but feel compassion for him. I know his weakness, his lack of confidence as king; and most of all, I witness his constant fear of papal retribution. Oh, Peter, God never meant for us to live in such fear of man, such anguish."

"Nay, quite so," Peter agreed. "You and I were blessed with strong, protective, and loving fathers; but Jamie had no living father, no guidance—only his ungodly regents and tutors, nothing to inspire him to honor and greatness. Quite the contrary. They encouraged his debauchery so they could distract him, gain power over him. It is a sad commentary. The doorstep to a king's palace is a slippery one. Give me a stable gate any day."

Katherine laughed. "Spoken like me own dear cousin," she said, expressing herself in the informal language their fathers still used.

"But Peter, I feel I was a positive influence on Jamie in the early days at Linlithgow and Stirling; but now, I cannot seem to help him, to encourage him to stand strong as King of Scots. He seems so desperate to please the Privy Council and the hierarchy of Rome. And, Peter, we are all looking over our shoulders."

"Do not take his failures to yourself, dear Kate," Peter said softly, the old familiar tenderness he once felt for his cousin returning warm and sweet to his heart. "You have done what you could, lass. It is time—time to come home."

Chapter 26

For I know the thoughts that I think toward you, saith the LORD,
thoughts of peace, and not of evil, to give you an expected end.

Jeremiah 29:11

IN THE KING'S PRIVATE LIBRARY at Crawfordjohn, a servant prepared a table of refreshments for the visiting guests. The young king motioned for Sir John and William to be seated at the table, then dismissed the servant, who quietly quit the room.

"So," the king began, waving a hand in the air, "I say, Sir John, ye must have some important business to discuss with your king— riding from Carmichael this morning." He broke off a portion of warm bread from a loaf and added a slice of cheese.

"Aye, we have come with a request to present to our king," Sir John stated.

"We can speak while enjoying this refreshment, aye? So," continued the king without waiting for a response, a hint of irritation in his tone, "what is on your mind this day, Sir John?"

Serving himself some oat cakes and fruit jam, Sir John nodded his agreement. "Aye, we can do that, to be sure." He paused, finishing his oat cake, then looked directly into the king's eyes, knowing he must be careful with his words.

"I understand that negotiations are underway to find a queen for Scotland . . . and a wife for ye, of course. Is this so?"

The king took his time in answering Sir John's query. He took a long drink of spiced cider, then replied. "Aye, it's so, and has been for quite some time. As ye well know, this takes a lot of political maneuvering on the part of me advisors, the Privy Council, ye kin. I have little to do with the process—or the outcome, more's the pity."

"Are the negotiations near completion then?" queried Sir John.

"Why do ye ask, Sir John? I would question your interest in such mundane matters. The negotiations to find a queen are dull and taxing, to say the least, but a necessary affair for the Privy Council to handle."

"Choosing a queen for Scotland is an important decision," William offered.

"Perhaps so," replied the king, turning to William, "but not a decision in which ye need to trouble yourself. It is none of your affair, after all. Surely, ye men must have something more on your mind."

William felt the rebuke and paused, knowing this was Sir John's battle and that he best remain silent. "Quite right, quite right," William nodded in agreement. He took some refreshment from the table and waited for Sir John to take up the conversation.

"I shall be plain and to the point then," Sir John stated with an air of authority. His years as a commanding officer under James IV's reign gave him the boldness to speak to this young monarch as though he were a son to be chastened. The arrogance of the young king had vexed him.

"The purpose of me visit to ye this morning is to ask that ye release Katherine from her . . . situation as your mistress . . . since ye will be marrying a queen sometime soon. I want to bring Katherine home . . . to Carmichael."

The king drummed his fingers on the table as though bored with Sir John's request. "I see, I see," he said coolly. He brushed a hand over his riding habit, signaling the two men that he would rather be riding his mount.

"In truth, I have grown rather fond of Katherine—have been since we were children—but she paid me no mind, preferring the company of Somerville . . . until I received my majority as King of Scots, that is. And when I summoned her as the king, she complied, as all subjects must," he added. "What say ye to that, Sir John?"

"What I have to say to ye is this. If ye think Katherine accepted your summons because ye were king, that ye could offer her the luxuries of court, all that entails, ye are wrong in your assumption, sire," Sir John said sternly, his eyes steely with anger.

The king seemed to shrink from Sir John's harsh response, knowing very well that Katherine had accepted him as his consort for reasons other than what privilege and wealth could offer. And because of his fondness for her, he had wished to please her, putting himself in a precarious position.

It had not been for love that she had come to him, but only to influence him. He understood that now; but because he truly loved her, he complied many times to her sweet entreaties. To the young, self-indulgent king, the reality of her lack of love for him and her obvious disregard for all that he had done for her, all that he could give her, seemed not to persuade her at all. If she were only of royal blood, he would have married her, given her anything she desired; but Katherine did not truly love him, and he knew it.

Her sympathy for the Reformation and her grief every time a heretic was sentenced to death were proof of where her loyalties really lie. He must let Katherine go, or eventually, he would be questioned about her allegiances. Even though he was king, he might face excommunication, be eternally damned if he were not in total agreement with the Pope of Rome. He cared deeply for Katherine's welfare, fearing for her future with him and for his own reputation as a devout follower of the Roman Church. He must let her go home before her sympathies were discovered and brought into question.

His son by Katherine, Sir John's own wee grandson, would someday come to court when he was old enough to leave his mother, as was customary with bastard children. These illegitimate children of the king received privilege and position, but they would never be considered in the accession of kings.

The king rose from the table laden with refreshments and walked to the long window overlooking the gardens. In the distance, he could see Peter and Katherine sitting on a bench beneath a flowering apple tree, the branches gently swaying above them in the warm spring breeze.

An overwhelming sadness washed over him, like the incoming tides of the cold North Sea. He knew then, he must let her go, empty his heart of her, somehow forget that she had slept beside him, borne him a son, and melted his heart with her tender entreaties. Aye, he must find the strength to send her away.

Of course, he reflected, watching the two cousins laughing together beneath the tree, he could disregard Sir John's request. After all, he was the king, the highest authority in Scotland, save the papal hierarchy at St. Andrews. He could demand that she stay at Crawfordjohn, waiting for him to come to her. But she would despise such an arrangement.

The young king knew her too well. He was no fool. She would become unhappy, and perhaps, come to despise him as well, rejecting him for his disloyalty. He could not stand such a thought. He would let her go while she still cared for him, before the life-altering marriage would take place.

He thought of her compelling and winsome ways, her kindness and caring, her devotion to God, and her steadfast convictions. Katherine had inspired him to be a better man, to go beyond his base humanity and weakness. She challenged him as no other woman had; and without Katherine, life at court would never be the same.

He had other mistresses—some of noble birth—but none so endearing and intriguing as this fair-haired daughter of a country soldier. Without Katherine to comfort him, to be the assurance he so desperately needed, what would he do?

A queen would be chosen for him, a political alliance that would further the financial prosperity of Scotland and convince the hierarchy of Rome that Scotland would remain loyal and faithful to the papacy. Aye, indeed, he would marry a woman he did not know and endeavor to turn his affections toward her, his queen. Then, perhaps in time, he would come to love her.

The king turned to face the two men who had risen to their feet in deference to their standing sovereign, waiting patiently for him to speak. The time had come, and the young king knew it; and at the same time, he hated the very thought of it. For Katherine's safety and for his own good, he would acquiesce to Sir John's request. He would send Katherine away. Now, before he changed his mind and sent the three men away instead.

But what would he do without her sweet presence? How would he make it through the dreaded nights of terror and fear? None of his other mistresses could comfort him as Katherine did. They all paled and faded into nothingness when Katherine was near him.

"As you wish, Sir John," the young king said flatly. He sighed deeply, then continued. "I will release Katherine and send her to Carmichael House in a fortnight when I return to Linlithgow Palace. I will send an escort with all her things," he said, his voice wavering slightly, "the gifts and trappings I have given her while at court. I wish for her to have them."

Sir John had prepared himself for a lively debate with the king over his request for Katherine to be released from court. He was pleasantly surprised that no argument followed. He looked at the king, a question in his eyes, wondering if he had heard correctly or if there were some other attachment to the king's immediate response.

"Ye are surprised, Sir John." The king chuckled softly, but no mirth was evident. "I can see it in your face and in your speechless manner. Aye, as ye have heard, I will marry soon; and, all things considered, life at court will change, and, well, Katherine has served me well. She deserves a chance to marry, to find someone . . . someone who will love her as I have." He held Sir John's gaze, daring him to dispute this claim, but Sir John only nodded, not rising to the bait.

Pausing momentarily, Sir John responded carefully. "I thank ye, sire, and, aye, I did not expect ye would release Katherine so . . . ah . . . so willingly."

"It is not willingly that I return Katherine to your household, Sir John. As I said before, I am quite fond of the lass, but the time has come for me to wed. It is expedient that I release Katherine at this time—for her own happiness and for the future of Scotland and the chosen queen."

"I believe it is the wisest choice for both of ye, and for the bairn as well," Sir John said. "Wee John will be carefully and lovingly cared for at Carmichael, I can assure you."

"I have no doubt of that, but you do realize that he will come to court when he is of age. After all, Sir John, he is my son, even though a bastard; but I will do the proper thing by all my children, see that they have royal positions in the realm."

"Aye, I understand. It is the way of the . . . the way of kings."

A slight frown crossed the king's features. He was fully aware of Sir John's implication—*the way of kings*—but chose to ignore the insinuation. He had other things on his mind and would address these matters while the Carmichaels were here in his presence.

He turned to William and said, "Please be seated, William. I have an important matter to discuss with both of you, but particularly with William."

Chapter 27

He that handleth a matter wisely shall find good:
and whoso trusteth in the Lord, happy is he.

Proverbs 16:20

THE TWO MEN RESUMED THEIR former seats, and the king sat behind his ornately carved desk, pouring himself a tankard of spiced wine. He assumed a casual posture, settling himself into his leather chair and looking at one man, then the other.

"Some talk has come to my ears of a man riding through the countryside in various disguises," the king began. "The purpose of this rider is to interrupt the efforts of the magistrates, to stop these ongoing and illegal meetings of the so-called Reformers." He gazed purposefully at the faces of his guests, endeavoring to read their expressions at his words.

"I am wondering," the king said, turning to William, "if in your riding about the lands of Carmichael and beyond, if ye have heard of this man or, perhaps, even seen a stranger in numerous covers riding about the countryside?"

William remained quite calm—not a muscle moved—and his face revealed nothing to suggest he was involved. "Aye, I have heard of him," William said in all truthfulness. "From what I understand, the rider does no harm, just disbands the secret meetings of the gatherings. Is this not a good thing? Ye don't wish for these secret meetings to continue, isn't that right?"

"Not disbanded or interrupted before the leaders are taken into custody," the king bellowed in sudden anger. He pounded a fist on the top of his mahogany desk. "Ye understand my meaning, William Carmichael; and if ye are wise and see this man, ye will tell him this— that if he is caught, he will be hanged! Do ye understand?" thundered the king.

The room rang and crackled with the obvious threat. William paused, reasoning how to answer the king. "If indeed, I come across the rider in my rounds about Carmichael," William replied calmly, "I shall certainly inform him of your warning."

"See that ye do!" commanded the king, his anger quite evident.

"Are there no witnesses to this man's identity?" William queried.

"No proven witness to his real identity has come forth," answered the king in a calmer tone. "He is clever; and since he uses various disguises, never riding the same horse, he can disappear before the magistrates get to the meeting place. But if this provocation continues, this Reformation Rider, as they call him, will surely be caught."

"I understand your concern," William said in a mild tone. Sir John remained impassive, not entering the conversation.

"We are taking strong measures to discover who this man is," continued the king. "And if he is discovered—or should I say, *when* he is discovered—he will face a merciless court."

Silence hung in the room, like the threat of approaching doom.

"Indeed!" the king said, his voice rising as he spoke. "This man has even snatched condemned heretics from their guards, and the heretics disappear completely. Poof! Vanish! Off to England or the Continent, I assume; but be assured, William, we will find him, hunt this betrayer down. He cannot stay hidden forever. Eventually, someone will discover his identity or betray his trust. After all, he must have accomplices, people who help him."

The king looked steadfastly into the rugged, handsome face of William Carmichael but could discern nothing in his easygoing manner. Not a bead of sweat appeared on his brow, not a shadow over his countenance. Then for one fleeting second, he thought he recognized a mocking look in his eyes, but it vanished as quickly as it appeared, leaving his countenance undisturbed by his questioning.

"I understand your concerns," William replied, "and will not hesitate to warn our people of this person."

A disgusted look crossed the king's youthful features, and he shoved his chair away from the desk as though he wished to distance himself from the two men waiting quietly in his study. There was something about the men that unsettled him—a sense that they could see into his soul—and he did not like the feeling of such transparency. He respected Sir John, but he had an uneasy feeling about William. But what was it?

In an abrupt change of subject, he said, "Now that spring has come, I will be expecting you and Peter to bring several of my chosen stable mounts up to Linlithgow for the spring festival, as usual. I shall send my grooms from Linlithgow to inspect my horses in your stables and see which are ready to use for the event."

"As you wish, sire," William said. "Ye will find your horses healthy and in show form."

"Aye, by the way, William," the king said, adopting a more congenial tone, "ye and Peter do an excellent job of training my mounts. I am well pleased with the way the horses perform, how regal they appear, surpassing the entire stables at both Linlithgow and Stirling. Ye shall be rewarded handsomely."

"It is a privilege to work with your noble steeds, aye, indeed. When I be away, maintaining watch on the borders of Carmichael, Peter has proven to be an excellent trainer, exceeding all me expectations. Since he was a bairn, he is always happiest when tending the horses."

"That's so, sire," Sir John agreed. "Peter would rather sleep with the horses than in his comfortable room at Carmichael House."

A reluctant smile tugged at the corners of the king's lips. If he were not a king, he would desire to be as Peter was—a trainer and keeper of horses. But . . . he *was* a king.

"We already be preparing the horses for the spring festival," offered William, hoping the subject of the king's equestrian interest would deflect the talk of the mysterious rider.

Hearing about his mounts stabled at Carmichael seemed to brighten the king considerably, and he waved away his suspicions concerning the shadowy rider of the Scottish Lowlands. Surely, it could not be William Carmichael, as some had suspected—not his own Master of the Horse at Carmichael House.

The king rose from the desk, motioning for the men to follow him into the gardens. It was time to speak to Katherine about returning to Carmichael. Perhaps, he thought with a measure of hope, she had grown accustomed to living at court and would miss all the trappings of her royal status as his consort, having all her heart desired in the way of servants, clothing, and jewels.

But deep down in his heart, he knew she would not stay and that all the worldly goods and kingly prestige would not change her heart toward him. Ah, yes, Katherine would return to Carmichael, and he would marry a queen, a woman chosen for him by his advisors, a woman approved by the Pope, a woman he did not know and certainly did not love.

Chapter 28

When a man's ways please the LORD,
He maketh even his enemies to be at peace with him.

Proverbs 16:7

IN THE EARLY AFTERNOON, THE three Carmichael men mounted their horses and bid farewell to the king and Katherine. The parting was amicable enough, but an underlying strain dampened the goodbyes. In a fortnight, Katherine and wee John would return to Carmichael escorted by the king's royal guardsmen. The matter was settled.

The meeting with the king had gone reasonably well, and Katherine's release from court was assured. However, there was the obvious insinuation by James V that he, or at least his advisors, suspected William of the covert activities connected with the Reformation efforts of the Scottish people. Who else was so familiar with the Valley of the Clyde and could disappear to places hidden from the magistrates?

The men were subdued, deep in their own thoughts as they rode northward through the radiant sunshine of early spring. The air was cool but refreshing, the fields alive with shades of greens and yellows that carpeted the hillsides and riverbanks. Drifting on the gentle breeze was a cacophony of sweet smells—colorful, blossoming wildflowers and spicy herbs that reminded Peter of Jenny at his first encounter with her, the lass lying unconscious in the heather, auburn hair covering her face.

Since that time, his thoughts of her were an everyday occurrence. He decided to part company with his father and uncle near the hamlet of Symington. He would stop at Shieldhill Castle, hoping that Jenny would be free to spend some time with him before evening shadows covered the valley.

Approaching St. John's Kirk near Symington, Peter turned northeast toward Biggar and Quothquan, only three miles away, while Sir John and his father continued northwest toward Carmichael. An air of tension had settled over the two brothers, an obvious disquiet, causing Peter to speculate on what the king had said in the library to bring this unusual strain between them.

* * *

At Shieldhill Castle, the large, brass key turned in the lock with a resounding thud, securing the oak-lined library from any intruders. From a high shelf, Edward Chancellor lifted the wooden case that concealed the forbidden Bible Testament. For months now, he had been secretly reading the translation; and for the first time in his life, the words in English, instead of the Latin liturgy spoken by the parish priest, held some meaning he struggled to understand.

A passage of Scripture taken from the book of St. John, chapter fourteen and verse six, had kept him up late into the night hours, pricking his heart and sending a certain fear and trembling to his soul. What could it possibly mean? Was Jesus overlooking his very own mother, bypassing the Queen of Heaven, counting her unable to save or answer prayer? The words of Jesus played over and over in his mind. "Jesus saith unto him, I am the way, the truth, and the life: no man cometh unto the Father, but by me."

He was certain Jenny assumed he had destroyed the missive, and he let her think so. If it were discovered that he still had the Testament in his possession, he would be the one facing charges of heresy. The words on the pages had not burned his fingers as his parish priest had warned, but instead, burned a curiosity in his heart that would not allow him to destroy the book.

A gentle rapping at the library door sent a sudden chill from his stomach to his heart, and he hastily replaced the Testament in its hiding place, trying to recover a semblance of calmness. What if it were the priest, the magistrates? They had come only once during the mandatory searches, apologizing profusely, knowing he was a devout papist, and barely glancing at the books on his library shelves.

The sweet voice of his daughter spoke through the heavy oak door. "Papa, it is me, Jenny. I need to speak to you for a wee moment. I am sorry to disturb you. Will you open the door?"

Her father had lately taken to locking the library, a habit he had only recently acquired. She wondered at this, but assumed he wearied of frequent interruptions by the servants and decided to secure his privacy by locking the door.

"Coming, me daughter," he said, turning the key in the lock. The door swung open, and Jenny stood in the hallway, Peter Carmichael at her side. Edward Chancellor gazed at the young people, sighed wearily, and motioned for the couple to come in.

"Good afternoon," Peter began in way of a greeting. He was only a few feet into the library when he said, "I was in the neighborhood, or close enough, so thought I would stop by to see Jenny . . . if you don't mind, that is."

"Aye, Papa," Jenny quickly added. "Since Peter was close by and the afternoon so delightful and lovely, we thought to walk in the gardens for a wee bit—enjoying the spring flowers, perhaps looking at the new foals."

"I must say, young Carmichael," Chancellor said, "ye are a persistent man. Your jaunts into Biggar to buy supplies for your stables seems to coincide with Jenny's music lesson in that town, aye?"

"Well, I cannot deny," Peter agreed with a grin, "that it is more than a mere coincidence, sir, but we are accompanied by Jenny's governess, and, well, I am fond of your daughter, sir. I would like your permission to spend more time with her."

"You mean to court her?"

"Aye, sir, I would like to court her with your permission."

"Ye are bold, young Carmichael. What do ye have to offer a lass such as Genevieve? Ye are a man who keeps a stable, who works with horses. Genevieve has been carefully raised, educated, and can move among the best in our country's society."

Peter felt his face grow warm at Chancellor's assessment of him. Besides raising a daughter who was well-educated with a sizable dowry, Chancellor had also beaten her until she ran from home, and Chancellor himself was a sour and bitter man, Peter thought. He would not say this, though, or he would never win the favor of Edward Chancellor.

"With all due respect, sir, I, too, have been carefully raised and educated with the best of tutors in all aspects of mathematics, architecture, languages, and present-day cultural trends. I prefer working with horses, for I am best suited to that. At the right time, I have an inheritance equal to what you possess here at Shieldhill Castle. I am well able to provide for a wife and family when the Lord sees the time is right."

"Is that so?" Chancellor said with a measure of unbelief. "And will you raise your children with the blessing of your priest and Rome?"

Hesitating for a moment, Peter answered discreetly, "I am aware of your religious and political beliefs, sir; and with the present unrest in Scotland concerning the reforms suggested for the Church, I am in full agreement that the Church needs radical reforms. And by what measure that takes, it is certainly out of my hands. As ye have said, I am only a lowly horse master." Peter paused in his reply, and Chancellor snorted his disdain.

"Is that all you have to say," Chancellor said with a note of sarcasm in his voice.

"If God grants that I should one day have a family of my own," Peter continued, "I will follow what Scotland has deemed as true worship." Peter waited for Chancellor to respond, feeling his heart pounding in his chest.

It was a long shot, Peter thought, but he felt certain that one day, Scotland would fully embrace the Reformation, that the Roman Church would lose its stranglehold on the Scottish people, and that the hierarchy of St. Andrews would lose its power over the believers. He trusted his answer would satisfy Jenny's father. He was certain Edward Chancellor would never believe that Rome would lose its authority over Scotland. After all, the Church of Rome had been in power for over one thousand years.

"Very well," Chancellor said, "you may see Jenny on occasion, but do not consider this a courtship. Go now, smell flowers, and look at horses; but remember what I say."

"Yes, sir," Peter said humbly, "I will remember. Thank you for your time, and I apologize for the interruption."

Chancellor waved them away, saying nothing.

The two young people quietly closed the door behind them, then walked leisurely past the servants, through the dooryard, and into the gardens, where—looking around them and seeing they were alone—they turned to each other, laughing and skipping through the fragrant herb garden. Peter whooped with delight, assured that God was working and that someday, He would answer their prayers and cause Edward Chancellor to grant his permission for a real courtship.

Chapter 29

They have taken crafty counsel against thy people,
and consulted against thy hidden ones.

Psalms 83:3

EVENING SHADOWS LENGTHENED, STRETCHING ACROSS the Valley of the Clyde like ghostly specters, hovering over the tree-lined wagon road, then stealthily vanished into the gloaming. Sir John and William reined their weary mounts to a stop in the dooryard of Carmichael House, glad to be home again.

As the two travelers dismounted, stable lads came running to take the horses to the stables to be groomed and fed. William's mount, Shadow, and Sir John's Sebastian, whinnied and snorted, pawing the ground, shaking themselves, happy to be free of their burden and ready for a supper of oats and hay.

Walking toward the double doors of the central tower, Sir John detained William with a vice-like grip on his arm. "William, we must talk."

"I kin, brother, but first, let us eat some supper. Coira will be serving the meal soon, and I am starved. I would have thought that Jamie would have served us more than just a simple refreshment before we left."

"He was distracted, or surely he would have ordered the servants to prepare a meal. Probably never even thought of it after me request to release Katherine from his court. It took him by surprise. Took it hard, very hard."

"Aye," William agreed, "that he did."

The two men entered the keep, where delicious smells wafted from the kitchen into the expansive hallway. Coira appeared in the doorway and placed both hands on her hips.

"Well, I say, it's about time ye two vagabonds came home. I be holding supper for half an hour. Just wash up, and I'll lay your meal out on the table in the dining room. Go now!"

The brothers left the hall, grinning at Coira's obvious lack of fear for her cheeky admonition. "Are ye sure Coira doesn't run Carmichael House entirely?" William asked, chuckling behind his hand. "So bossy she be in her old age, but . . . of course, canna do without her."

"Aye, to be sure," Sir John said pausing, opening the door to his private chamber. "Coira has run the house for years! Still treats me like I was still a wee lad, like she is me mother. Happy she'll be to know Katherine will be returning with wee John. She has missed her like her own daughter."

The brothers smiled knowingly, shaking their heads, then separated to wash up.

Coira placed steaming dishes of seasoned vegetables and roasted lamb on the long plank table, bustling about as Sir John and William returned to the dining room for their supper. She set a bowl of stewed apples laced with cinnamon and honey on the table between them.

"How was our Katherine and the wee one, Sir John?" Coira queried.

Eyes twinkling, Sir John said, "They be fine, Coira, and ye will be pleased to hear that Katherine is released from court. She will be returning to Carmichael in a fortnight. What think ye of that?"

"Praise be to God forever!" Coira said, clapping her work-worn hands. "So long have I prayed for this happy news. This old table will be full of life and laughter, to be sure, and I be happy to be cookin' and carin' for the lot of ye."

"I know ye will, Coira, but wee John will add more work for ye as well."

"Never ye mind about that, Sir John. Katherine is not like those lazy noble ladies who can't lift a finger. A brae lassie she be. And ye kin, there be nothing like a wee laddie prattling about the house, aye, lifting your spirits and bringing barrels of love along wi' the work, that so?"

Tucking a lock of silver-white hair that had escaped from her starched muslin cap, the trusted old housekeeper shuffled from the dining room, wiping tears from her eyes with the corner of her apron.

The two men ate in silence for some time; then William pushed his plate away and leaned back in his chair, opening the subject he knew was on Sir John's mind. *May as well get this talk over with*, he thought. It was not always easy to please God and his brother, too. Sir John should know that his intention was not to cast suspicion on the good name of Carmichael or his clan.

During the mandatory searches by the royal guards, no substantial evidence had been discovered, and nothing of significance pointed to William as a participant in the covert meetings of the believers.

Everyone living in the valley knew that William patrolled the lands of Carmichael and the surrounding area, sounding an alarm if anything were amiss. It was common knowledge, and the landowners were grateful for protection of their livestock and property.

"I kin what ye are thinking, John," William began. "The king be suspicious of the rider who goes about the countryside, warning the people. He suspects it is me, aye?"

Shoving his own plate aside, Sir John filled his tankard with cider and leaned forward, facing William across the table. A glint of anger surfaced in his usually calm demeanor, and he said, "William, ye kin that ye are the guilty one. I canna say that I have seen ye, and perhaps I do not want to see all that ye are doing for the Reformers, but I kin that it is ye."

"Perhaps it be another rider," suggested William with a glint of mischief. "There be other men taking up the cause of Reformation."

Sir John's fist came down hard on the oak planks of the table, rattling the trenchers and tableware. Coira came hurrying from the kitchen, but Sir John motioned her away with a wave of his hand. She raised her eyebrows and quickly backed into the kitchen, noting that the brothers were in a private discussion.

"Blast it all, William!" thundered Sir John. "This be not your private cause. Nay, no point in denying that the king and his Council have ye in their sights." He pounded the table again. "I forbid ye to continue this alleged treasonous activity. Ye will be discovered, and then what? Do ye hear me?"

The space between them crackled with tension, but William remained silent; only his eyes spoke, pleading for Sir John to understand. Remorse for the danger to Sir John and their clan was evident, etching his face with both determination and regret. He was caught in some middle ground that offered no way out. He gazed steadfastly at his older brother, a man he loved and respected above all others, a man who had been like a father to him. He reached a hand across the table, waiting, saying nothing.

The two men stared at each other in a lengthy stand-off; then Sir John softened, sighing deeply, then reached his hand across the table to clasp his younger brother's hand in a conciliatory gesture.

"Do ye remember . . . we promised never to allow anything to come between us. We be brothers," said Sir John, grief in his voice. "Let me remind ye of this." He withdrew his hand and wiped it across his brow. "I kin ye have passion for the right cause, William, but ye must learn to trust God and not take the sword into yer own hands. Jesus said, 'My kingdom is not of this world: if my kingdom were of this world, then would my servants fight.'"

After a long pause, William said, "Aye, be remembering our pledge, to be sure, John, but I canna believe we canna take up arms to further the cause of reformation, to protect ourselves from hatred and violence."

"King Solomon reminded us," said Sir John, "that, '*the king's heart is in the hand of the Lord, as the rivers of water: he turneth it whithersoever he will.*' God is still in control, even though it may not appear that He is."

"God's men were also men of purpose," William added, objecting to John's passive attitude. The idea of such inaction caused his aggressive nature to rise.

"We are men of purpose, William, always have been. We be Men of the Broken Spear, but that does not mean we should take up arms in a spiritual conflict."

"Och, John! Ye should consider Gideon, David, and Joshua then. We cannot just sit on our hands and do nothing when innocent men and women are being arrested and burned for heresy. From where I sit, brother, to me, doing nothing is worse than death."

"William!" Sir John said, rubbing his temples in frustration. He paused for a moment, calming himself. "I do not pretend to understand how to proceed with this Reformation. Perhaps, as we pray, there will be radical reforms in Rome, and we need not put our hand to it. But if not, we must move forward with caution. Ye kin I have no fear of men, but I do fear what will become of our children, our clan. *'Every way of a man is right in his own eyes: but the Lord ponders the hearts.'* Our own methods are not always the right way."

William scoffed at his words. "Radical reforms in the Church of Rome? Ha! Are ye serious? That time has passed with the persecution of the believers. Our own St. Andrews, the epitome of the papal authority in Scotland, is filled with corruption. How can ye even suggest that reforms will happen when the cardinals and bishops are the ones who need reforming?"

Sir John cradled his head in his hands, propping his elbows on the table. His voice was low, almost a whisper. "'To do justice and judgment is more acceptable to the Lord than your sacrifice, William."

"I canna understand ye, John. Ye expect me to stand by without even attempting to rescue those condemned of heresy? With warmer weather, the secret meetings will resume, and the magistrates will be waiting, seeking revenge on the dissenters of the papal Church. There will be no justice for any of them."

"All men who serve God out of a true heart desire to fight, to right the wrongs; but William, it may not be with the sword that ye are to fight. I be convinced, the people of God be standing on the brink of something we canna understand."

"What do you mean?" asked William.

"For one thousand years, the Popes of Rome be reigning over the world. I read in the Revelation prophecy of ages and times, of churches, of seals, of one thousand years of tyranny and corruption. I feel we are looking forward to a blank page, not knowing what we should do, how we should move forward. 'Tis why I move with caution. I be desperate, desperate to understand, but it be closed to me."

William shook his head, his frustration almost palpable. "Ye and I, John—Men of the Broken Spear—we struggle to understand the prophecy. I feel I am pounding at a locked door; but I say, it doesn't take much to understand that Jezebel of Thyatira will never repent. Calls herself a prophetess, causing people to ere, to worship men and idols. She seduces the innocent and kills the believers. I see this as the fallen and broken religious system that Rome has become. We must forsake it, John."

"Forsake it in our hearts is one thing, William, but to physically oppose it is quite another. A literal sword will never conquer this spiritual beast. It must be by the hand of God."

"We will never agree on how it's to be done, John, but understand this: ye are still the head of this family, the chief of our clan, and I will honor your request. I promise to stop any suspicious activity, at least for this present time. If the day comes when I canna comply, I will leave Carmichael for your sake, for the sake of our family, for the clan."

"Nay, nay, perish the thought! I do not want ye to leave, William. Nay! Ye kin we are brothers. Ye and me—we possess a bond stronger than most men." He exhaled a long breath, pushed his chair back and stood. "I grow old and weary of war and fighting, William. I pray for peace, for reconciliation, for the time when I gather me feet up in me bed and bid farewell to this life."

"Dinna talk like that, John. Ye have long years ahead, and we must hold fast to the pledge between us. Katherine will be home soon, and Peter is happy, doing well. It is enough—enough for now."

William stood as well and walked around the table to stand before Sir John. The two brothers faced each other; and for the moment, opinions and differences fell away. They grasped each other in a strong embrace that needed no words.

"Hold fast, William," Sir John said, tears glistening in his eyes.

"Aye, John, above all that we understand—hold fast."

Chapter 30

From the mountains and hills, let us gather the few,
Who will stand for the right, and dare to be true.

Evening Light Songs

IT WAS A TIME OF great spiritual darkness, a time when the papal powers of deception and tyranny seized entire nations, holding them in the grip of fear and bondage. It was a time when men's hearts failed them for fear of what was to come. But then, the clear, reverberating sound of a single trumpet began to break apart the great and terrible stone of offense.

Light and hope sprang from the darkness, piercing the gloom of a long millennium of fear and anguish. God had not forgotten. He remembered His people and had set in motion a great awakening that was sweeping across Europe, reaching unto the distant lands of bonny Scotland.

And in the Valley of the Clyde, summer crept across the meadows and hills like a shy maiden, slowly giving way to the long, sun-drenched days of June, a time when wild yarrow and sweet vernal grass swayed gently in the warm breeze. Seasons would come and go as always since the beginning of time, even during dark and desperate days.

The lowlands of Scotland were clothed with wildflowers, sprinkling the meadows with a plethora of color. Spring run-off swelled the brooks, sending icy water tumbling over the moss-covered rocks in a continuous cadence of sound. The Falls of Clyde increased in volume, making pools that swirled and churned, exposing rocks long buried beneath the earth.

At Crawfordjohn, after a reluctant farewell to Katherine and her escorts, King James V of Scotland mounted his favorite stallion and rode out for a hunt, pushing his habitual melancholy into the dark recesses of his heart. Katherine was gone—and he had let her go. He must put her out of his mind, his life.

The royal guard of the King of Scots accompanied Katherine and wee John along the wagon road to Carmichael, enjoying the pleasant ride through the June morning. Someday, wee John would return to court, but now, Katherine and her son were free to return to the home she loved.

The leave-taking from Crawfordjohn and the young king brought a measure of sadness for Katherine, knowing Jamie was often lonely and distraught over the many pressures of ruling the kingdom. His loyalties were divided, and he was not certain whom to trust. She prayed that the chosen queen would prove to be a true helpmate and would offer the troubled King of Scots a sense of confidence and well-being.

Several weeks after the arrival of Katherine and wee John at Carmichael House, the homecoming was celebrated by a clan gathering. Neighbors, tenants, and the entire household at Carmichael who had known Katherine since she was a child were included in the festival-like occasion. Long tables of Katherine's favorite foods were placed about the central courtyard, and a mixed group of clan musicians accompanied the happy homecoming. Dogs barked; children laughed; and the guests of Clan Carmichael greeted the homecoming party with expressions of genuine pleasure.

From the wagon road surrounding Kirk Hill, a rider on horseback slowly made his way down the incline, then reigned up short, stopping some distance above the keep, overlooking the ongoing celebration. His dark eyes swept over the people, searching for someone. Seeing Katherine moving among the crowd, he turned his horse as though to leave, but Sir John had discovered his approach and waved a hand, signaling for him to join the gathering.

The rider paused, uncertain, until he noticed Katherine moving away from the crowd, looking toward him, watching, waiting, gesturing to her father to fetch the rider to join them. The rider motioned toward the orchard, and Katherine nodded, then excused herself from her guests. She followed the path to the orchard, now in full bloom, and waited by the old bench beneath the pear tree where she had last seen Robbie Somerville.

He had dismounted and was slowly walking his mount through the newly tilled earth beneath the fruit trees. He halted a few feet away from Katherine, tying his pony to a branch. Then he turned toward her, his face inscrutable.

"Katherine," he said, softly speaking her name—that name so sweet upon his lips, her likeness forever etched upon his heart.

"Dearest Robbie," she said, her voice faltering with emotion. "It is good to see you again."

Seeing his stalwart figure standing in the shade of the old pear tree, she remembered their last meeting on this very spot, trying to explain that her desire was to refuse the king's summons, but that she had found no way to avoid the royal command without leaving Scotland as an exile; but Robbie refused to understand, even though he was well aware of such a summons. Their parting was painful, unresolved.

After a long pause, he said. "I came at your father's invitation—to let you know that Lady Somerville sends her love, but she is unable to attend your . . . your homecoming."

"Och, this was not my idea of a homecoming party, Robbie, to have a celebration. Papa thought this would be a good time for a clan gathering. We always have a gathering in early summer, you remember. Everyone is invited, and they all seem . . . so happy."

"I see."

"And how is your mother . . . Lady Somerville?"

"She is doing well but has a lingering cold. Otherwise, she would be here, wishing you well."

"I'm sorry to hear she is not well. She was like a mother to me when I was growing up. Please give her my love. I will ride over one day soon to visit."

Robbie nodded, then cleared his throat. The space between them was tight with tension, and the effort at small talk did not lessen the cool atmosphere.

"Is your brother here also?" Robbie asked, making another attempt to ease the tension.

"Nay, he is not. Papa was hoping he would be released from his post in the Hebrides to come home; but unfortunately, his company would not spare him. I miss him so very much. Someday, he will be the Laird of Carmichael, but his duties in the royal guard keep him occupied."

"I believe I understand," said Robbie. He lifted his hat and bowed slightly. "I am happy for your return to Carmichael, Katherine, for Sir

John and your family." Hesitating somewhat awkwardly, he said, "I will bid ye farewell for now." He lifted her hand politely and kissed it, his lips trembling at the touch, then abruptly turned away, preparing to leave.

Katherine laid one hand on the sleeve of his linen shirt, detaining him. The linen was of fine quality, clean and soft against her hand, and his brown leather jerkin smelled of wild earthy things—of horse, crushed mint, and creeping green moss.

"Wait, Robbie, please. Won't you stay? I want us to be . . . friends. I don't want this invisible wall between us. Perhaps you will never forgive me for my decision not to oppose that time at court with Jamie, but that part of my life is over now. Jamie will choose a queen very soon. Please, Robbie . . . we can still be friends, be neighbors, can't we?"

He turned to face her, bending over her slight form. His eyes softened, and tears glistened in his eyes. He cupped her chin, raising her face to his. "Nay, Katherine, nay. We canna be mere friends."

"But why, Robbie? Why can't we be friends?" Tears filled her own eyes, and Robbie could see the pleading in their depths.

His touch was soft and gentle, and he moved his hand to caress her cheek. "Because," he said with a husky voice, "I love you, Katherine. For as long as I live and breathe, I will love you. It must be more than friendship for me. It is that simple. But Katherine, it will take time—and who can say what will happen."

"It is not that simple for me, Robbie! Your love for me is based on the old days—days before I left for the king's court, before wee John was born. You are remembering times gone by when your heart was knit with mine. I have changed, and doubtless, you have changed, too. You cannot possibly love me as I am now. I am a different person, but we can try to be friends."

"Then answer me this, Katherine. Do you love Jamie Stewart?"

"Aye, I love Jamie—the affection of a friend. He understood that it could never be more. That is why he let me go. I could never return the love he so desired." She paused, drawing in a deep breath. "Jamie pursued me continually during summers at Cowthally Castle while under Lady Somerville's protection. He just wouldn't give up. But, Robbie, I have only ever loved one man."

"One man? Dare I hope that . . . that it was me?" His eyes grew soft, remembering.

She covered her face with her hands and began to weep. "Aye, Robbie. It has always been you—you and no other—but now, I have ruined everything. Since there was no avoiding the summons to court, I felt I could do something to influence Jamie, to aid the Reformation, to spare the accused heretics, spare them from death at the stake; but Robbie, it was never enough, never enough. I felt God would help me, spare me from my obligation as the king's consort. I was so naïve and foolish. But I tried, Robbie, truly I did. The powers of the kingdom were against my efforts."

Robbie nodded, dropping his head.

"I am so sorry for hurting you so," Katherine said weeping.

At her words of remorse and seeing her hot stinging tears, he drew her into his arms, holding her close. She heard the steady beating of his heart and wept in earnest, spilling her tears on his leather jerkin, holding tight as though she would never let go.

"Hush, lass, hush. Forget all the sadness, the pain, the regret. We both have changed in many ways, but we have learned, you and I." He whispered against her ear, parting the sunny tresses with his lips.

"When you left for the king's court, Katherine, my heart was broken. I didn't know if I would ever see you again; and if I did, how would I react? How would I stop the pain of losing you to Jamie Stewart? But time has proven to be a healer; and if ye still love me—still want me— canna we begin again? God can help us. It is not all ruined, as you suppose. Jamie did listen to you, I have heard. Remember, Katherine, he loved you, too."

They sat on the old bench beneath the pear tree until Katherine's tears subsided and she grew calm. "I'm sorry, Robbie. Your jerkin . . . it is spoiled."

"Sorry for the tears? God created tears, so we could work through our pain, our sorrows. Dinna fash yourself, lass."

"Aye, I suppose God created tears like a floodgate for our grief and heartaches. It must be God's way."

"Aye, indeed. Tears are the bleeding of the soul, the healing balm for our wounds. They purge the heart of things too hard to bear, cleansing our heart of bitterness and resentment, allowing it to heal, to recover. Aye, lass, it is so. Recovery takes time, and I am still recuperating. Who can say what the future will hold for either of us."

In the courtyard below the orchard, boisterous laughter and singing floated up from the gathering. And on the wide lawn, a variety of games so loved by the local clans were in progress, challenging the more daring of the players. Smells of roasting mutton and locally raised geese turned on the spit, sending delicious and tempting odors wafting on the breeze.

Sir John greeted his tenants and neighbors, while Zebulon, his wolfhound, followed at his heels, sniffing the fragrant odors of cooking meat. Only William was missing, having taken several of the king's horses to Linlithgow for the spring festival. He mentioned to

Sir John that he would lodge with the family of the martyred Henry Forrest, alluding to concern over the welfare of Forrest's sister, Lorna. Sir John had raised his eyebrows but said nothing.

As the gloaming crept stealthily over the Valley of the Clyde, the last of the guests climbed into their wagons and mounted their steeds for the journey home. The day had been a joyous occasion for Clan Carmichael and their neighbors, and for one day, the dark threats of the papal powers were forgotten.

Peter had invited Jenny and her father to join the gathering, but Edward Chancellor declined the invitation. However, he permitted Jenny and her governess to attend. When Peter returned to Carmichael after escorting Jenny home to Shieldhill Castle, he joined Katherine and Sir John to sit in the terraced courtyard, watching the night sky dotted with a million stars, more than one could imagine. They talked of the clan gathering, of the various humorous incidents during the games, and how the delicious food was so enjoyed by everyone.

As the misty gloaming turned to darkness and the watchers on the terrace prepared to seek the warmth of the fireside, suddenly, the sky lit up with a spectacular display of light and color. Sir John and Peter rose to their feet, wondering at the awesome splendor of the heavens flashing fire and ice. Katherine stood close to her father, amazed and terrified at the same time.

A giant green smudge of light began to appear in the north, moving slowly at first, then dancing and shimmering across the heavens, skipping and bouncing across the darkened realm of space as though trying to speak to the watchers on the terrace.

"Och, Papa," Katherine said, trembling beside Sir John. "I have never seen the lights so bright before and moving so rapidly! Are we in danger?"

"Nay, lass. We be safe. God is in control, even of these strange and fearful lights. The Psalmist writes, 'The heavens declare the glory of God; and the firmament showeth his handywork.' Be seeing these colorful lights many times in me life, but as ye say, not as bright and bold. Appears they be close in our valley. Some be frightened of the lights, thinking God is angry and might strike men from the Earth with this strange fire in the sky."

"Aye, they do seem very close, almost unfriendly," Peter said with a measure of awe and wonder. "Like something is about to happen. Seen them before, but not so unearthly, so forbidding."

"Old Celtic legends speak of the lights," offered Sir John. "Stories passed down through the ages, some very frightening—like warriors fighting, serpents devouring men, heathen gods seeking vengeance. On and on they be. But dinna fash yourself, children, we know the Creator of all things; and for reasons we canna understand, warnings come through unusual events in nature. In past times, the lights have appeared before a great battle, and sometimes after a great and terrible bloodshed, like they be mourning the dwellers of Earth."

"Truly, Papa, I am frightened," said Katherine trembling. "Perhaps God is warning the believers of something terrible to come. Do you think it could be?"

Sir John placed a strong arm around Katherine, drawing her close to his side in a protective gesture. The lights continued to flash and dance in unpredictable patterns, seeming to almost touch the treetops.

"Who can say, lass? There be many reasons we see the lights tonight, but we must not fear. Whatever happens in the days to come, we know that God is with us, encouraging us to be His brave followers. He will strengthen us for what is to come. The psalmist says that God has set a faithful witness in the sky, like the moon, established forever."

"Aye, Uncle," Peter said as his eyes swept over the night sky. "I believe we will face a greater battle than we could imagine, but God has promised that His Kingdom will stand forever. He says in the book of Daniel that His Kingdom will never be destroyed."

Amazed at the fearful display of dancing lights in the deep purple sky, Katherine watched the battle in the heavens, like invisible giants shooting arrows of light into the endless expanse of space.

"Do you feel these strange lights are portraying this?" Katherine asked, still trembling.

"I believe God is telling me that I will have a part in this battle," Peter said. "Patrick Hamilton's death at the stake was not in vain. I have come to understand this. God is using his testimony and the brave Reformers to bring back the light, to break apart this terrible stone of darkness and deception. Aye, and it is a fearful thing, just like these lights."

"Surely, God will bring the Gospel of light and truth to our land, to our people. And I believe He will use the 'Men of the Broken Spear' to bring it about," said Katherine with renewed hope.

"To be sure," Peter agreed. "And God is counting on us to be strong, to be ready, to stand firm for the light of the New Testament truth, those truths most surely believed among us."

"Aye, me children," said Sir John lifting his arms to the flashing lights in the heavens. His prayer was simple. "O magnificent Lord Jesus, Creator of the universe, whose majesty is revealed to us this night; O, Lord, let it be so, let it be so!"

Afterword

WHILE RESEARCHING MY FAMILY ROOTS, I discovered some fascinating stories that piqued my interest to the point that I spent several years gathering facts. This captivating glimpse into sixteenth century Scottish history compelled me to write this series.

As I dug into historic accounts, I noted some interesting parallels and events taking place in our modern society. The players differ; the methods change; but the causes are nearly the same—that of obtaining freedom, freedom from tyranny, from the religious hierarchy so jealously guarded and protected by the systems of men.

The story of Peter, Katherine, William, and Sir John Carmichael and their family connections provided the catalyst for the *Stone of Destiny* book series. We gathered these historical accounts from events taking place in late medieval times. The title "The Broken Spear" appears on the Carmichael family crest. The surname of Carmichael originates from a barony found in Lanarkshire, territory granted to the Douglas Family by Robert the Bruce in 1321. William de Carmichael witnessed the charter in 1225. In 1384, Sir John de Carmichael held a charter for the lands of Carmichael from William, Earl of Douglas. The Barony of Carmichael was confirmed on the head of the family in 1414.

Sir John de Carmichael of Meadowflat fought with the Scottish mercenaries sent to France to help the French army against the English invasion of Henry V at the Battle of Baugé, he is said to have broken his spear while toppling the unfortunate Duke of Clarence from his horse, an action which led to the duke being killed by Sir Alexander Buchan. Thereafter, the English became so demoralized that they fled from the battlefield. The "Broken Spear" became the Carmichael family emblem.

Where details are lacking, I step into the story, filling in the gaps and weaving what is a believable and probable account, using the facts I have collected and the recorded history of the Carmichaels.

In *The Broken Spear: Reformation Rising,* we begin our story with the death of Patrick Hamilton (1504–1528). He was a Scot, a leading Protestant reformer, a charismatic thinker who preached the Gospel to the common people. He was eventually arrested, tried as a heretic by Archbishop David Beaton, and burnt at the stake at St. Andrews. In the wake of this tragedy, we meet Peter Carmichael, our protagonist who was caught up in the fires of the Reformation that swept across Europe.

While Peter's story is taken from historic accounts, his involvement with Genevieve Chancellor is from my own imagination. We do know that the Chancellors and the Carmichaels were close neighbors; the family seat of the Chancellor family is located near Biggar, Scotland, where Shieldhill Castle remains today as an upscale hotel and events center. In some instances, names and locations have been changed to augment the storyline.

Interesting glimpses of Katherine's involvement with young King James V of Scotland are named in *Memorie of the Somervilles: Vol 1, 373-386,* the Somervilles being an influential clan who entertained

Katherine and young King James V at twelfth-century Cowthally Castle, Camwath, their baronial estate in Lanarkshire, Scotland. The castle is now a protected ruin.

A more detailed glimpse into the King of Scots' pursuit of Katherine, a reluctant subject, is found in the ancient book of *Scot Lore*, Vol. 1, pages 290-291. It describes the young king's pursuit of Katherine, and Lady Somerville's attempt to protect Katherine from the king's unwanted advances. When Katherine was released from court as mistress from King James V, John (Robbie) Somerville took Katherine as his wife.

A plethora of books have been written on the Protestant Reformation, some that include Peter's involvement in the slaying of Cardinal Beaton. Researching the background of the Protestant Reformation is the best way to understand the complexities of such a world-changing event. God Himself orchestrated the coming together of the key Reformers, and along with the invention of the printing press, the catalyst for Reformation was in place.

When eyewitness accounts are available, they are certainly preferable to accounts written hundreds of years after the fact. *The History of the Reformation in Scotland* by John Knox is a direct and personal account of events during the Reformation years. The text has been updated since the Scots' language and spellings can be difficult to understand, but otherwise, the book is an accurate chronicle of events experienced by Knox himself.

Numerous resources can be found online with information on events leading up to the Reformation. A word of caution concerning online information: many online resources are written from a modern-day perspective far removed from the original context.

I also gathered information from Carmichael Clan history, the archives of generations of clan activities during those turbulent years of papal inquests and heretic burnings. Many accounts are listed in the public domain.

I chose to use proper English for this series, using only a few well-known phrases easily understood by most readers. The language of the ancient Scots is a mix of cultural dialects within geographical locations and social contrasts. For instance, the use of "me" for "my" and "dinna fash yourself" for "don't fret yourself" were everyday language of the Scots. The charming and melodic turn of a vowel is unique to the Scots, making the speaker easily identifiable. *The Edinburgh History of the Scots Language* by Charles Jones (Edinburgh University Press, 1997) provides a detailed description of the syntax, phonology, morphology, and vocabulary of the Scots' language from the earliest time to present day.

I am not attempting to write an account of the Protestant Reformation, neither a scholarly examination of the theology of the Reformers, but follow one family's involvement in those extraordinary times of spiritual upheaval. In contrast to academia's hypotheses, I, the writer, envision the impacting scenes that happened between the lines, imagine those tender and stirring words never recorded in history, remember love known only in secret, and write about the honor and integrity of those whose brave deeds were never valued or remembered . . . except by God.

—*Ruth Ann Ellinger*

Resources Bibliography, and Historical Notes

Principle Characters

Katherine (Elizabeth) Carmichael

b. 1515–d. 1552

a.k.a. Elizabeth Carmichael

Daughter of: Sir John Carmichael of Meadowflat, Captain of Crawford

Wife of: Sir John Somerville of Cambusnethan

Natural offspring: John Stewart (1531-1563), Prior of Coldinghame

Mistress of King James V of Scotland by order of the king (1530-1535)

According to Fraser in *The Lennox* Vol. 1 (p. 420), Katherine Carmichael married "young Cambusnethan," Sir John Somerville, in 1537. It was this young man who married Katherine Carmichael, daughter of Sir John Carmichael, the third of Meadowflat.

Cowthally: Lord Somerville's seat in the parish of Carnwath

Note:

> Katherine, daughter of Sir John Carmichael of Meadowflat, captain of Crawford, was one of the mistresses of James V. In that curious book, "The Memorie of the Somervilles," published in 1815, 2 vols., from the original manuscripts,

many interesting notices are given of the royal visits to Cowthally, Lord Somerville's seat in the parish of Carnwath; and especially of the flirtations of James V with "Mistress Katherine Carmichael," the captain of Crawford's daughter, a young lady much about sixteenth years of age, admired for her beauty, handsomeness of person, and vivacity of spirit.

Alluding to "Mistress Katherine's" connection with the king, the author thus concludes an admirable defense of her. 'Thus far I have digressed in vindication of this excellent lady Katherine, that it may appear it was nether her choice nor any vicious habit that prevailed over her chastity, but an inevitable fate that the strongest resistance could hardly withstand.

The Scottish Nation, Vol. 3 (488-489)

James V of Scotland, King of Scots

b. 1512-d. 1542

a.k.a. Gudeman of Ballengeich—a name he chose when riding incognito throughout the countryside.

Son of James IV of Scotland and Margaret Tudor of England (sister to King Henry VIII of England)

Husband of:

1. Madeleine de Valois (married 1537)

2. Marie de Guise (married 1538)

Sir John Carmichael

b. 1489 (approximate)-d. 1567-1579?

Third of Meadowflat, Carmichael Estate, Lanarkshire, Scotland

Captain of Crawford Castle

Peter Carmichael

b. 1522 (approximate)-d. 1556?

Birthplace: Lanarkshire, Scotland

Son of James Carmichael (William) and Margaret Kincraigie

In 1546, Peter was one of the murderers of the infamous Cardinal Beaton and for his crime was sent to the "galleys," where he shared penance with John Knox. He was imprisoned in Mont St. Michel but later escaped disguised as a monk.

James Carmichael (William)

b. 1494-d. ?

Birthplace: Balmedie, Lanarkshire, Scotland

Son of John Carmichael of Meadowflat and Elizabeth Janet Bruce

Brother to Sir John Carmichael, the third of Meadowflat, and Gavin Carmichael

Genevieve Chancellor

A fictional character

For Further Reading on Carmichael History:

https://en.wikipedia.org/wiki/Clan_Carmichael
https://clancarmichaelusa.com/about-clan-carmichael/clan-history

Resources

Bainton, Roland. *Here I Stand: A Life of Martin Luther* reprint. Nashville: Abingdon Press, 2013.

Cargill, R.W. "Torchbearers of the Truth: Patrick Hamilton." BelieversMagazine.com http://www.believersmagazine.com/bm.php?i=20100805 (accessed August 1, 2010).

Chambers, Robert. *Traditions of Edinburgh*. London: W. & R. Chambers, 1868.

Donaldson, Gordon. *Scottish Kings*. New York: Marlboro Books Corp., 1967.

Foxe, John. *Fox's Book of Martyrs*. John Day, 1563.

Harvey, William. *Scottish Life and Character in Antidote and Story*. London: Sterling: Eneas MacKay, 1927.

Hetherington, W.H. *History of the Church of Scotland*. New York: Robert Carter and Brothers, 1881.

Hillerbrand, Hans J. *The Protestant Reformation* revised ed. London: Perennial, 2009.

Howie, John. *The Scots Worthies*. Edinburgh: Banner of Truth Trust, 1870.

Knox, John. *The History of the Reformation in Scotland*. Edinburgh: Banner of Truth revised ed., 1982.

Lutzer, Erwin W. *Rescuing the Gospel: The Story and Significance of the Reformation*. Ada: Baker Books, 2017.

MacCulloh, Diarmaid. *The Reformation* reprint. Westminster: Penguin Books, 2005.

MacKay, Dr. James. *Pocket History of Scotland*. United Kingdom: Paragon, 2002.

MacLean, Fitzroy, *Concise History of Scotland*. New York: Beekman House, 1970.

Morton, H.V. *In Search of Scotland*. New York: Dodd, Mead & Co., 1934.

Ritchie, John. *Reflections on Scottish Church History*. Edinburgh: Sands & Co., 1927.

Scots Lore. Glasgow: William Hodge & Co., 1895.

Also by Ruth Ellinger

The Wildrose Trilogy:
The Wild Rose of Lancaster
Wild Rose of Promise
Sword of the Wild Rose

*Women of the Secret Place: A Collection of Inspirational Stories and
Personal Moments with God*

All available through your favorite retailer.

Coming Soon . . .
The Broken Spear & The
Serpent: Reformation Reckoning

August, 1547

St. Andrews, Scotland

FOR OVER A YEAR, THE Reformationists held the besieged castle of St. Andrews by force. The zealots had wrestled it from the hands of David Beaton, archbishop and papal authority over all of Scotland. Then, they had unceremoniously assassinated him, hanging his body over the castle wall.

Now that the same castle fortress lay in stony ruin, the Reformationists' dreams of spiritual freedom appeared to be over. They had not expected the French to bring their heavily armed war ships mounted with massive cannons to blow the stone fortress to a pile of smoking rubble. But it had happened, and now they were marked as outlaws of Scotland and the Crown.

Outside the rain-drenched wall surrounding the castle, Genevieve Chancellor and William Carmichael waited with the restless crowd, searching the muddy grounds for some sign of Peter. The royal guard would be bringing the prisoners out to board the slave galleys waiting at the quayside, where the cold waters of the North Sea slapped at the sides of the wooden galleys.

William was there, hoping for an opportunity for a rescue. Jenny stood nearby, jostled by the crowd, trying to get closer to the line of prisoners. She slipped repeatedly on the slick, mud-trampled ground, barely able to keep her footing. If only Peter could glimpse her, know that she was there, she could urge him to hold fast to courage and not lose heart. She must find him.

As the captives rounded the outside wall, William saw with dismay that Peter was chained in heavy, salt-encrusted irons. There was no way he could free him from the restraints fastened to the prisoners, each captive's leg fettered to his fellow. There was nothing he could do to help Peter now. He knew that his son was hoping that by some miracle, by some Divine intervention, he would mount a rescue as he had done so many times before.

Through the crush of the crowd, Peter glimpsed his father and nodded slightly in recognition. William's tall, straight figure was mounted on a swift Galloway pony, swathed in his crofter's disguise. Great sadness welled up in Peter's heart, knowing his father would not be able to save him from his desperate plight; and no doubt, he would not see his father again unless God intervened.

All through the night, William had ridden his pony through the pelting rain, praying for an opportunity to rescue his son, but the milling crowd and the royal guard made it difficult to move more than a few feet through the churning throng of onlookers. Peter signaled to his father, pointing to his chains. It was over. There would be no rescue.

After all this time, all these years, Peter thought, were his night terrors returning to haunt him once again? The chains fastened on his wrists and ankles rubbed and dug into his flesh, and he understood without a doubt that this was no dream. This was an unbelievable reality!

The armed French guard escorting Peter and his fellow Reformers to the waiting ship prodded the weary prisoners along, unconcerned with their bloody wounds or their festering wrists and ankles caused from the chafing irons.

And then Peter saw her, stumbling along with the people trying to keep up with the followers and the family members of the captured men. He could see Jenny's tear-streaked face—that beautiful face that he loved—her auburn hair tumbling about her as she was jostled and pushed along by the unruly crowd, some of whom were elated at the capture of the Reformers, while others appeared defeated and silent.

Along with his co-conspirators, Peter was shoved on board the wooden galley, John Knox chained next to him, pulling him along the bloodied floorboards. Peter's last glimpse of Scotland, his beloved homeland, was of Jenny on the shoreline, her hand waving, hair blowing in the wind, throwing kisses and signaling him with a raised fist holding aloft the triumphant sign of a broken spear.

For more information about
Ruth Ann Ellinger
and
The Broken Spear: Reformation Rising
please visit:

www.ruthellinger.com

For more information about
AMBASSADOR INTERNATIONAL
please visit:

www.ambassador-international.com

Thank you for reading this book. Please consider leaving us a review on your social media, favorite retailer's website, Goodreads or Bookbub, or our website.

From the peasant revolt in Northern England, which threatens the very lives of her beloved father and brothers, through a loveless marriage, and finally to the political intrigues of Henry VIII's court, Anne's courageous and steadfast faith sustains her. But when her own life is threatened, can Anne's faith hold true?

Fiona's world is a carefully built castle in the air that begins to crumble as she watches her brother march away to join in the English invasion of France.

Robbed of the one dearest to her and alone in the world, Fiona turns to her brother's silver cross in search of the peace he said it would bring. But when she finds it missing, she swears she will have it and sets out on a journey across the Channel and war-ravaged France to regain it and find the peace it carries.

The Legions have left the province of Britain and the Western Roman Empire has dissolved into chaos.

With the world plunged into darkness, paganism and superstition are as rampant as ever.

Young Indi has grown up knowing nothing more than his gods of horses and thunder; so when a man from across the sea comes preaching a single God slain on a cross, Indi must choose between his gods or the one God—and face the consequences of his decision.

www.ingramcontent.com/pod-product-compliance
Lightning Source LLC
Chambersburg PA
CBHW020416260626
47156CB00007B/2413